HEARING THINGS ...

On his way to the closet to get a mop, Mark thought he heard a soft hiss.

He stopped and listened, his forearms tingling as goose bumps rose on the skin. The only noise was the ticking of the clock in the living room.

As he began mopping up the spill, he caught another faint sound. This time he could have sworn that a man's voice whispered, "Fool."

Refusing to stop again, he reasoned that he must be hearing his conscience speak to him. He knew now that Lara hadn't knocked over the first cup of coffee. The expression on her face when he'd accused her should have told him that from the start. Those big baby blues had looked so innocent. His behavior to her was inexcusable. He would have to try to apologize.

He sped up the mopping. Normally, he dreaded apologies, but this one felt urgent. He wasn't sure why—and maybe he didn't want to know—but he had to see Lara as soon as possible.

Dear Susan —
  Thank you for supporting
the Berkley/Jove authors.
    Best wishes!

Eternally
Yours

Jennifer Malin

www.geocities.com/jennifermalin

Jennifer Malin

JOVE BOOKS, NEW YORK

This is a work of fiction. Names, characters, places, and incidents are
either the product of the author's imagination or are used fictitiously,
and any resemblance to actual persons, living or dead, business
establishments, events, or locales is entirely coincidental.

ETERNALLY YOURS

A Jove Book / published by arrangement with
the author

PRINTING HISTORY
Jove edition / January 2002

Visit our website at
www.penguinputnam.com

ISBN: 0-515-13238-1

A JOVE BOOK®
Jove Books are published by The Berkley Publishing Group,
a division of Penguin Putnam Inc.,
375 Hudson Street, New York, New York 10014.
JOVE and the "J" design
are trademarks belonging to Penguin Putnam Inc.

PRINTED IN THE UNITED STATES OF AMERICA

10 9 8 7 6 5 4 3 2 1

Chapter 1

A SHARP TRIPLE bang startled Lara Peale. She jumped, and a dollop of carmine-red paint catapulted from her brush onto the front of her shirt.

"Damn it!"

It's only the door knocker, she realized.

Letting out a sigh, she rubbed her eyes with her free hand. She *had* to get around to changing that heavy clump of green-tinged copper. Not only did the noise always scare her out of her wits, its snarling lion's face unnerved her whenever she came home after dark.

"Just a minute," she shouted, doubting that her voice would carry through to the front of the huge old house. She wondered who could be calling. Her friend and fellow teacher, Diane Golden, often dropped in unannounced—but Di had just started a summer job.

All of Lara's other acquaintances normally phoned before coming over.

She slopped some linseed oil on a rag and swiped at her top. The effort only smeared the paint, creating a tonguelike shape that curled across her chest. She hoped she hadn't gotten any in her hair. With certain paints her blond curls soaked up the color and retained it for days.

The knocker exploded again, giving her another jolt. After half a decade in the house one would think she'd be used to that noise. Dropping the rag on the studio floor, she muttered, "Hold your horses."

She grabbed her unfinished painting and took it over to the closet. An original feature of the room, the nook was a joke as far as storage went. Less than a foot deep, the space couldn't hold much more than the single canvas she now slid inside. For once it served a purpose, keeping her work out of sight. She never liked showing her paintings until she had them as near to perfection as possible.

When she reached the foyer she could see a form through the curtains, still waiting on the porch. Whoever her visitor was had patience. *Too bad.* Since her ex-husband had moved out six months before, she preferred keeping mostly to herself. Di often tried to coax her into going out, but Di was married—like all of their friends—and now Lara was always a third or fifth wheel. In any case, she needed this time to herself to get all of the things done that she'd put off during five years of marriage.

She opened the door about a third of the way and raised her eyebrows. Her visitor was an unfamiliar man, a very good-looking one. About thirty years old, he had thick, black hair, slightly in need of trimming.

His big brown eyes gave him an almost childlike look of innocence—which she figured must be deceptive, since he was probably a salesman about to give her his pitch.

"Yes?" she asked, inching the door open further, to about halfway.

"Are you Lara Peale?" He cleared his throat. Apparently remembering he held a card, he jerked his arm out. "I'm Mark Vereker . . . from the Falls Borough Historical Society."

"Oh!" She blinked with surprise. Though she'd known the society would be sending someone over, she had imagined their representative would be some sort of town elder, not this young, virile guy. "Well, come in. Please."

As the man entered he handed her his card, but the heaviness of his stare distracted her from reading it. She looked up and saw that he had focused on her bare legs.

He yanked his gaze upward but not before she felt a wave of embarrassment over her clothing. Knowing she'd be painting today, she had slipped on an outfit she wouldn't normally wear in public: an old pair of somewhat scanty blue gym shorts and a clashing yellow halter top.

"I apologize for my appearance." She bit her lower lip and told herself it didn't matter what he thought—but it did, because the guy had the power to sway the society in favor of her request or against it. "I didn't realize someone would be stopping by the house so soon. I just turned in the application for the grant the other night. The historical society is more efficient than I expected."

"I should have called first." He rubbed his forehead, evidently embarrassed, too.

"No, it's okay." She led him into the main parlor, where she felt self-conscious again, this time because of the emptiness of the room. The only objects breaking up the large space were a stepladder and a wooden table holding a pitcher of iced tea and some disposable plastic cups. A lot of furniture had gone with her ex-husband, and she'd been lax about replacing it. Money had been tight since she'd bought out Ron's share of equity in the house.

"I'm sorry it took me so long to answer the door," she said, moving toward the table. "I was in the middle of painting. I'm an artist . . . well, especially when I'm not teaching high school."

He hovered near the entrance. "Maybe I should come back another time."

"Oh, no. I'm anxious to get started on my projects, and I can't get into any of the bigger ones without the grant." She reached for the pitcher, making an effort to smile. Being friendly to strangers hadn't been a priority lately, and she felt somewhat out of practice. "Iced tea?"

"Uh, yes, that would be nice." The expression on his face looked the way she imagined hers did. An uneasy tick tugged at one corner of his mouth.

Good, she thought while she poured. He didn't seem like the type to want to make small talk.

When she handed him the cup her fingers brushed his, warm and pleasantly smooth. His gaze caught hers. He really *was* a handsome devil.

Her visitor turned to survey the room, striding away from her into the center. "You have a beautiful home.

Not many houses of this era are so well preserved, especially before the owner has had help from us."

She watched him until her stare drew his eye, then glanced down to sip her iced tea. "Seeing the results of the funds you've contributed must be rewarding."

"It is." He smiled, this time without reserve. The topic must have been close to his heart.

She felt a pinch of curiosity. "How did you first hook up with the historical society?"

"My roommate in college told me about it—which was odd enough, since the society didn't interest him. But his aunt was a member, and he knew I was upset that my parents' colonial farmhouse had been torn down by a developer. Anyway, I went to one of the meetings and immediately liked what they were doing. Helping to preserve other old buildings was a good channel for my personal frustration."

"That's great." She studied him more closely. The guy cared about what he did. She admired that. "Of course, this one isn't in any danger of being torn down. Maybe I shouldn't even have applied for the grant."

"No, I'm glad you did." He began a slow walk around the room, taking in its features. "The society's main goal is to conserve older buildings in the community. The more homeowners we can get involved, the better."

For the next few minutes he scrutinized his surroundings while she stood by in silence. She considered pointing out that her plans didn't involve the parlor, but she didn't want to seem impatient. Clearing her throat, she said, "Sounds like you love your work. Do you earn a living this way or is it strictly a hobby?"

"A very big hobby." He glanced at her and focused back on the ceiling. He'd been completely absorbed in the house since he'd arrived—except for the one peek he'd taken at her legs. "Fortunately, I've had some success with two books I've written on local history. . . . I see this is an original gas chandelier."

"Yes, my husband's grandfather converted it to electricity—*ex*-husband's, that is." She frowned, hoping she hadn't stressed her marital status too obviously. "Mark Vereker," she said, looking at his card again. "Hmm. And you say you're an author? You wouldn't happen to be related to the Victorian poet, Geoffrey Vereker, would you?"

"Yes," he said. His lip curled. The question seemed to irritate him.

"You're kidding! I was just reading some of his poems last night." By the look on his face, she guessed he was sick of being asked about his ancestor—but in this case she couldn't resist. Stepping closer to him, she said, "I'm no poetry aficionado, but Geoffrey Vereker is my favorite. I like to read his poems before bed."

Engrossed in examining a wall panel, he didn't bother commenting on her statement. "This wainscotting is remarkably detailed. And I noticed the millwork on the staircase in the foyer as well. The wood is a wonderfully warm shade."

She regretted having to drop the subject, but the man had come here for another purpose. How ironic that *she* would be the one to get chatty. "Yes. Fortunately, most of this room has never been painted. For generations the house was owned by my ex's family, and they're all very conservative about change. In fact, he wouldn't let me so much as move a stick of furniture. Of course, that was when there *was* furniture."

Still inspecting the woodwork, he asked absently, "How long have you been living here?"

"Five years—during which I've come up with a thousand ideas for improvements." She set down her iced tea on a window seat and waved an arm about the room. "Now that the place is all mine, I'm going to change *everything*."

He gave her a strange look, verging on a frown. "Ms. Peale, I hope—"

"Oh, please. Call me Lara. You sound like one of my students, and the last thing I want during the summer is to feel like a teacher."

"Lara, then. And, uh, I'm Mark." He gave her one of his nominal smiles. "You do understand that houses of historical significance have to be renovated with a . . . a degree of respect?"

"Well, of course I do, Mark." She laughed at his misplaced concern. "Don't look so worried. I have a bit of an eye for decorative art."

He pressed his lips together.

"As I mentioned earlier, I'm an artist—in case it isn't obvious." She gestured toward the paint stain on her shirt.

That parted his lips, but he must have realized he was gaping and snapped his jaw shut. She hadn't meant to draw attention to her chest, but she felt a tingle of excitement over his instinctive reaction.

As he turned away from her and looked toward the windows, she suppressed a grin. "This is only the latest of many articles of clothing sacrificed in pursuit of beauty and truth."

"The floor-to-ceiling pocket windows are magnificent," he said. "Do they still draw up into the wall above?"

Her smile dwindled. She chided herself for her lapse into schoolgirlish giddiness. Maybe she'd been alone at home for too long. "Most of them do, but that one on the right doesn't work."

He stepped closer and spent a moment squinting up at the window in question. "Did you realize there's a piece of paper jammed up there?"

"No, I didn't."

"Maybe that's the problem." He turned and glanced around the room. Setting his drink down on the table, he asked, "Can I use that stepladder?"

"Sure."

While he moved the ladder, she went over to the window and gazed up, spotting the paper. Yellowed and crumpled, it appeared to be an old letter. "I wonder how that got there. I never noticed it before—and I do dust once in a while."

"It does seem strange. The only thing I can think is that it must have somehow slipped down from the room above. There may be access to the window mechanism from upstairs." He climbed up and stretched to reach the top edge of the window. A tug on the letter freed it fairly easily, but suddenly he shuddered and had to catch himself against the wall.

She reached out to hold him steady by the leg, distinctly aware of the warmth of his thigh through the thin fabric of his pants. "Are you all right?"

"Yeah, I'm fine. The coldness by the window got to me." He handed the letter down to her. "The temperature outside must be dropping sharply."

As she took the folded parchment she felt the chill, too. The abrupt change seemed peculiar, but her contact with him preoccupied her more. Beginning to feel

awkward, she let go of his leg and pretended to be engrossed in his find.

"M.A.S.," she read from the address side as he
made his way back down. Gazing at the elaborate, old-
fashioned handwriting, she wondered who M.A.S.
was—maybe an ancestor of her ex. Ron's last name
was Sulley. Curious, she asked her guest, "Do you
mind if I open it now?"

"Go ahead. I'd like to know how old it is."

She unstuck a misshapen wax seal and unfolded the
stiff paper. "Damn. There's no date. Maybe the contents can clue us in. Would you like to hear it? It's
short."

He shrugged. "Why not?"

She cleared her throat and read the note out loud:

My dearest M,

   *Pray put me out of this wretched state of un-
fulfilled desire. An exotic flower such as you cannot be sensible of how much suffering she inflicts
on the man she beguiles and then denies.*

   *Your lips are like a rose on the morn it blooms,
fresh and glazed with dew. Every inch of your
skin is as perfect and pure as a lily. Open your
petals to embrace me, and our love will flourish
fully, as Nature intended.*

                          Your own ever-patient G

"Well!" She gave Mark a wry grin. "'G' doesn't exactly sound patient to me."

He raised his eyebrows but didn't reciprocate her
smile. "No, he sounds pretty much like a snake."

"Do you think so?" She looked back down at the
beautifully crafted handwriting. The letter gave her a

weird feeling—maybe because it had seemed to come out of nowhere—but something about it appealed to her, too. "I kind of like the note. No one writes stuff like this anymore. It's gratifying to see a man express his feelings in words."

The curl returned to Mark's lip. "Maybe genuine feelings, but the sentiments in that are drivel—the words of a womanizer trying to get a virgin into his bed."

"Maybe." After her failed marriage, Lara considered herself pretty cynical about love, but apparently she still had a soft spot for romance. She touched the ink of the man's initial, imagining how much "M" must have wanted "G" when she read his pleas. "I wonder who they were. Doesn't this glimpse into the past make you want to know the whole story?"

He gave her a long look, and his expression softened. "In a way. That is, I can understand how you feel. The houses I research make me feel that way. There are usually only scraps of information available about the people who lived and died in them—just enough to make me more curious. Lots of times the only history recorded about a house comes from letters like that one. Can I have a closer look?"

"Be my guest."

He took the note from her and skimmed its contents. When he'd finished, he smirked. "I still think these are empty words, but it's always interesting to uncover a piece of the past. Something like this is the nearest you can come to going back in time."

She smiled. "You're right. I think that's kind of what I was doing when I read the letter—reliving a moment from the past."

He stared at the note for a moment longer, rubbing

his thumb over the signature, like she had done. Then he shook his head. "'Open your petals . . .' What a ridiculous thing to say."

"*I* think it's rather poetic."

"Well, then, the letter will make a nice keepsake for you." He held the piece of paper back out to her and started looking around the room again. "Anyway, we'd better get down to business. Why don't you tell me your plans for this place?"

"Okay." As she took the paper from him, another chill went through her. The wild thought occurred to her that maybe the note was haunted. As much as the discovery had piqued her curiosity, something about it made her vaguely uncomfortable, too. Why hadn't she found it before?

Dismissing the crazy idea, she set the paper down on the window seat next to her iced tea. "Just give me a moment to gather my thoughts."

"Of course." He reached inside his jacket, then patted his other pockets. "I think I've left my notepad in the car, anyway. Let me run out and get it. I'll be right back."

Trying to clear her head, she followed him to the front door and watched him dash out to his car. He'd parked on the side of the road instead of in her driveway—a considerate gesture, she thought. The way he moved looked athletic, but who could tell with that suit he was wearing? The fact that she was taking so much notice of his physical attributes surprised her. When was the last time she'd given a guy a second glance?

As he opened the passenger-side door, she reflected that she'd never met an author before—or the descendant of a Victorian poet. Those things particularly intrigued her about Mark Vereker . . . though, admittedly, she'd noticed his good looks right off the bat, too.

He leaned into the car, and she moved away from the door, irritated by the direction of her thoughts. For months Di had been nagging her about starting to date, and it seemed that her friend finally had her thinking about men.

That, however, was as far as she wanted to go.

Her resolution hardened as she walked back into the parlor. Somehow over the years of marriage her hopes and dreams had deteriorated into pain and a sense of helplessness about her situation. Now she was single and free again, but the hurt still lingered, along with something like guilt. She had vowed to live her life with a man, and she hadn't been able to keep her promise. She would never try it again. As for dating, she hadn't yet figured out how that might fit into her future. All she knew was that she wasn't ready for it now.

She glanced out the front window and saw Mark Vereker pulling back out of his car, holding a writing pad. In another moment he would be coming up the walk. She had to pull herself together and present her plans for the house to him in a positive light. If she got this grant from the historical society, she could finally build a *real* studio.

Combing her fingers through her hair, she took a deep breath. Ron had always made it difficult for her to pursue her art—maybe out of some sort of jealousy. Now that he was gone she intended to dedicate herself to her work, and revamping the studio would be the first major milestone in her new life. Making a good impression on Mark Vereker today could mean a huge difference for her in the future.

Too nervous to wait for his knock, she walked back into the current studio. Maybe she *would* try softening up her guest with some small talk. So far, making conversation with him had been surprisingly easy.

Though he hadn't responded well to her questions about his ancestor, she thought the poet might still prove a good choice of topic. She would probably fare better if she expressed her admiration for Geoffrey Vereker instead of asking Mark for information about him. The poet had to be a great source of pride to the family, and Mark would be flattered to know she was a serious fan.

Chapter 2

THE LATE GEOFFREY Vereker, who in life had
won modest fame with his poetry and utter notoriety
with his womanizing, floated around his haunt on a
summer afternoon, utterly bored with his existence.
Ennui, he'd long ago concluded, was his personal hell.
Life for him had been an ongoing chase after adventure in one form or another, and the afterlife had
proven the same—only with far fewer successes.

He glided down Main Street in Falls Borough, the
town where he'd been born and raised. Though his
haunt ranged to any place he had traveled during life,
he found himself coming back to his hometown more
and more frequently. What did it matter where one
wandered when one could do so little *anywhere*?

A pretty redhead walking out of Town Hall caught

his attention. *Ah, here is some excitement worth pursuing.* Geoff drifted closer to her for a better view.

She turned in his direction and sauntered toward him. Tall and elegantly dressed—for *her times,* in any case—she was a little slimmer than he preferred. As she approached him he sucked in his breath, admiring her green eyes. Her complexion was fair and faultless, precisely as he liked—though he rather wished she had long flowing locks, instead of the short modern coif she sported.

Reaching an electric traffic light, she stopped and waited at the crosswalk.

Geoff inched up beside her to study her profile.

All at once she put a hand up to her mouth, as if suddenly recalling something. She turned away from the light and strode toward him—promptly walking through him.

"Oh!" Shuddering, she nearly stumbled in her spiked high heels. She directed a horrified glance over her shoulder, but her gaze sliced through him. Shaking off her discomfort, she hurried on her way.

Geoff hovered behind, scowling to himself. This was the extent of his contact with women! He could inspire only fear in mortal females, and he had never met a female spirit—or a fellow male one for that matter. Though he occasionally might have sensed another ethereal being, making contact loomed beyond his abilities.

Well, if he'd learned one thing in the last century, it was that pining away only made his circumstances seem worse. He let out a great sigh and floated off, choosing the direction opposite the way the redhead had gone.

Having been out of town for several months, he decided to check up on a favorite local beauty. He'd first noticed the woman the previous autumn on the day her husband had moved out. Taking in the scene at the house, Geoff had been titillated. Divorcées had always intrigued him because of their worldliness. Soon he'd found, to his delight, that this one often read his poetry! From that moment on, the lovely blond had held a special place in his heart.

As he neared her residence today, he spotted a strange man in front of the house. A jagged stab of jealousy ripped through him. A mortal man could do what he could not—touch the lovely divorcée. Still, it remained to be seen whether the woman actually *liked* this fellow. Trying to stifle his fears, he floated closer to see what would happen.

The man looked to be fetching an article from one of those motorized carriages people drove these days. As he pulled back out of the vehicle, Geoff glided over next to him. When he got a good look at the fellow, he started.

A Vereker! He would have known that profile anywhere—and because it had shown up in his own hometown, he felt doubly sure. That the man who could potentially steal his divorcée from him might be a relative didn't lessen his resentment. Over the years he'd run into many of his descendants and few of them had impressed him. Though occasionally one dabbled in writing or another fared well with the ladies, none had seemed to encompass enough of his own personality to interest him much.

The man stood up straight and revealed his full height, a good six feet. As he stepped onto a slate walk that led to the house, Geoff conceded that the fellow might have some presence. Though his drab attire obscured his physique, a long, easy stride showed he was in shape befitting a relative of Geoff's. In fact, the ghost rather thought he saw a bit of himself in the man's sweep of black hair and wide-set brown eyes. The mortal's nose was stronger and straighter, but he rested easy, knowing that the fair sex had always admired his own rather delicate nose.

As he watched his flesh-and-blood counterpart climb up to the porch and rap at the door, he wished with all his soul that he could trade places. What would he do if his descendant managed to get where he himself could not with the divorcée? He wondered if there were any possibility he could enjoy the experience vicariously.

The twinge of distaste he felt at the thought told him it wasn't likely.

To Geoff's displeasure, the mortal opened the door himself, signifying some degree of intimacy with the divorcée.

"Lara?" he called.

So her name was *Lara*. He had wondered what to call her. That her name should be similar to that of Petrarch's Laura seemed fitting, for Geoff could imagine this woman being his own earthly muse . . . if only he could still write. As it was he had no access to an ethereal pen and paper, and he couldn't usually manipulate physical objects unless in a fit of extreme rage.

After a moment's hesitation the mortal Vereker let himself in, stepping slowly, clearly tentative.

Geoff made a wry face. The fellow must not have been on completely familiar terms with the lady, despite seeming somewhat expectant of a welcome.

"I'm sorry," a feminine voice sang out from a room beyond. "Here I am."

The ghost followed his descendant into a barren drawing room. The lady emerged from a door in the back, and Geoff gaped. She was even more lovely than he had remembered.

On the upper half of her body, she wore a sleeveless bodice, fitted closely enough to demarcate the pertness of her breasts. Her eyes were among the bluest he'd ever seen. He had always liked the way her golden curls suggested a hairstyle more attuned to his century than the current one. But what truly tormented him now was the glory of her legs, flaunted under a pair of those shockingly short pantaloons that modern women wore in warm weather. Good Lord, but he wished he had been born a century later!

Biting his fist, he forced himself to stand back so as not to give her a blast of unexpected coldness. But if he'd had any doubt before, he felt certain now that he couldn't bear to see his mortal counterpart have her when *he* could not.

The fellow was—for some unimaginable reason—observing the ceiling. He pulled his gaze down and nodded to the lady.

Geoff frowned at the indifferent greeting. Didn't his descendant know that a man should always make a woman feel like she was the sole object of his attention?

In return the lady flashed him a smile that made her face radiant and—Geoff thought with pain—boded well for the recipient.

His descendant didn't even seem to notice, looking back up at the ceiling. As he observed some unfathomable feature of interest there, the fool actually strode away from her into the center of the room.

Geoff stared, amazed that it looked as though he

might be spared the anguish of further jealousy after all. What was wrong with this fellow? Could it be that he was dutifully leg-shackled? But no, a glance at his left hand showed he wore no wedding band.

Uncertain what to think of the mortal, Geoff resolved to stay and watch what transpired. The fellow was now turning about the room, apparently surveying the walls. Though he seemed disinterested in the lady, Geoff would not take any chances. If his descendant made a move on his Lara, he swore he would foil the man's efforts.

Mark Vereker made a slow pass around the parlor, only half seeing the antique crown molding he meant to study. The proximity of Lara Peale behind him was too distracting for him to concentrate on anything. She must have been eager to hear what he thought of the house, but with her so close to him he couldn't even think straight. The woman was so gorgeous and glowing with life—so unlike himself these days—that he felt in danger of making a fool of himself.

He glanced back at her and she beamed at him. She had sunny California looks that seemed out of place in this old Victorian on the East Coast. He tried to return her smile but felt his lip twitch. The attempt must have looked ridiculous.

Turning back to the ceiling, he wondered what to make of her. She seemed kind of flaky—which didn't surprise him with her being a creative type. His ex-girlfriend Karen had been an interior decorator and could get pretty eccentric at times.

The thought of Karen made him stiffen. After they'd split up, he'd promised himself a long break from women. Now, only a month and half later, here he was getting worked up over another artsy type—another *divorcée*. He'd seen what sort of baggage could come with that. After eight months of dating him, Karen had gone back to her ex-husband, a man she'd never had a good word about. The last thing he needed was another woman recovering from a marriage.

Lara walked around to his side and cleared her throat, obviously trying to get his attention. "It's so strange that I was reading your ancestor's poetry just last night and then today *you* walk into my house."

"Hmm." Purposely not meeting her gaze, he tried again to focus on the architecture of the room. The poet had always been a sore spot with him. As a child, he'd been disgusted that the one famous person in his family had gotten that way writing sissy love poems. These days his opinion hadn't changed much. He'd recently tried reading some of old Geoff's work again and found it nauseating—especially after his experience with Karen. At the moment he wasn't too enthusiastic about love.

"Do you feel a draft?" Lara rubbed her bare upper arms.

"Maybe a slight one." He frowned. "That's strange. When I ran outside, it seemed to have warmed up again."

She hesitated, then shrugged. "Anyway, I mentioned earlier how much I love Geoffrey Vereker's poems. You must be very proud to be related to him."

He made no comment.

"The vivid imagery he uses is what grabs me," she went on. "For me, reading his poetry is something like what we were saying about reading old letters—not like going back in time in this case but stepping into another world for a moment."

She obviously didn't realize her effusions were wasted on him, but he wasn't about to tell her. He had no desire to dally here arguing with her about what constituted worthwhile reading. Her love of trite poetry only convinced him more thoroughly that she must be a bit of a flake.

Glancing around, he said, "Well, I guess I've seen most of the parlor. Shall we move on to another area?"

"Oh. Sure." She went to one of the window seats and retrieved her iced tea. Her legs were slender and beautifully shaped—but he forced his thoughts on what she was doing. He noted that the padded surface of the seat didn't seem like the safest place to keep a drink. If she spilled sugary tea all over the antique wood, she'd have a real mess to deal with.

He turned toward the back of the room, where a set of pocket doors stood partly open. "Do those lead to a second parlor?"

"Yes, and that's the scene of my master plan." She darted in front of him and gave him a wide grin. "My ex's family always used this next room as a library. Unlike in here, most of the wood is painted with a thick caramel-like stuff that sucks up light like a sponge. But I plan to open up the space and convert it into a *real* art studio. Right now it serves as a makeshift version."

"Open it up?" The phrase put him on the alert. He wondered if she wanted to knock out any walls—not always a good idea in a house this old.

"Wait till you see what I have in mind."

Grabbing hold of one of the pocket doors, she put all of her sparse weight into pulling it the rest of the way open. She smiled again. "Come on through to the studio."

He followed her into the second parlor, where she motioned for him to join her at a large drawing table. As she rushed to push aside strewn layout papers and art books, he looked around the room, shocked by the mess.

Aside from the table and two wooden stools in front of it, the main furnishing was a large red couch, not old enough to be called antique but enough to have grown shabby. A scarred end table beside it held a lamp that also had seen better days. Two of the walls sported built-in bookcases coated with the dark varnish she'd complained about. About half the shelves held books, while the remainder overflowed with tubes of paint and other art supplies.

On the far wall a pair of floor-to-ceiling windows stripped of treatments allowed sunlight to fall on an easel and a cluster of canvases, the visible ones primed but unworked. Stained drop cloths littered the floor, and occasional streaks of pigment had escaped onto the light-and-dark parquet.

He could feel his blood pressure rising as he took in the disorder. Such a great house deserved far better care.

A familiar odor drifted to his nose, and he sniffed at the air. Recognizing the smell, he scowled. "You're not using linseed oil in here, are you?"

She nodded. "I usually work in acrylics, but at the moment I'm also doing an oil painting. I figure I have plenty of time with the summer off from teaching."

"My God, you could burn the place down." He stooped and gathered up the rags. A year ago one of the most impressive houses in town had burnt to the ground in a fire that started due to the same sort of debris. "Linseed oil can heat spontaneously. You can't leave these lying around."

"Don't worry." Frowning, she took the rags from him and set them on the corner of the drawing table. "I know enough to dispose properly of oily rags, but I was in the middle of using these when you came to the door."

He glanced around the room again. "Where's the painting you were working on?"

"I have it in the closet at the moment."

"That doesn't seem like a good place to keep it."

She clenched her teeth. "I'll take it out when you and I are finished with our interview."

He didn't care if he was annoying her. She obviously didn't understand the value of a house like this, not only materially but historically. And if she didn't see the light after living here for five years, he doubted he could explain it to her. Closing his eyes, he took his notepad and pen into one hand so he could massage his temples with the other.

"What is it—headache?" she asked. "I may have something I can give you."

"No, thank you," he snapped. He tossed his things onto the area of the drawing table that she'd cleared. "Can we sit down and talk about your ideas for the room?"

She blinked at him but eventually took a seat.

As he pulled out the other stool she slid a sketchbook from a corner of the table into the center. Her arm brushed up against his, and his skin tingled.

He nudged away, bothered that he could still be attracted to her now that he'd seen how careless she was. Again he was reminded of Karen. As far as his ex had been concerned, her interior decorating took precedence over any practical considerations—and in the end, she'd used the same lack of logic in personal decisions. From what he'd seen today he gathered that Lara Peale was cut from the same cloth.

"Since you don't feel well, I'll get straight to the point." She flipped through her book to a draft of a floor plan. "Though the windows in here are large, the dark wood neutralizes the light. To make the room suitable for a studio, I'll need virtually a whole wall of glass. What I plan is to knock out the outside wall, build a small addition, and line the new wall with French doors. Since the roof over the addition will jut out from the house, I'll install skylights, too. Wait— I've got sketches of how I expect the end result to look."

As she began searching through the pages again, he held up a hand to stop her. "Don't bother. I'll tell you right now that you can't knock out an exterior wall. Frankly, I'm shocked you'd want to. Would you really sacrifice two original pocket windows for cheap contemporary doors?"

She pursed her lips. "I admit I had reservations, but, all considered, the need for serviceability won out. I'm not going to throw out the original windows. I thought I'd use them for something else."

"Like when you've torn down a wall in some other part of the house?" He couldn't prevent a note of scorn from seeping into his voice.

"Yes." She stared at him for another moment, then looked down and snapped her sketchbook shut. "Well . . . you sound firm in your disapproval of the studio wall—the biggest of my ideas. Does that mean if I decide to go ahead with the plan, you won't recommend me for the grant?"

"You *can't* go ahead with the plan."

Her focus shot back to his face, her blue eyes huge with apparent disbelief.

"Lara, this house is listed on the National Registry of Historic Places. The whole block is, in fact. You're not *permitted* to change the facade. Since this is a corner lot, that wall faces a street, which makes it particularly important. I'm afraid you'll have to limit your ideas to restoration and decoration."

"Restoration and decoration?" She scrunched up her nose. "The place will look the same as it always has."

"The same as it was *intended,* actually—with all the original splendor restored."

"That's not enough." She sprang from her stool, revealing—much as he had feared—an artist's temperament. "I need *change*."

"There are plenty of things you can change in here. You could paint, install carpeting, even refinish the wood." He got up and walked to the bookcases along the back wall. "Stripping these would do a lot to lighten the room."

"Not enough." Crossing her arms over her chest, she paced away from him, then turned back. "Look, it's clear that we can't work together on this. I'm sorry I wasted your time. Forget about the grant."

"Your getting the grant is almost a sure thing. This house would make an excellent investment for the society."

"But only if I don't build the addition?" She tapped her foot on the hardwood floor.

"You *can't* build the addition, with or without us." He gave her a hard look. "You're not thinking of going ahead with the idea anyway?"

"That's no concern of yours."

"The local historical board has set guidelines for what can and cannot be done—"

"This house is *mine*," she interrupted. "The historical board owns no part of it. They—or you, for that matter—have no say in what I do."

He twisted his mouth, disappointed in himself. He should have approached this matter with more tact. At this rate she would never see his point. Adopting a tone of patience, he said, "Lara, I know you must understand that this house has historical significance, or you wouldn't have contacted the society in the first place."

"I've changed my mind about that." She reached into the pocket of her shorts and drew out his card, glancing at the front. "Mark *Vereker*. I can't believe you're related to that wonderful poet."

He snorted. *What nonsense.* He didn't live up to that hack? For her to say so without reading a single chapter of his books proved how rash she was.

She held the card out to him. "Your ancestor would be ashamed of you. You have no vision whatsoever."

Heat accumulated under his collar. He snatched the card away from her. "Well, I'd choose taste over vision any day—and if you consider old Geoff's maudlin clichés visionary, that's just an example of your lack of taste."

As he pulled back his arm, his elbow hit the bookcase behind him. Though he barely jarred it, a book dropped from a high shelf and skimmed his head. Startled, he fell against the case with a thud. The case pivoted and ground along the floor, and he landed beside it on his rear end.

A hole had opened up in the wall—no, not a hole but an entrance. Unhurt but stunned, he lay sprawled, staring into the doorway to an unlit hidden chamber. Cold air drifted out of it, adding an eerie quality to the discovery.

"Oh, my God." Lara stooped next to him. "Are you all right?"

He pushed himself up into a sitting position, his attention anchored on the exposed opening in the wall. Peering into the darkness, he asked, "What is this?"

Lara stood slowly and took a step backward as though she expected a monster to jump out and attack them. "I don't know. I always thought the kitchen stairs were right behind that wall."

He hoisted himself to his feet and brushed off the seat of his pants. Leaning through the doorway, he said, "It's pitch-black in here, though judging by the echo, there's a fair amount of space. Amazing—we've found a secret room. Do you have a flashlight?"

"Not on me." She hesitated. "Mr. Vereker—as long as you're not hurt—I believe you were about to leave."

"Well, I wouldn't mind a chance to see what's in here." He turned around and found no encouragement in her expression. Somewhat daunted, he added, "Even in my business, I don't run across hidden rooms every day."

She glanced toward the opening, rubbing her upper arms. "Why is it so cold in there? Do you feel that horrible chill?"

He shrugged. "Maybe it leads to a cellar or tunnel—which is why I don't want to walk in without a light. Who knows what the footing is like? You must have a flashlight around here. Why don't you go and get it?"

"Why don't *you* just *go*?" she threw back.

He frowned. "You don't really mean that, do you?"

"I'm afraid that I do." She pursed her lips. "You

should be glad that you won't need to spend any more time putting up with me and my terrible *lack of taste*. As I told you, I'm withdrawing my application for the grant. Now, I'm sorry about your head. I must have left that book sticking out when I put it back this morning."

She bent to pick it up, and he glanced at the cover. To add insult to injury, the book that had hit him was a volume of Geoffrey Vereker's poetry.

Straightening back up, she looked him in the eye. "As long as you're not hurt, I have to insist that you go."

He matched her gaze for a long moment. "Listen, Lara, I know we have our differences, but can't you look past them for five minutes and give me a chance to explore something as extraordinary as this?"

"I'm afraid not. I'm too busy to waste another five minutes of my time."

He looked away from her to the dark entrance next to him. The opportunity for him to glimpse inside was slipping away, but if she didn't want him around, there wasn't much he could do. Now he wished more than ever that he'd presented his views about her house more diplomatically.

Racking his brain, he came up with a last-ditch attempt to change her mind. "You know, going in there by yourself after I leave could be dangerous. Even if the footing looks all right, the floorboards may be half rotted. You really should have someone with you when you investigate."

She glanced at the hole and quickly looked away. "I'm not going to investigate—not now anyway."

"What?" he asked in disbelief. "You're not *dying* to see what's in there?"

"Frankly, the only thing I'm dying for is some time to myself. I have a painting to get back to—and a lot of work and planning to do regarding my house."

He shook his head, frustrated by her attitude. "Instead of coming up with so many plans for this house, maybe you should take some time to appreciate it. Your lack of interest is unbelievable."

Her jaw dropped. "As is your interference in my business."

"Do you know what I would give to have an opportunity like this of my own, what I'd give just to have my parents' house back *without* any secret rooms? If this place had been passed down to you from your parents or grandparents, maybe you'd understand. But no, this beautiful home simply landed in your lap. You say your ex's family never changed a thing here. What would they think of your recklessness now? Don't you care about anyone else's feelings?"

She let out a humorless laugh. "Oh, now you're on very thin ice. You have no idea what you're talking about."

"But I do. I've seen how careless people can be."

"Have you? Well, I've seen a lot of things, too." She strode to the drawing table and picked up his notepad and pen, holding them out to him. "Here. Now get out of my house."

The anger in her eyes convinced him he'd said enough—probably too much. *How* did *she end up with this house?* he wondered . . . but now wasn't a good time to ask. He took his belongings from her and stashed them inside his jacket. Being thrown out of someone's house was a new experience for him, and he didn't know what to say.

"Okay, then," he muttered. "Good-bye."

He walked out of the studio without looking back, leaving her amid the mess of art supplies and smelly rags.

Geoffrey Vereker smirked to himself. As far as he was concerned, the encounter between the mortals couldn't have come to a more perfect conclusion. The little he'd seen of his descendant had done nothing to impress him. The man had denigrated both Geoff's poetry and his current favorite, Lara. Knocking a volume of his own work onto the fool's head had brought him some pleasure, but this altercation meant far more to him. Now he had Lara all to himself again . . . at least until she met another earthbound man.

He watched Mark walk out to his motorized carriage and climb inside. As the mortal started up the engine, he looked back at the house one last time, and Geoff followed his gaze.

Lara's face appeared at the window of the front door. The next second the curtain closed.

The ghost frowned to himself. He looked back at his descendant, who dropped his gaze, his brow furrowing.

Could it be that he has an inkling of what a fool he's been? The comments Mark had made about Lara's apathy had indeed gone beyond the pale. From what Geoff had overheard when her former husband left, the man had spent his days lazing about while she went out to win the bread—so much for maintaining his treasured family home and caring about his heritage.

True, Lara's plans for the house were misguided, but what did Mark expect from a member of the impractical gender? A man was meant to guide a woman, not insult her, as he had done. Perhaps her disinterest in the hidden room had been somewhat surprising, too—but not what one could call *uncaring*. Geoff, too, had wondered what was in there, but not enough to look for himself. Something about the room disturbed him, just as it seemed to unnerve her.

While the ghost floated above, anxious for his descendant to leave, Mark spent another moment looking back toward the house. Surely the man wasn't contemplating an apology!

Go home, Geoff tried to will him, *go home.* But his thoughts didn't seem to affect the mortal.

After what seemed like ages, Mark finally looked ahead at the road and drove the carriage away.

Geoff breathed a sigh of relief. Fortunately for him, his good-for-nothing descendant didn't know when to eat his words. He only hoped the fellow had as little conscience—and taste in women—as he appeared to. If the ghost had his way, he would never see Mark Vereker again.

Chapter 3

THE NEXT MORNING Lara slipped into a tank top and a pair of tattered cutoff jeans. The outfit was as atrocious as the one she'd worn the day before, but she didn't care. She wasn't likely to get another surprise visit today—in any case, not from anyone in the historical society. After the send-off she'd given Mark Vereker yesterday neither he nor his colleagues would ever drop in again.

The phone rang, startling her. The first thought she had was of Mark—but only because he'd been on her mind. She walked to the nightstand where she kept the phone and waited for the second ring before she picked up the receiver.

"Hello?"

"Hi!" a woman's voice greeted her.

"Oh, hi, Diane." She let her body relax. Of course it wasn't Mark.

"Listen—I'm on my way to work," her friend blurted, "so I can only talk for a minute, but I've got a proposition for you."

Lara rolled her eyes. She braced herself for one of Diane's blind-date recommendations. "What sort of proposition?"

"How about a week in Cape Hatteras in a beautiful house on the beach?" Despite her hurry, Di spared a second for a dramatic pause. "Jerry's brother and his wife rented the place with another family, but now the other people have backed out. We're heading down next Sunday, but there's still an extra bedroom available. We wondered if you'd want to come."

A vacation on her own with two couples didn't sound ideal to her. "Thanks, but, as you know, I've earmarked all my time and money this summer for art and renovations on the house."

"A week isn't much time to spare, and you won't need to spend a dime on accommodations. Jerry and I will treat you. If you don't come, we'll be paying for half of the house rental anyway."

"That's very generous, but—"

"Not really. I'll enjoy myself more with you there. The guys will probably be out fishing a lot of the time. I'll need you around to keep me company."

Lara knew the men would be on hand enough of the time to make her very conscious of being the only single one there. "I appreciate the offer, but I'd really rather get some work done here. You'll have your sister-in-law to hang out with."

"Well . . . I don't want to twist your arm." Di hesitated. "You sound kind of down today. Is everything all right?"

"Yeah, I'm just ticked off because of an encounter I had with some guy yesterday."

"Really?" Her friend's tone perked up immediately. "What guy? A *good-looking* one?"

"Well, yes—but that doesn't matter." Lara gave her an abridged account of what had happened. She ended it complaining, "The nerve of him nitpicking over my paint rags and practically *forbidding* me to go through with my plans! I almost felt like Ron was back in the house, ordering me around."

Di took a moment to absorb the story. In a quieter tone, she said, "It's a shame the guy was rude, but are you sure he doesn't have a point—about the National Registry, I mean? Maybe there are other ways to improve your studio without knocking out that wall."

Lara sighed, acknowledging an issue she'd been avoiding since Mark had brought it up. "I may have to think about that—but you know how much this project means to me. Anyway, I'd better let you go. Aren't you supposed to be in the store by ten?"

"Yes, and they're not going to be thrilled when I ask them for a last-minute vacation, either. I'll talk to you before we leave for Hatteras."

They made their good-byes quick. Lara hung up and sat on the bed, thinking about the point Di had made. She suspected that part of the reason she'd been so mad at Mark was because some of his arguments made sense, as much as she didn't like them. But to give up on expanding the studio seemed out of the question. If she only redecorated, the space would still be inadequate. Besides, the new studio sort of symbolized her new start in life.

Unsure what to think, she settled for deferring her final decision. Without the grant she couldn't afford to do the work yet, anyway.

She went downstairs to get started painting before eating breakfast. Remembering the secret room, she stopped outside the studio door. She wished she didn't know it was there. Pitch-black and unnaturally cold, the place gave her the creeps. She didn't like that her house had kept a secret from her all these years—more than one secret, actually. That letter stuck in the parlor window had made her feel funny, too.

Nevertheless, she wasn't about to let irrational fears keep her from getting any work done. If she wanted to be independent she couldn't cower in her own house.

Swallowing her fear, she stepped inside the studio. Her gaze automatically shot to the secret entrance. After Mark had left she'd been too uncomfortable to go near the bookcase and try to move it back into place.

She drifted slowly toward the rear of the room, trying not to let her gaze stray to the open entrance. Unfortunately that didn't stop her from feeling the chilly draft seeping out again.

Backtracking back a few feet, she stared at the black gap and bit her lip. Despite herself she couldn't help believing that something creepy lurked in there.

She took a deep breath and walked closer to the entrance. Instead of looking inside, she gave the bookcase the hardest shove she could and reduced the opening by about half. After a few seconds of recovery she pushed again, this time closing up most of the hole.

On her third try, the case caught on the jamb. Though she struggled to force it completely shut, her feet slid out from under her. The heavy door wouldn't budge.

Breathing hard with the effort, she took a step backward and rubbed her arms. "Damn, it's cold in there. I don't like that."

A sudden pounding noise made her jump.

She clapped one hand over her heart and closed her eyes. Someone was at the front door again.

Letting out her breath, she hurried through to the parlor, more eager than usual to receive company. Today she would gladly do without the seclusion she normally enjoyed.

When she opened the door she found herself face-to-face with Mark Vereker. Dressed in casual pants and a polo shirt, he looked more at ease than he had the day before—and even more handsome, too.

"Hello, Lara." He gave her one of his halfhearted smiles.

She leaned against the door and crossed her arms over her chest. "Forget something yesterday?"

"I deserve that cool greeting," he said without missing a beat. Despite her annoyance with him, his chocolate-drop eyes appealed to her. The steadiness of his gaze made him look the picture of sincerity.

"As a matter of fact, I did forget something." He kept his focus glued on her. "Diplomacy. I came by to apologize."

A softness in his tone made her think he meant what he said, but she didn't quite trust her judgment. As much as she'd tried to build independence in the last six months, part of her still longed for attention from a man. Her ex-husband had rarely given her much. On top of that, she couldn't deny she was attracted to

Mark, despite his lack of "diplomacy." If she didn't watch herself, she might find herself forgiving him.

She frowned. "I hope you haven't come to try to tell me again what I can and can't do with my house."

He shook his head. "Not at all. What I want is to try to undo the damage I did yesterday. I can't pretend that you and I are in agreement, Lara, but I don't want you to think I'm a complete jerk."

"And why should you care what I think?"

"For one thing, I'm a history buff and you have a fascinating old house. I'm especially intrigued by that secret room of yours." A hint of a grin tweaked his face, slight but with an amazing effect. All at once he looked impish and overwhelmingly appealing, like the type of guy she would have fallen for in high school.

Determined to escape his spell, she pretended to be engrossed by a butterfly that landed on his foot. She noticed that the dock shoes he was wearing were slightly scuffed. Today she didn't feel so self-conscious next to him in her paint-stained clothes.

Her gaze wandered up to his shirt. The short sleeves revealed a pair of well-proportioned arms.

She forced her focus back to his face and rewound to what he was saying. He recognized that he'd been overbearing yesterday. She suspected that she hadn't been entirely reasonable either—not that she was going to admit it. But it might be better not to burn her bridges with the historical society yet, in case she came up with another plan for the studio that they would find palatable.

"Okay," she said. "I mean, apology accepted."

He looked surprised, then his grin deepened. "I was hoping you'd say that. In fact, if you have a minute, I have a little token of friendship I'd like to give you. It's right out in the car. I'll get it."

"That's not necess—" she started, but he was already running down the front steps and out to the street.

As he went around to the far side of the car, she stepped onto the porch and let the screen door close behind her. When he came up the walk again he held a large briefcase, stuffed to capacity. He climbed to the porch, looking downward. Finally he opened the briefcase and pulled out a large book. "I brought you a copy of my latest."

"Oh . . . I couldn't." Almost against her will, her gaze slid to the cover photo, a shot of a gorgeous gingerbread Victorian house. "Thank you, but I can get my own copy. I intended to already."

"*This* is your copy. See?" He opened to the title page, where she glimpsed her name scrawled in a masculine hand. Before she could read any further, he snapped the book shut. "Now you have to accept it."

She didn't know whether to feel pleased or bribed. "I . . . I'm not sure what to say. You shouldn't have."

He shrugged. "It's nothing. But I hope some of the houses in it will appeal to your artistic sense. After you've had a look, I'd like to hear your impressions."

"Well, okay. Thank you." She broke down and smiled. Taking the book from him, she resisted the urge to open it back up and read the inscription. "Would you like to come in? I could make some coffee."

"I don't often turn down coffee in the morning."

She held the door open for him. "This will give you a chance to see a little more of the house—not that the kitchen is much to look at. I'd better warn you that it was remodeled in the nineteen-fifties and remains in that decade to this day."

Leading him through the main hall, she purposely hurried past the studio. He lagged behind a little, taking in the decor, but when she stopped at the kitchen door to wait for him he quickened his pace and caught up.

"Have a seat." She nodded toward the dinette set, a metal-rimmed relic she'd picked up at a yard sale. While he sat down, she set his book on the table, which, luckily, was clean this morning. Opening the refrigerator, she pulled out a container of ground coffee. "Maybe you and I can agree on this room. Pretty hideous, isn't it?"

He glanced over the straight white rows of cabinets and the worn linoleum floor. Focusing on two large windows on the outside wall, he said, "There's plenty of space and light."

"True." She pressed a filter into the coffeemaker. "It has all the warmth of an emergency room."

"I wonder what's under the linoleum." He tapped his foot. "The construction is really solid. Even if the material's in bad shape, it might be an improvement over this."

She paused between scoops of coffee to look down. "You might have something there. I'll rip it up this afternoon."

"Are you serious?"

"Whatever's underneath can't look worse than this. I'd start the job right now, but my matte knife is dull. I need to buy some new blades."

"I think I have a utility knife." He leaned down to open his briefcase. The bag was so full he could barely squeeze his hand inside. He pulled out a fat white envelope and set it on the table next to his book, then tried again.

Surprised, she watched him rummaging. She hadn't taken him for the spontaneous type. From what she'd seen the day before, he fought change tooth and nail—like Ron.

She frowned to herself and switched on the coffeemaker. First he brought her a gift, now he was jumping at her whim. She couldn't help but suspect he was trying to get on her good side so she'd change her mind about the studio.

"Here it is." He pulled a utility knife from the bag and slid out the blade. "Do you think this will work?"

"As long as the blade hasn't been used too much. Are you sure you don't mind lending it to me?" She made a wry face. "I might return it to you dull."

"Actually, I thought I'd start the job for you now—if you really do want to rip up the floor." He lifted his brows in an unspoken question.

She stared at him, not sure how to interpret this. If he was trying to indulge her, she wondered how far he'd take the game. She waved the back of her hand over the linoleum. "By all means, take a stab at it."

As the coffeemaker began to trickle and fill the room with the aroma of a Sumatra brew, he walked to the outside wall and stooped near the corner. She stepped up behind him and peeked over his shoulders, momentarily distracted by the V shape of his back, a form Michelangelo could have sculpted.

He slit into the linoleum and peered under the corner. Until that moment she hadn't quite believed he would do it.

"There's another layer," he said over his shoulder.

"Cut it."

Now that she knew he meant business, her curiosity kicked in. As he bent forward a second time, she shifted along with him. She could feel the heat of his cotton-covered thigh next to her bare shin.

He pulled the first layer back, revealing an even uglier pattern below. Cutting a small slice into it, he wrested the corner loose and yanked it. Only after the third layer did he reach the bottom. Leaning closer, she got her first peek at the original brickwork floor.

"Wow." She squatted next to him for a better look.

"Nice." He turned to her and smiled. "Are you sure you want to get rid of the linoleum? If I cut much more, we won't be able to put it back down."

"Oh, please." She laughed. "Slice away."

He turned back a large portion of the first layer, using the knife whenever a spot got sticky. Together, they rolled the piece back across the room until the dinette set got in the way.

"Can we move this?" he asked, nodding toward the table. "Or will it be too heavy for you?"

Having struggled with it before, she knew exactly what effort the move would take. "I could handle one end, but it would be asking too much of you. You didn't come here expecting to take on a home improvement project."

"How do you know?" He grinned and stepped to the far end of the table. "Can you get that side?"

Realizing she wouldn't be able to do the job on her own, she decided to accept his help. But his comment made her wonder what he *had* come expecting. As they struggled with the heavy piece, the envelope he'd left on it caught her eye.

"What's in the package?" she asked between grunts.

"My new manuscript." He shuffled backward into

the empty adjoining dining room. They set down the table, and he brushed his hands together. "Actually, I was hoping you'd take a look at it . . . and consider letting me include your house."

Learning that he had a second reason for coming doubled her suspicions. She should have known that the urge to apologize wouldn't have been enough to bring him back. Now she saw his real purpose, hidden within this proposal. His books had a historical slant, so he would ask her to put off renovating until after his photo shoot.

She dodged his gaze. Though she understood his concerns about the house, she didn't like his attempts to pressure or charm her into changing her views. He had no idea what her plans for that room meant to her. That room, more than any other, exemplified her ex-husband's stubbornness. Though Ron had designated it her work space, he'd never even allowed her to put a drawing table in it. With him gone now, she wanted a full-fledged studio—and she was going to have it, one way or another.

Starting back toward the kitchen, she said, "I'm sorry. I can't see it working."

"Why not?"

She went to the coffeemaker and poured two cups, listening to his footsteps as he followed. "You and I don't have the same vision for this house. A project like that would cause a lot of tension I'd rather avoid. . . . Milk and sugar?"

While she opened the refrigerator, silence loomed. She grabbed the milk and turned around to face him.

His eyes looked big and sad, like a lost little boy's, and she felt a pang of regret. As an artist she loved to share beauty, and she knew her house had potential for a lot.

"Both, please," he said.

Apparently he couldn't deny that they would have problems working together. She fixed his coffee and handed it to him. Picking up her own mug, she sat down on one of the dinette chairs, now stranded without a table.

He took the seat opposite her. "There's another reason I stopped by."

"Yet another? They're beginning to add up."

His mouth tugged at the corners, and he looked down into his mug. "I've been wondering ever since I left here yesterday about the secret room. Were you able to get around to exploring it?"

"Oh, that." She felt herself stiffen and tried to hide her reaction by sipping her coffee. "No, I wasn't. I was caught up in work all day yesterday."

He raised his eyebrows. "I'm shocked. I thought for sure that once you'd had time to get over our, um, disagreement, you'd change your mind about taking a peek."

Her face felt numb, as if the blood had drained from it. She couldn't come up with a response.

"Look," he said. "If you're worried about spiders or mice, I'd be glad to check it out for you. I have a camping lantern out in the car today. I brought it just in case the opportunity arose."

His offer tempted her. Finding out what the room held might help her get over her silly fears. But she didn't like the idea of his taking on the role of big man, braver than her, protective of her, knowing what's best. Put in a position of dependence, she might end up being influenced in other areas—like in her plans for the house. Her freedom from Ron had been hard-won, and she wanted to guard every shred.

She got up and stepped to the counter to add milk to her coffee. "It's not that. I just . . . I don't have the time today either."

"You don't have a couple of minutes to look around?"

"You know very well it would take more than a couple minutes." To avoid his gaze, she watched herself stirring. "I mean, probably. Just moving the bookcase back out could be a struggle."

"It wasn't yesterday."

"Yes, but you almost got hurt when you triggered the door." She lifted her mug and peered over the rim at him. "What if something like that happens again? That book seemed to fall out of nowhere onto your head. Who knows what other accidents are waiting to happen behind the bookcase?"

He studied her for a long moment. "I don't understand why you're so reluctant. There's probably nothing back there but an empty room."

"In which case we'll have wasted our time, something I can't afford to do. I have a lot of work around here, and now we've started another project on top of everything." She gestured toward the floor. "I can't leave the kitchen like this. I'm going to have to spend the rest of the day ripping up linoleum."

"It's really not that big of a job. Don't forget you have me to help."

"You've already done too much."

"I've hardly done anything—"

"Yes, you have." She set down her coffee and finally met his gaze straight on. "Look, Mark, you came over here with an autographed book for me; you of-

fered to feature my house in your next one; you even
helped me start tearing up my kitchen floor. That adds
up to 'too much.' I don't want to feel obligated to you,
like I need to change my plans for the studio because
I *owe* you or something."

"That's absurd." His eyebrows crunched together.
"I'm not trying to build up a debt for you—as if that
were possible. I may have hoped my book would give
you alternate ideas, but I certainly didn't think it
would *oblige* you to change your mind. The same goes
for including your house in my new manuscript. And I
helped with the floor because I wanted to see what was
beneath it, the same way I want to see what's in the secret room."

He looked her in the eye, apparently telling the
truth, but she wasn't sure it made a difference. She
chewed on her lip. "I don't know. Maybe another
time."

"I don't believe this. Aren't you even the least bit
curious?"

She shrugged. "I have other things on my mind. I
appreciate your offer to help—I really do—but I just
wouldn't be comfortable accepting it."

"Well . . . if that's how you feel, there's nothing I
can do about it." He got up and went to the sink. Setting his mug down on the drain board, he turned back
to look at her. "I guess I'd better go and let you get
back to your projects."

She drew in a deep breath and exhaled. "I'll tell you
what: when I get time to check out the room, I'll call
you and let you know what I find."

"I suppose if I can't explore it with you, I'll have to
be satisfied with that." He went back to his chair and
picked up his briefcase, reaching inside. "I'll give you

my card again. But if you change your mind about letting me help, please let me know. You'd be doing *me* a favor."

Taking the card, she set it down on the counter. She wished she didn't have to disappoint him, but the fact that she felt so sensitive to his response reminded her to be cautious. The man made her feel vulnerable. "We'll see. I can't promise anything."

A hint of a frown creased his forehead. "No, of course not."

Looking away from her, he fiddled with some papers in his briefcase and tried to stretch the buckle far enough to latch it closed. The effort was clearly hopeless.

"Is something the matter?" she asked.

He shook his head. Giving up on the briefcase, he grabbed it by the handles. "Something you said just reminded me of something."

"What did I say?"

"Don't worry about it," he said—but the mood between them had definitely changed. He turned toward the hallway and strode out of the room.

She followed him to the front door, hurrying to keep up. What had she said to make him go cold? Her only guess was that a combination of all the strife between them had gotten to him. And, of course, his plan to bribe and charm her hadn't gone exactly as he'd hoped.

He opened the door himself, stopping at the threshold to face her. "There's one thing about you I don't understand, Lara. You call yourself an artist—and judging by the way you announced your profession yesterday, you seem to take pride in your field. But you have this beautiful house, and you can't seem to see the art in it. I'm not just talking about your plans for the studio. You're not even curious about the secret room. Is that the way you would want your work to be viewed?"

She stared at him, too astonished to speak. On one hand, he seemed to have a point—but a house wasn't a work of art, not essentially. A house was built for shelter. Aesthetics played a secondary role.

Before she could form an answer, he pushed through the front door and darted down the porch steps.

As she watched him get into the car, her shock gelled into irritation. Whatever his point, who was he to criticize her—to try to tell *her* about art? His sudden lecture for her was nothing more than sour grapes. She hadn't given him his way, so he wanted to get back at her.

With all of this alternating cajoling and jabbing, he was as controlling as Ron, though in a less obvious way. Well, she wouldn't let either of them compromise her dreams. Maybe she could get a loan to renovate her studio. Today was Saturday, but she had a good mind to apply for a building permit Monday morning as soon as the town offices opened.

Turning away from the door, she swept back through the hall. This time if he looked up as he drove off, he wouldn't catch her watching, the way he had the day before. She didn't care enough to watch him go.

When she reached the kitchen the sight of the floor hit her like a slap in the face. Why on earth had she started another project? If *he* hadn't come over, the stupid idea never would have occurred to her.

She sank into one of the dinette chairs and leaned

back, closing her eyes. Her one consolation was the thought that she'd probably never see Mark Vereker again. After the way he'd tried to manipulate her, she didn't care if she broke her promise to call him about the secret room.

When she opened her eyes, a glimpse of something white over in the dining room caught her attention. Beside the book Mark had given her, his manuscript lay, forgotten in his hurry to leave.

"Oh, no." She jumped up and ran to the front door. Naturally he had left.

Her shoulders slumped. She shook her head to herself, then retraced her way to the rear of the house.

Back in the dining room, she glared at the fat envelope. So much for not seeing him again. She wasn't about to lift a finger to return the manuscript—but she had an idea he might feel differently about getting it back.

Chapter 4

By THE TIME Lara got up on Monday morning her anger had cooled, and she'd regained some of her sense. She still felt determined to build her studio the way she wanted to, but she wasn't eager to take out a big loan to do it. Her mortgage payments already kept her strapped for cash. In fact, she doubted a bank would even approve additional credit for her.

As she got dressed, she wondered if she could earn the extra money somehow—maybe get a summer job, like Di had with the clothes shop. But how much could a job like that earn her? It would probably take a lifetime of summer retail work to save up the sort of money she needed.

The phone rang, and she picked up the cordless receiver from her nightstand and pressed the button. "Hello."

"Hi, honey," her mother said at the other end of the line. Her voice sounded slightly edgy.

"Hi, Mom. What's wrong? You sound funny."

"Nothing much, but I've run out of my sinus prescription, and my head's killing me. Your father's working today, so I can't get to the drugstore. Is there any chance you could go for me?"

Her mother belonged to a rare breed of suburban women who didn't own a car. Growing up in the city she'd never needed one, and, after marrying and moving to the suburbs, she'd gotten her license but rarely drove. Lara couldn't imagine always being dependent on other people to take care of errands like this, but her mother claimed she was too nervous to deal with the stresses of traffic.

"Sure, Mom," she said. "I've got some other errands to run in town anyway. I'll pick it up and stop by your place in an hour or so."

"Thank you, dear. I'll make something for lunch."

"Okay. Sounds good."

After they hung up, Lara took her purse and fetched her checkbook from her desk so she could pay her property taxes. She'd been putting off the huge bill until the last minute, and now she would have to stop at Town Hall in person to pay before the deadline. Of course, the taxes were virtually going to wipe out her checking account.

She frowned. Maybe she would have to get a summer job just to make ends meet. *Forget trying to renovate the house.* The thought depressed her. Sometimes she felt like she *needed* a decent studio just to keep herself sane.

Twenty minutes later she was waiting for a receipt at the appropriate window in Town Hall when she noticed something on the felt board behind the clerk. This office also handled building-permit applications. Applying for hers seemed precipitous since she had no money for the renovations, but a stubborn streak in her swore she was going to get it. She *had* to. Maybe she'd play the lottery or appear on a game show and win the top prize. Maybe she'd borrow part of the cost from her parents. In any case, she'd find a way.

"Can I have an application for a building permit, too?" she asked the clerk.

"Sure," the woman said. She went to a file cabinet and came back with several sheets of paper, along with a clipboard and pen. "You can sit over in the waiting area to fill these out, then return them to me."

Lara sat down and trudged her way through the mercilessly long form. Near the end of the application she came to an oddly worded question she didn't understand. She went back to ask the clerk, but now another woman stood at the window chatting away with her, obviously a personal friend.

After a few interminable moments, the clerk looked past her friend's shoulder to Lara. "Are you ready to turn that in?"

"Actually, I have a question." With the other woman beside her practically breathing down her neck, Lara pointed out the section she didn't understand.

"Oh, you don't have to answer that," the clerk told her. "That's for office use. It looks like you're finished. Let me check for you."

Lara handed her the forms. While she waited for the clerk to look them over, she could feel the other woman's gaze on her. Uncomfortable, she avoided looking in that direction.

"Don't I know you from somewhere?" the woman finally asked her.

Lara turned to face her. Tall, slim, and attractive, she had stylishly short red hair and wore a sleek, dark-green business suit with a short skirt. Her catlike green eyes looked vaguely familiar. "Yes, I think so . . . but I'm not sure where we could have met."

"She's Lara Peale," the clerk interrupted. "She was married to Liz Sulley's cousin, Ron. You know Liz— my old high school friend."

Surprised, Lara looked back at the clerk, who didn't appear familiar at all. Sometimes the town of Falls Borough could be too small for comfort.

"You're right, Paula," said the redhead, and she turned toward Lara again. "Paula and I went to a New Year's party at Liz's a couple of years ago, and you and your husband were there. Do you remember us? I was wearing a long black dress."

"Oh, y-yes," she said, recalling the party but not her or the clerk specifically. "You're right. That's it."

"So you're divorced now? That's too bad."

"It happens," she said, not eager to discuss her personal life with a stranger.

"I see you got the house in the divorce," the clerk noted, still looking at the permit application. "I remember Ron had a big old Victorian. Lucky you. But why would you want to build an addition on that big place?"

"I have a room I want to expand," she said through clenched teeth. She got her checkbook back out of her purse. "I'm sorry, but I'm in a hurry. How much do I owe you?"

"Just the twenty-five dollar application fee for now.

You'll be billed for the rest if they approve your request."

"Is everything else in order?" Lara asked as she scribbled out a check for the sum.

"Ye-s . . ." she said, still reading the forms. "There is one thing, though. Maybe you should talk to the historical society about—"

"Thanks, but I already have." By this time all she wanted was to get away from the two busybodies. "Well, my phone number is on the application, so if there are any questions, I'm sure they'll call me. Thanks for your help."

Before either woman could ask another impertinent question or make an unwanted suggestion, Lara slid the check under the glass and turned to go. Catching the redhead's eye, she said, "Nice seeing you, er . . . I'm sorry. What was your name?"

"Karen."

"Right—Karen. Take care."

She walked away quickly. As she turned out of the office door, she heard the redhead say just within earshot, "What a bitch."

Lara snorted and shook her head to herself, moving on her way but inwardly steaming. The woman was probing her for information about her divorce—the most painful experience she'd ever gone through— and yet *she* was the one who was a bitch!

During her walk down the block to the drugstore she thought up half a dozen clever comebacks she wished she had shot back at the redhead. If she met one more nosy stranger this week, she'd tell them just where they could go!

*   *   *

When Mark got up that morning and saw sunlight streaming through his window, he decided to walk into town to the office-supply shop. Since he'd left his manuscript at Lara's the other day, he needed to print out a new copy, but he'd run out of paper. Going back to pick up the old one had crossed his mind, only to be dismissed. He and Lara continually rubbed each other the wrong way. Since he still had his computer files, he'd worked from them over the weekend.

He went downstairs to the main floor of his apartment, a place he loved because the building had been converted from an old schoolhouse. While he made coffee and fixed himself a bowl of cereal his final words to Lara replayed in his mind. In hindsight, he saw that he shouldn't have brought up her ex-husband's family. Alluding to her divorce had been a cheap shot. He'd gotten carried away, annoyed by her attitude about the secret room and further agitated when she'd used the phrase "I can't promise anything." Karen had said the same thing on more than one occasion when he'd tried to pinpoint where he stood with her. Shortly after the final time, she'd broken up with him. She'd said she needed time to get over her divorce before she could handle another relationship.

A week later she was back with her ex.

As he sat down to eat, he wondered if he'd been extra hard on Lara because she too was a divorcée—and an attractive one. She neither looked like Karen nor had her personality, but the few traits they had in common made him wary of her.

During his walk into town, Lara kept coming back to his mind. The inconsistencies in her personality bugged him. Her lack of appreciation for her home didn't seem to fit in with her chosen profession. He hadn't actually seen her paintings, but her well-used "studio" showed how much time she spent on her art. How could she have no talent or taste? Or was his attraction to her making him look for a way to believe there was more to her than there was? He really should have asked to see some of her paintings when he'd been at her place.

He reached the office-supply shop and picked up a package of paper, then dallied for a while. As he browsed the aisles the thought began to nag at him that he should use the manuscript he'd left at Lara's as an excuse to visit her again. If she had any sense of aesthetics at all, she had to be capable of seeing reason about her house. Maybe her problem with it boiled down to disliking the Victorian style—but if so, then why didn't she move somewhere else? And he still couldn't explain her indifference about the secret room.

His questions continued to bother him, and by the time he paid for the paper he'd resolved to go and see her again. The only thing he didn't know was when he'd feel up to facing her. He started for home, debating how soon he could stop by without being too much of a pest.

"Mark!" a familiar feminine voice called from behind him before he'd gone half a block.

Karen. Without looking, he knew it was her. For an instant he considered pretending he hadn't heard, but that would have been childish—and probably useless.

Slowly he turned around and saw her hurrying toward him. She looked clumsy mincing in her high heels and mini suit. The contrast of Lara's casual dress and graceful movements flashed in his mind. She seemed so much more down-to-earth than his ex. They really couldn't be much alike.

"Hi!" Puffing from the exertion, Karen smiled up at him. "I'm so glad I ran into you."

"Hello," he said, wondering why she wanted to talk to him at all. They hadn't had any contact in weeks, and he felt oddly detached from her, as if she'd become a stranger. Maybe he was finally coming to realize that he'd never truly known her in the first place.

"I was just visiting my friend Paula at Town Hall, and an interesting thing happened. By any chance, have you met a Lara Peale in connection with the historical society?"

He stared at her, startled. His surprise quickly evolved into annoyance that Karen hadn't even asked how he'd been doing. She'd dumped him less than two months ago, but she acted as though they were on perfectly friendly terms. "Yeah. Why—how do you know her?"

"Well, I met her briefly at a party a couple of years ago, but that's beside the point. She was in Paula's office just now, and she mentioned having talked to the historical society about her house." She pushed back her short-cropped, dyed-red hair, though every strand fell back into the exact same position. "Frankly, Paula and I thought she was lying to us. I had to check with you."

Had Lara complained about him? But what did it matter anyway? His impatience with Karen outweighed his curiosity. "Why do you even care, if you hardly know the woman?"

She raised an eyebrow. "You seem defensive. How well do *you* know her?"

He frowned. If he hadn't known better, he would

have sworn she was jealous—but that was ridiculous. "I've barely met her. As she apparently told you, she has business with the society. She applied for a grant for some work she's doing on her house."

"I see. That must be why she was applying for a building permit."

Lara had applied for her permit? Once again, he was stunned. Where had she gotten the money for the addition? He tried to hang on to the tiny bubble of hope he had for her house, telling himself that maybe she'd come up with another plan.

"Mark?" Karen interrupted his thoughts. "I was asking what you thought of her house."

"Oh, it's very nice—in good condition." He really had no desire to get into the topic with her. "I'm sorry. I can't stay and chat. I have an appointment in half an hour."

"Wait a minute," she said before he could get away. "If you're going to be working with that Lara Peale, there are a few things you should know about her. Paula was telling me that the woman's poor ex-husband lost his shirt to her in their divorce. Apparently, his family had owned their house for generations. Now it all belongs to her."

Of course he knew this, basically, but the remark struck a nerve with him, especially after the news he'd just heard. Lara's house really would have been better off in the hands of her ex . . . but why Karen thought she had to warn him about the situation was a mystery. What could *he* do about it?

"I'm not sure I see your point," he said.

She looked at her fingernails, glossy pink and an unlikely length. She seemed so artificial to him now; he no longer trusted her. "If you're interested in her, Mark, I'd think twice before getting involved. I mean,

I guess she's attractive, if you like the earthy type—
but she sounds like a gold digger."

He could hardly believe what he was hearing, considering the source. Karen, who had returned to a man
with a drinking problem and a tendency for compulsive
gambling, was now trying to advise *him* about rela-
tionships. He almost told her off but decided she
wasn't worth the energy.

Looking past her, he said, "As far as I can tell, the
only money Ms. Peale is after is a grant from the society to build an art studio—and, actually, she's probably withdrawing her application."

"An art studio?" She raised her thin eyebrows. "That
would be a commercial venture, wouldn't it? It's funny,
because the permit she applied for was residential."

The news surprised him, but he didn't know for sure
whether Lara sold her work or not. He wasn't even familiar enough with zoning laws to know how rigid
they were. If she sold a piece of art here or there, he
guessed it wouldn't matter, as long as she didn't run a
full-blown gallery on the property.

"I'll have to ask some of my friends on the zoning
board about it." Karen tapped her chin with her index
finger, a fake gem gleaming on the tip. "They might
want to look into the case. I guess the historical board
might give her some flak, too, considering her request
to tear down that outside wall."

So she *did* still plan to tear down the wall. It took all
his will not to react. How on earth had she come up
with so much money so quickly? Now it looked like it
was too late to talk to her again, like he'd been considering. After this, he definitely couldn't reason with
her calmly. The situation was hopeless, he realized.
Hopeless.

He looked down at his watch. "One o'clock. I'm sorry. I've got to go."

"Oh, no problem." She gave him a funny, twisted smile. "I have a new client to meet, anyway."

"Hope it goes well." Without ceremony, he turned away.

As he started up the street she called after him, "Keep in touch, Mark! I miss hearing from you."

"Yeah, right," he muttered to himself without looking back.

He fumed the whole way home. Karen's sticking her nose into his business was irritating enough, but Lara's recklessness really upset him. She couldn't even have taken a week to think over the points he'd made? No, she had to rush down to Town Hall today—even though she had so much to do she didn't have time to look at the room with him on Saturday. She had no problem coming into town and filling out all the forms required for a building permit!

When he got home he slammed the printer paper down on his desk. The bang made him cringe. Louder than he'd expected, it had probably given his neighbors a start.

Telling himself to relax, he went to the refrigerator and got himself a beer. At least he seemed to be getting over Karen. He could truthfully say that today she hadn't appealed to him in the least. She'd seemed so phony with her claims of missing him and her concerns about his involvement with Lara. He wondered if she was a little jealous. After all, how happy could she be reunited with that idiot she'd divorced?

He popped off the cap and took a swig, walking into the living room. His aggravation over Lara was harder to dismiss. She'd completely ignored his warnings. To think he'd spent the last two days going back over their conversations and trying to convince himself she might be more than a pretty face. Amazing what thinking with one's brain fixed below the belt could do for a man's intellect.

Planting himself in front of the TV, he noted that the whole mess could have been worse. If he hadn't found out so quickly how shallow Lara was, he might have done something truly stupid, like asking her out. For the first time he acknowledged that the idea had been in the back of his mind, as much as he'd denied it. What was wrong with him anyway?

He picked up the remote control, making a mental note to stay away from previously married women. What was that saying about used cars? *Why take on someone else's problems?*

None of it mattered, he thought with another gulp of beer, now that he saw Lara for what she was. Perhaps Karen's interfering had done some good.

He remembered his ex's musings about consulting the zoning board, and he felt a little funny. He was the one who'd let it slip that Lara intended to build a studio. As much as he opposed her plans, he didn't like the idea of being a rat.

A twinge of guilt nagged at him. Sighing, he slumped back on the couch. Maybe he'd pick up his manuscript after all and see if she brought up the subject of the house. If nothing else, visiting her again would give him one last shot at seeing the hidden room.

Meanwhile, Karen's inquiries would probably stall the processing of the permit. If he was really lucky, the zoning board would straighten Lara out, and he could forget about this whole mess.

Chapter 5

LARA DABBED ACRYLIC color onto a still-life painting of fruit, trying hard not to glance over her shoulder. She usually lost herself in her work, but lately she couldn't get past the feeling that someone—or some*thing*—was watching her.

Trying to capture the shadow of a pear, she took consolation in the fact that Di would be here for lunch any minute. Unfortunately she couldn't count on her friend to rescue her from her isolation every day, especially since Di would be going away to Cape Hatteras on Sunday.

Little prickles rose on the back of her neck. She spun around—naturally, no one else was in the studio. Everything looked normal except for the bookcase, still jutting out slightly from the wall. Since she couldn't get the damned thing back into place, she

wished she had the nerve to peek behind it. Maybe
then she could shake off the creepy feelings she'd
been having since discovering it.

She just couldn't bring herself to look.

Getting up, she started putting away her supplies in
order to break for lunch. She wondered if Ron might
know something about the secret room—not that she
would bother to ask him. If he hadn't known about it,
he'd only insist on taking a look. The last thing she
needed was her ex-husband at the house berating her
for the changes she'd made so far. For years her salary
had paid off *his* home equity loans, and he'd never
even given her a say in the decor. The fact that she
now held the deed wouldn't matter much to him either.

She went to the kitchen and put on a pot of coffee.
While she was making sandwiches, a soft rap came at
the back door. Looking up, she confirmed that it was
Di.

"Come on in." She reached over and undid the
latch.

"Hi," her friend said as she entered. She set her
purse down on the counter and pushed her long, dark
hair out of her eyes. "Hey, the floor looks great. When
you told me about the bricks, I imagined a bunch of
crumbling clay, but these are in really good shape."

"Yeah, a few of them could use replacing, but over-
all it's not bad."

"Not bad at all." Di walked into the center of the
room and looked around in all directions. "The kitchen
seems so much warmer. It's hard to believe that someone thought this should be covered up with a hideous
linoleum pattern."

"At least the material was easy to tear up." Lara

sliced the sandwiches and set them on plates. "Thanks for coming over today. How's the job going?"

"Okay." Her friend stepped up to the sink and retrieved two mugs from the dish rack, taking them to the coffeemaker. "The work's not exciting, but my discount should help me build up a decent wardrobe for school this fall."

They exchanged a few more pleasantries and carried their lunches into the dining room. Lara had never moved the table back into the kitchen, it being too heavy for her. Instead she'd dragged the dinette chairs across the hall so the whole set now stood there.

"What happened here?" Di asked, nodding toward Mark Vereker's manuscript, which lay spread over half of the table. Three days after he'd forgotten it, he still hadn't contacted her about it—not that she wanted him to.

"Oh, I'm sorry about the mess. This belongs to that guy from the historical society. Remember I told you he left his manuscript here the second time he stopped over?" She set her plate down at the clear end of the table. "My curiosity finally got the best of me, and I was looking at it this morning."

"Oh, right." Di took the place across from her. The signed copy of Mark's last book was also on the table, and she flipped it over to the back cover, looking at his picture. "Wait a minute, this is him—Mark Vereker?"

"Yeah, why?"

"I went to school with this guy!"

Lara laughed. "You're kidding."

"No. How strange. I guess I'm not surprised that he turned out to be a writer. He was a whiz in English class. I have to say he always seemed nice back then, too—not at all the ogre you describe." She looked more closely at the photo. "He's even better looking than he used to be. Are you sure he's as bad as you say?"

"I only told you what happened between us. You can judge for yourself." Lara bit into her sandwich.

"Well, maybe he's been under stress lately. He may have a tight deadline to meet or something. Who knows? Did you happen to find out if he's married?"

"Oh, please. He and I could barely say two words to each other without one of us flying off the handle."

Munching on her sandwich, Di skimmed through the bio beneath the photo. "There's no mention of a family here. I'll bet he's single."

Lara gave her a warning look. "Don't even start."

Her friend ignored her. "So, what did you think of his manuscript?"

"The part I read was pretty good," she admitted. "I got through the first chapter during breakfast, and I hated to stop. Instead of just listing the features of a house, he sort of sketches the life in it during the past. He made the story so interesting I felt like he'd swept me back in time."

"I remember our English teacher once trying to get him to submit a short story of his to a magazine." Di sipped her coffee. "He must be very talented."

"What a coincidence that you went to school with him—well, maybe not, in such a small town." Lara's peek at Mark's writing had made her wonder what more there was to him, but she didn't want to show too much curiosity. "You say he didn't seem like a hothead back then?"

"Not at all. He was a very sweet guy. I guess the pressures of the world have soured him, just like the rest of us." She grinned.

Though the comment was made jokingly, Lara thought it could be true. Preoccupied, she chewed on a bite of her sandwich. Certainly she herself was no longer the carefree girl she'd been ten years ago.

"I'll bet you just caught him during a couple of bad days," Di said. "I think you should make a play for him."

Lara barely managed to swallow. "You're crazy. He's arrogant and manipulative, and he's made it clear he thinks I'm irresponsible and apathetic. He obviously can't stand me, or he would have come back for his manuscript by now."

"Maybe he's afraid you don't want to see *him*."

"I don't."

Di picked up her mug and swirled her coffee around. "But you said you liked his writing, and I'm telling you he isn't really a bad guy. I'd think an artist and a writer would go well together—two creative types. Why don't you take the manuscript over to his place? Seeing him on his own turf may give you a different perspective."

Lara felt an unexpected tug of temptation. Mark's writing had already shown him in a different light. She would have liked to see that pensive, soulful side of him in person—but she wouldn't admit it to her friend. She shook her head. "No way."

They sat and chatted for another half hour, then Di had to run back to work.

After seeing her friend off, Lara returned to the dining room, and the manuscript caught her eye again. Putting off clearing the dishes, she took a seat and picked up where she'd left off that morning. Before long she had finished the second chapter. Mark's power of description intrigued her.

She straightened the papers carefully and slid them back into the envelope. She'd been wrong when she'd told him he had no vision. His imagination matched— or even beat—that of his ancestor.

The book he'd given her still lay where Di had left it. Recalling that she'd never read his inscription, she stretched her arm out across the surface and slid it toward her.

Opening to the title page, she read what he'd written:

> *Dear Lara,*
>
> *The reason I like writing so much is because it gives me time to* think *before I make a statement. If I could rewrite the words I spoke to you yesterday, I swear I'd come off sounding helpful instead of pompous. Since I can't, I can only apologize and hope you'll accept this book—my attempt to prove that I can be circumspect on occasion. If the writing does nothing for you, I hope at least the photos will appeal to your artistic sense.*
>
> *Sincerely,*
> *Mark*

She put her hand up to her mouth. The words seemed so sincere, but she wasn't sure if she was ready to excuse him, when his second visit to the house had ended as poorly as the first.

Getting up to clear the dishes, she thought about her own behavior toward him. Hadn't she been just as stubborn about her views as he had been about his? He had no way of knowing the studio meant so much to her. And his own feelings about his parents' house had probably made him react badly to her ideas.

After loading the dishwasher she went back to the studio, but the room felt cold and lonely. She'd had enough isolation for one day. Maybe her silly fears of being haunted were signals that she'd passed the stage of needing space after her divorce. Having a social life didn't sound quite so intimidating as it had six months ago. She wasn't exactly sure what she wanted, but she knew she had to get out of the house today.

Deciding to go for a drive, she headed for the bedroom to grab her purse. On her way to the kitchen stairs she spotted Mark's manuscript again. He'd made a gesture of apology to her after their first tiff; maybe this time it was her turn. Though she was tempted to read the whole thing before giving it back, this seemed like the perfect time to stop by his place.

She hunted through her organizer for his business card to see if his address was on it. It was, and she recognized the name of the apartment complex. The converted schoolhouse always caught her eye when she drove by.

Fifteen minutes later she entered the vestibule at the building and searched the names above the rows of mailboxes. M. VEREKER stood out quickly, and she pressed the buzzer above it.

After a minute the intercom speaker crackled to life. "Hello?"

His voice sounded gruff, as if he'd been interrupted. Until that moment she hadn't felt nervous. Maybe she hadn't thought he'd be home. Now that she had him on the intercom she wondered if he might be busy.

"Hi, Mark." She moistened her lips. "It's Lara Peale. I've got your manuscript."

The pause that followed made her bite her lip. *I never should have come.*

"Come up the stairs," he said finally. "Turn right at the top. I'll meet you in the hall."

So he wasn't going to ask her in. Feeling daunted, she took her time climbing the stairs.

The hall of the second floor still looked like part of an old elementary school. Emerging from the stairwell, she turned to the right.

Mark poked his head out of the first door, his expression bland. "It's this one. Come on in."

Though she'd received her invitation after all, he didn't look happy about issuing it. She wished again that she hadn't come but forced a smile as she stepped inside.

The smile wavered when a frowning redheaded woman stepped up beside him and gave her the once over. It was the obnoxious friend of the clerk at Town Hall! Today she wore a sleek burgundy-colored business suit, again with a short skirt. In comparison Lara felt like a frump in her paint-stained T-shirt and jeans.

Mark cleared his throat. "Lara, this is Karen Ridley." He looked to the redhead. "Oh, I'm sorry. You said you've met, didn't you?"

"Yes." The woman glanced at him then looked back at Lara. "Suddenly we keep running into each other."

"What a small world—or town, at least." Lara looked back and forth between the two of them and got the feeling Karen was more than a friend. So he *did* have a girlfriend. Di would be disappointed. Strangely, she felt displeased, too.

"Karen was just leaving." Mark stood holding the door open, his features stoic. It appeared the two of them weren't on such close terms after all. Maybe they were ex-lovers.

The redhead faltered for a second or two but eventually succumbed to the hint. She reached up to a shelf on the wall and grabbed a clutch purse that perfectly matched the color of her suit. Walking to the door, she said to Mark, "I'll drop off that shirt of yours soon."

"Whenever." He pressed his lips together.

She looked to Lara, her catlike green eyes narrowing into slits. "Have a nice day, Ms. Peale."

"You, too," she murmured, her composure broken.

Mark shut the door as soon as the woman had exited. For a moment he didn't turn around.

"I get the feeling I came at a bad time," Lara said.

He let out a sigh but still wouldn't look at her.

"Did you and Karen, um . . . once have a thing?"

He turned around and gave her a smirk. "You guessed it."

She felt a little sick to her stomach—and more awkward than ever. Judging by his behavior, he seemed to be carrying a torch. She swallowed. "Maybe I should go."

"No, it doesn't matter." He glanced at her, then walked past, looking at the floor.

"Here." She held the envelope out to him. "I had another errand in town today, so I brought this with me."

"Thanks." He made another face, not quite a grimace but not a smile either. Taking the manuscript, he said, "You didn't have to bring this by. I was going to print out another copy."

"Oh."

There was an uncomfortable moment of silence, then he said, "Can I make you a cup of coffee?"

"Are you sure I'm not intruding? If you're in the middle of something, I'll go."

He shook his head, tossing the package onto a small bistro table that fit snugly into the wide front hall. Across from the table an archway opened, the edge of a refrigerator showing around the corner. He stepped into the kitchen, out of her view. "I owe you a cup of coffee."

Not exactly an entreaty for me to stay, she thought, inching farther into the hall. He obviously hadn't gotten over that horrible Karen. *Why am I even here?* A guy hooked up with that nasty woman couldn't be the saint Di described.

On the other hand, maybe he'd *have* to be.

While he fixed the coffee, she scanned the towering walls in the front hall. Beside her hung a group of black-and-white photos, apparently shot in Paris in the nineteen-twenties or so. She moved forward to look at a larger print above the table and recognized Van Gogh's "Cafe Terrace/Night." Peeking into the kitchen, she admired the retro decor. Evidently Mark had varied tastes. She'd thought his place might look something like a Victorian museum.

"I'm surprised you came by. You could have just called." Standing at a small counter between the sink and stove, he scooped ground coffee into a filter. A prolonged view of his backside led her to decide he looked best in jeans.

"I knew I would be in the neighborhood." She sat down in one of the two chairs at the bistro table. Her statement, she told herself, was basically true. She *lived in* the neighborhood.

"Yeah?" He switched on the coffeemaker and

turned toward her. "What errands are you running today?"

"Besides bringing you your manuscript? Well, I've got to pick up a few things at the supermarket. I'm not good at keeping the fridge stocked. I end up having to hit the grocery store every other day."

He walked over to the table and took a seat across from her. "Did you get everything on your agenda done yesterday?"

It was strange for him to ask about just the day before, since they hadn't seen each other since Saturday, but her mind wandered before she pointed that out. She stared at a pair of unlit tapered candles between them, pushed off-center by his manuscript. A napkin holder and two coasters added to the cluttered surface. Wondering if he'd often made dinner for Karen here, she said, "Yes, I had to get a prescription for my mother and . . . do a couple other things. Believe it or not, I even have the kitchen floor completely uncovered now. All I need to do is move the dinette set back."

As soon as she'd spoken, she worried that he might think she was fishing for help from him—which she by no means wanted. She'd find a way to take care of the table on her own. She added, "My friend Diane has promised to help me do it."

"Karen mentioned she saw you in Town Hall," he said, practically on top of her words. A hard edge had crept into his voice.

Had Karen told him about the building permit? *That bitch.*

On the slim chance that he didn't know, she decided not to volunteer the information. Luckily she'd had more than one errand at the office. "Yeah, I stopped to pay my property taxes."

The coffeemaker let out a discordant sputtering, as if protesting her equivocal response. Breaking their shared gaze, Mark got up and went into the kitchen. His silence gnawed at her, and she raked her brain for another topic to talk about.

She cleared her throat. "I hope you don't mind, but I read some of your manuscript this morning."

For a long moment she heard only the tinkling of a spoon stirring in a china cup. At last he said, "Why should I mind? That's the reason I brought it over there."

Though his voice remained tense, she reached for the envelope and pulled the manuscript out onto the table. Flipping through the pages, she looked for a phrase she had particularly liked.

He returned carrying two large cups and saucers in a style made especially for cappuccino. Jaw clenched, he handed her one of the sets. "Milk, no sugar, right?"

She nodded, impressed that he'd noticed and remembered. Balancing the cup and saucer, she thought he must be an unusual guy. She regretted having to be evasive with him, but she doubted he'd have been happy if she had been frank.

"Lara, did you apply for a building permit?"

Damn it, Karen did tell him—of course. Poised to sip her coffee, she looked up at him. She didn't like the way he soared above her, staring down his nose. "Mark, I see no point in talking about that with you. I don't want to start another argument."

"Are you saying you did apply for it?"

"I'm saying I don't want to discuss it." She tried her coffee. The flavor was mellow, the temperature perfect. Too bad their conversation couldn't follow suit.

He stepped toward the other end of the hall, where

two armchairs faced what must have been the living room. His back to her, he asked, "So why didn't you say that before, instead of making up that lie about property taxes?"

"I didn't lie. I did pay my taxes yesterday. I didn't mention the permit because I knew you wouldn't like it."

He wouldn't meet her gaze or speak, but he turned partway around and leaned his back against the wall.

She set down her cup and saucer. "It's none of your business, anyway."

"Maybe not . . . but you know how I feel."

She frowned to herself. That damned studio wall seemed to mean so much to him that she actually felt a pang of guilt—but what could she do? None of the other rooms in the house were bigger or brighter.

Sighing, she asked, "Well, do you want to hear what I thought of your writing or not?"

"I don't know. I'm not in the best mood right now." He shook his head. "No, I think it would best for us to talk some other time."

She took a deep breath, trying not to feel affronted. After all, he hadn't asked her to drop in today—and his ex-girlfriend's visit had plainly upset him. Then again, he didn't have to take his bad feelings out on her.

Standing slowly, she said, "All right, but I don't know when. I can't promise you anything."

His eyes constricted. He looked so annoyed that she had to turn away from him. Tension hung heavy between them, almost like a third presence in the room.

She smoothed down her jeans, wondering why he was so mad. So she'd caught him at a bad time. Big deal. Nevertheless, she hated to leave on such a sour note.

"You write well," she blurted. Her exasperation made her sound begrudging even though she meant what she said. "On a good day, you might even go head-to-head with your notorious ancestor."

This time he definitely grimaced, looking off into the kitchen. "That idiot wrote nothing but tripe. His poems have nothing to do with real life. They're a load of adolescent fantasies. He was a middle-aged Romeo."

Clearly her effort hadn't helped. Now she had no choice but to leave. As she pushed her chair under the table with a squeaking noise, a sudden cold descended on her. She shivered and heard the cups rattle in the saucers. Hers turned over, flooding the surface with coffee.

"My manuscript!" Mark sprang forward and scooped up the scattered papers. He held the bundle away from his body, dripping milky coffee onto the hardwood floor. "Damn it, Lara. This is a mess, completely ruined."

"*I* didn't do it!"

"Right. Then who did?" He ducked into the kitchen and stepped on the pedal of a flip-open trash can, dropping his work in among the coffee grounds.

Her heart sank at the sight.

"The cup just turned over." She felt helpless to defend herself, especially since she didn't want to mention the eerie cold she'd felt as evidence of another, less earthly culprit. She had to be imagining things. "There was some kind of vibration. Maybe a helicopter flew over the building."

"Whatever." He snatched up a sponge from the sink and blotted the table. Excess liquid ran off the sides.

"Can I help?" she asked, embarrassed. Looking like a guilty party made her feel almost as bad as being one, and she *had* been next to the table when the spill happened. She glanced around for a roll of paper towels but didn't see one.

"I'll handle it." He picked up the cup, and she saw that the side was cracked. "I don't think you know how to care for things of value. You've demonstrated that more than once."

Her wave of guilt broke into indignation. How dare he accuse her of being careless—again? He knew nothing about her. It all came back to his disapproval of her plans for the studio.

She crossed her arms over her chest. "Well, excuse me for being *close to* a wobbly table. Excuse me for wanting to make improvements on *my own* house— and for trying to do you a favor by returning your manuscript. I should have saved myself the ride over here and thrown the damn thing out as soon as I realized you'd left it."

Pouncing at the door, she twisted the knob open and spun around to face him one last time. "I'm so sorry I disturbed you. You can go back to your sulking now."

Mark watched her slam the door and winced to himself. So she thought he spent his time sulking. Was that really the impression he gave people? Worse yet, was it actually true? Reflecting on the encounters he'd had with Lara, he realized he had been pretty moody—and he'd also been a part of too many scenes like this. When had he become so touchy?

He looked at the broken cup in his hand, one of a silly cappuccino set that Karen had given him for

Christmas. He had always thought the design was too feminine for a guy's apartment.

An abrupt rush of cold made him shudder. The table shook and the other cup tipped over. He snatched it up by the handle and saved half of the coffee, but the rest splattered all over the wall. "Damn it!"

He glanced around at the ceiling and other walls, almost expecting an earthquake to kick in. Everything besides the table stood exactly in place. The incident kind of spooked him.

For lack of a better explanation he adopted Lara's helicopter theory. He had no explanation for the cold that had coincided with the vibration, but he wasn't about to let his imagination run wild. The old schoolhouse often suffered from drafts, and he'd noticed more than usual in the last week.

He now held both cappuccino cups. The second one had suffered no damage, but he dumped the remaining coffee down the drain and threw both of them in the trash. Following them up with the matching saucers, he muttered to himself, "Good riddance." He should have tossed the stupid things out a month ago.

On his way to the closet to get a mop, he thought he heard a soft hiss.

He stopped and listened, his forearms tingling as goose bumps rose on the skin. The only noise was the ticking of the clock in the living room.

As he began mopping up the spill he caught another faint sound. This time he could have sworn that a man's voice whispered, "Fool."

Refusing to stop again, he reasoned that he must be hearing his conscience speak to him. He knew now that Lara hadn't knocked over the first cup of coffee. The expression on her face when he'd accused her should have told him that from the start. Those big baby blues had looked so innocent. His behavior to her was inexcusable. He would have to try to apologize.

He sped up his mopping. It occurred to him that he'd been making a lot of apologies lately, but for some reason, this one felt urgent.

Floating above, Geoff frowned to himself. He sensed a change of mood in his descendant. The ghost knew that when his own emotions ran high, his penetration into the physical world increased, and he feared that his condemnation of Mark might be seeping into the mortal's conscience and taking root.

He moved away, putting some space between him and the man. Though he hadn't been able to resist spilling the cups of coffee, he shouldn't have called Mark a fool out loud. He believed his descendant had heard the epithet and taken it to heart. If the scapegrace found it in himself to learn to appreciate Lara, it wouldn't do Geoff any good!

Backing out of the apartment, the ghost decided to follow his love interest home. What was he doing wasting his time with this jackanapes anyway?

Chapter 6

Lara stalked into her house, still seething from the encounter with Mark. The nerve of that guy! How dare he accuse her of not knowing how to care for things of value? She knew more about handling valuable objects than he ever would. Hadn't she taken a graduate course in the restoration of paintings? She'd been entrusted to work on masterpieces.

She slammed the door, triggering a scraping noise on the other side that ended with a thump. Before looking she knew the knocker had fallen off.

Reopening the door, she picked up the heavy lion's head. The oxidized-green snarl on its face seemed to mock her.

"What?" she asked. "Are you trying to prove his case?"

She saw that the ear had been nicked, and tears

welled in her eyes. A feeling of complete inadequacy pressed down on her. Taking extra care, she placed the knocker on an empty plant stand in the foyer. She had too much to do in this house, too many repairs, let alone the renovations. Ron had left over half a year ago, and so far she'd done little more than dream. At this rate she would never get on top of things.

She went to the studio and plopped down on one of the stools at her drawing table. Mark had been arrogant about his opinions and gotten mad at her for no good reason . . . not to mention the fact that he seemed to be hung up on his ex-girlfriend. Between his interfering and his moodiness, why did she even care what he thought?

Because she knew his opinions held a kernel of truth, regardless of the way he expressed them.

Gazing up at the far wall, she acknowledged that a lot of skill had gone into crafting the pocket windows. Once she'd removed them, she'd probably never find another place where they would fit and work properly.

She glanced around at the hundreds of old books in the room. Mark's writing had affected her, too. How could she dismiss his opinion after she'd glimpsed what insight and passion he could summon up when he made the effort? Having had a peek into his soul, she hated knowing he thought hers was empty.

The displaced bookcase caught her eye. She wished once again that she had the courage to look beyond the secret entrance. If she found some wonderful treasure—say, a beautiful Victorian vase—she could restore the piece to perfection. Then she could show off her work to Mark and prove to him how scrupulous she could be.

Or at least she could call him and brag about exploring her fascinating secret room.

She stood up and moved tentatively toward the rear of the room. Today the area around the secret entrance didn't feel cold. She took that for a good sign. The thought that a ghost might be lurking around the house had been eating at her for days. She kept telling herself she was foolish: She'd lived here for five years and, before Friday, nothing strange had ever happened. Still, she couldn't seem to shake off her fears. Even the coffee spilling at Mark's had felt like a supernatural occurrence to her.

Inching toward the bookcase, she paused, then stepped again, like a bride walking down the aisle . . . but unlike a bride she didn't go on to meet her destiny. She stopped short and eyed the bookcase, almost expecting to see it move.

A fluttering noise behind her made her spin around. Finding that one of her sketch pads had fallen from the table, she let out her breath. The pad had opened to a self-portrait, a discreet nude she'd done as a part of an anatomy study. Though she'd planned to throw it out when she finished, the sketch had turned out so well she'd kept it.

Her heart still pounding, she bent to pick up the sketch pad. But another noise behind her—this time a thump—made her start. Forgetting the pad, she whirled around.

A volume had tumbled out of the bookcase. She shuddered. What was with so many things around here falling all of a sudden? She hated to move lest something else drop out of nowhere, but she leaned over to see if the book looked damaged. It was a novel Ron had left behind called *A Ghost of a Chance*.

She shuddered. *I've got to get out of this house.*

Her first thought was to call Di, but she remembered that her friend had a dentist appointment this afternoon. For a moment she reconsidered going away on vacation, but being alone with two couples wasn't a great remedy for isolation. Stuck alone at the beach, she wouldn't be surprised if her ghost fantasies followed her, just as they had followed her to Mark's apartment.

A glance at her canvases reminded her that in the past when she'd felt agitated after arguing with Ron, one thing had always helped calm her. Like Monet with Giverny, she could retreat to the garden, even if hers wasn't so exotic.

She tucked a primed canvas under one arm. Picking up her box of acrylics with the other hand, she hurried through the kitchen and outside. She chose a spot in the yard that looked out over adjacent farmland and put down her supplies. Retrieving an old easel and stool she kept stashed in the shed, she set up to do a landscape.

As she looked out on the sunlit fields and touched brush to canvas, her anxiety began to fade. Translating the scene in front of her from three dimensions into two consumed her concentration. While the canvas gradually developed into an image, she lost herself in her work for the first time in days.

"How on earth do you do that?" a male voice asked behind her, startling her out of her reverie. *Mark,* she realized at once and avoided jumping out of her skin. Years of teaching high school had made her used to interruptions.

She looked over her shoulder and found him studying her painting, his lips forming a faint smile. Her heart thumped in her chest. She guessed he had un-nerved her after all.

"Do what?" Clinging to her productive mode, she dabbed her palette and blended touches of shading into the landscape. She noticed her irritation with him had faded, left behind somewhere as her work had transported her far away. Vaguely she wondered what he was doing here.

"That." He paused, then stepped closer. She could detect the heat of his body at her back. "Create warmth and depth from something hard and flat . . . make layers of acrylic look alive. You've got light that looks like it really glows and shadows that hold secrets I can almost make out. I can't comprehend how you've captured so much detail and atmosphere."

"I suppose it's similar to what you do with words." Compared to his comments, her statement sounded childish to her. She couldn't express thoughts the way he did. Thank goodness she could paint.

"What—make a fool out of myself?" he asked.

She stopped, surprised, then decided not to comment. Without meeting his gaze, she went on working.

"Lara, I'm sorry about this afternoon. I know you didn't spill that coffee. At the time I thought you did, but after you left, the same thing happened again with no one near the table."

She glanced at him out of the side of her eye. "Was a helicopter flying over the building?"

"I don't know. I guess one must have been, though I didn't hear a thing."

"I didn't hear anything the first time it happened, either." Frowning, she tried to get back to her painting, but she'd lost her concentration. The more she thought about all the little accidents that had been happening,

the less she liked the idea. She just couldn't dismiss
the spooky feelings she'd been having.

"I don't blame you for being mad at me," he said,
his voice soft. "I've been an idiot from the moment
you and I met."

"I'm not mad." She shifted on her stool to face him.
His eyes looked big, his gaze intent on hers. "If our
roles had been reversed, I probably would have
thought you had spilled the coffee, too."

"If so, I doubt you would have acted like a jerk
about it."

She tried to stifle a smirk, only half succeeding.
"Probably not."

"I want to make it up to you, and this time I'd like
you to let me know how I can." He moved closer, his
nearness prompting her breath to come quicker. "I
don't want to make you uncomfortable in any way. If
the best thing I can do is get lost, just tell me so and I
will."

Avoiding his gaze, she focused on her brush and
palette. She set them down and picked up a rag, wiping at the streaks and specks of paint on her hands. Immediately something came to mind that she hadn't
been able to do on her own. Now that he'd convinced
her he owed her, a favor wouldn't put her in his debt—
especially a favor she knew he'd be happy to do.
"Maybe you can help me explore that room."

"You're kidding."

She shook her head and looked away. The prospect
of entering the room intimidated her. To hide her
uneasiness she kept herself busy gathering up her
supplies.

"That's hardly any sort of penance. You know I've

been dying to check it out. Have you taken a peek yet at all?"

"No." Before he started making assumptions about her indifference, she decided to come clean with him. Better to be thought of as silly than apathetic. She met his gaze. "The truth is that the room gives me the creeps. I know I'm being stupid, but I've been having all sorts of eerie feelings since you stumbled across the secret entrance—in fact, since you found that letter in the parlor."

"Hmm." To her surprise, he didn't even crack a smile. "Finding a room in your house that you had no idea existed is enough to freak anyone out. I've had some weird feelings myself lately, and I don't even live here. But there's no reason to be afraid. Why don't we take a look when you're ready to go inside? The sooner we can demystify this, the sooner you'll feel comfortable again."

"Okay." Swallowing, she glanced up at the sky. A cover of dark clouds had begun gliding in. "It looks like we're in for rain anyway. I'll pack up now."

While she put away her paints and brushes Mark stowed the easel and stool in the shed. He ran out to his car to get a flashlight, then met her again as she was carrying her things to the back door. Taking her supply box from her, he fell into step beside her.

"You said you've had 'all sorts' of eerie feelings." He darted ahead and opened the door for her. "I'm curious. What exactly do you mean?"

"Oh, I've been feeling cold drafts, seeing coffee cups spill by themselves, books falling—you know, typical ghostly stuff." She'd tried to sound light, but her voice came out shaky. Looking at him, she asked, "What's been going on with you?"

"Nothing worth mentioning." He wouldn't meet her gaze. "Let's face it: This sort of thing is easily explained. When you live in an older building, drafts and creaks come with the package. Once we've looked into your secret room and seen how mundane it is, our imaginations will stop running wild."

Unless the room is so creepy that it only makes matters worse. She kept the thought to herself as they reached the studio. While she put away her canvas and supplies, Mark went to the bookcase and studied the edges.

"I have no clue how this works." He ran his fingers along the crack between the bookcase and the jamb. Looking toward her, he lifted his eyebrows. "Should I try opening it?"

She nodded and stood back as he slipped his hands into the gap and inched the bookcase away from the wall. After a second of sticking, the mechanism clicked into action and the door ground across the floorboards. The automated motion made the house seem to have a will of its own. A chill drifting out of the blackness added to the spooky effect.

Mark picked up his flashlight and flicked the switch on. He turned around to face her. "Are you ready?"

"Wait." Her instinct was to cower—but she couldn't go on living in fear of her own home. Determined to follow through with the exploration, she unplugged a floor lamp next to her and moved it over near the entrance. Jamming the plug into a closer outlet, she tilted back the shade and turned on the light. "Okay."

He pointed the flashlight into the room, which was already somewhat brightened by the lamp. Peering around his shoulder, she could see an unfinished hardwood floor. The far wall, maybe eight feet away, had wooden paneling like the studio's but unpainted. From where she stood the room looked empty and seemed ordinary except for the coldness emanating from it.

"There's nothing in here." Mark stepped behind the bookcase, and she sucked in her breath. He moved away from the entrance, dropping out of her sight. She froze, staring into the black, waiting for the sound of his voice or the flashlight beam to reassure her. For all she knew, right beyond the light the floor might fall away into a pit.

"Hey, there's a fireplace," he called, his voice echoing, "and a window covered up from the outside. Come on in, Lara. You've got to see this."

She let herself breathe. Nothing weird had happened, apart from the continuing draft. "Okay, but first I'm going to prop open the door. I don't want to take any chances of getting stuck in there."

Scanning the room for something large enough to hold the mechanical door, she fixed on the couch. She wouldn't trust anything smaller. A little embarrassed, she asked around the bookcase, "Can you help me for a minute, Mark?"

He emerged without the bookcase trying to trap him in, which made her feel somewhat better. When he saw her standing at the far end of the couch his lips twitched, but he suppressed the smile. Coming around to her side, he helped her push until the opposite end slid in between the bookcase and wall. He kicked off his shoes and climbed over the cushions to get back into the room. Grinning, he held out a hand for her to grab.

She slipped out of her sandals and stretched to reach him, climbing onto the couch. The warmth of his fingers felt wonderful around her icy ones. Though she could have sat on the arm and swung her legs over the side, she let him take her by the waist and ease her down.

The comfort of his touch distracted her from her fears. For a moment they stood gazing into each other's eyes, his hands still at her hips. She thought he might kiss her—and that she would let him—but then he looked away, releasing her waist.

Karen, she thought with a frown. She felt disappointed, even though she shouldn't have. Moody and unpredictable, Mark certainly wasn't the best guy for her to pursue.

He leaned over to pick up his flashlight from the floor. Once he'd turned it on he took her hand again, but she didn't know whether he meant anything more than to try to keep her calm. The truth was that with him for company her fears were fading quickly— especially since nothing really eerie had happened. The room felt cold but not unnaturally so. Her main impression now was a keen awareness of being alone with him, alone with a man. She savored the touch of his fingers and fought a crazy urge to stroke them.

What a fool I am, she thought. *He has no interest in me, and I shouldn't care about him, either.* She forced herself to look away from their clasped hands and focus on the exterior wall. A faint pattering sounded from the other side. She realized it had begun to rain.

Following the beam of the flashlight, she took in the wooden panels, devoid of any hangings. The light played on the frame of the window and landed on a wide sill—a window seat. The glass panes above stood in place, but not a speck of light seeped in through the barrier on the outside.

"Why in the world would anyone wall up a room

like this?" she asked. Then a horrible thought occurred to her and she looked at Mark. "Do you think a murder might have been committed in here?"

"You don't see any skeletons lying around, do you?" He shot her a grin that eased her anxiety. Redirecting his attention to the wall, he said, "I doubt the room's origin is quite so diabolical. One possible explanation is that this house was a stop on the Underground Railroad. There are legends that it ran through the area."

"Really? I had no idea." Thinking out loud, she said, "I'll have to brush up on local history."

"This window should be possible to restore." He squeezed her fingers, and she closed her eyes, reveling in the sensation. "I wonder if the fireplace is functional. I'll bet so. This house has so many chimneys that an extra one would probably go unnoticed."

Telling herself not to act like a schoolgirl, she thought about what he was saying. The fireplace, fronted by a medium-size wooden mantel and slate hearth, looked intact. A strong intuitive feeling told her the chimney would work. She could picture a blaze crackling in the room, filling the small space with heat and soft, flickering light.

"A fire would be wonderful in this room," Mark said, his voice hushed and sultry. He seemed to be reading her mind. He looked down at her and their gazes locked. The light rain beat out a soothing patter, unbroken by any other noise. In this secret place that no one but they knew about, the rest of the world seemed far away. She saw him glance at her mouth and knew that this time he really was going to kiss her.

He bent and met her lips, his mouth warm and soft. She closed her eyes and let her other senses take him in. As he pulled her closer, she soaked up rapid impressions. He was tall. He smelled clean. His back felt warm and strong through the soft cotton of his shirt.

A rumble of thunder broke the quiet—as well as the moment. He drew away, staring at her, blinking as if surprised.

Her heart seemed to drop inside of her. She didn't want him to stop. The taste of him had only tantalized her. Now she wanted more.

"I'm sorry," he said. He looked away from her, spiking her with disappointment. Watching the beam of the flashlight, he pointed it at the floor and shook his head to himself. "I can't believe I did that."

She suppressed a sigh. Touching her lower lip, she murmured, "Don't worry about it."

He stared at her as if waiting for her to convince him. *Well, too bad.* If he hadn't gotten over his breakup with Karen, then he never should have kissed *her*.

She looked away from his puppy-dog eyes. "Maybe we should bring some more lighting in here so we can take a better look around."

"Good idea." His voice sounded strained. "Do you have an extension cord you could run in from the studio?"

"Sure. I'll be right back." Before he could offer—or *not* offer—his help getting her past the couch, she hurried to hoist one leg over the side. In her haste to pull her second leg up, she bumped her knee on the bookcase. "Ow!"

"Are you all right?"

"I'm fine," she snapped. She didn't bother to look back at him.

Once out of his sight, she took her time getting a

cord from the parlor. Her exasperation over Mark surprised her. Just that morning she'd told Di she wasn't
interested in him. Now she was pining over him.

When she got back, he'd come out into the studio.
He stood by the drawing table, holding her desk lamp.
Glancing at her, he asked, "Mind if I take this inside,
along with the floor lamp?"

"The more the merrier." Cynicism dripped from her
tone. Though she had told him to forget about the kiss,
she didn't want to forget it. She had to resist the urge
to demand to know why he'd withdrawn so abruptly.
To do so would have been stupid. She already had a
good idea the answer revolved around his feelings for
his ex.

She bent over and plugged in the extension.

After stringing the wire over the couch, he lugged
the floor lamp into the secret room. She passed him the
desk light and climbed in on her own, neither of them
speaking.

The rain pummeled harder against the house, and
Lara's mood deteriorated further with the weather. As
Mark flicked on the lamps and adjusted the shades, a
roll of thunder sounded, closer than before. She
crossed her arms and leaned against the arm of the
couch. "Maybe we should call it a night. The storm
seems to be getting worse."

He glanced around at the bare walls. Walking to the
fireplace, he stooped and looked under the mantel. He
ran his hands over the surface and knocked on the
wood in several places.

She rolled her eyes to herself. All he cared about
was her damned house. Now that he'd seen that the secret room held nothing of interest, she wondered if

she'd ever hear from him again. The way things had gone between them so far, she shouldn't even care.

Standing, he stepped to the window and squinted upward. He bent and tried to push it open. The frame seemed to be stuck in the casing, but after a second attempt, it skidded up a few inches. His third try freed the stoppage, and the window slid up into the overhead pocket. He ran his hands over the wall that obstructed the opening.

"The hole's blocked up with brick. That won't be easy to undo, but you might want to look into it if you want to use this room." He closed the window and turned around, giving the other walls a last glance. "I guess that's about all there is to see in here."

She stood and brushed off her hands. "So much for my fascinating secret room."

"Do you still feel creepy about it?"

She shrugged. "Not at the moment."

"Well . . . I'd better leave before the lightning gets any closer." Another rumble of thunder punctuated his statement.

Turning off the floor lamp, he carried it over to her. He leaned down to pull the plug from the extension cord, and she stepped back to get out of his way. While he wound the cord around one hand, she glanced around at the walls, inspecting them a final time.

The room looked absolutely ordinary. If the window could be unblocked, the space wouldn't seem so spooky. Viewing the part where the couch jutted through the entrance, she could see that with a few pieces of furniture it might actually be cozy.

Making these observations, she felt normal for the first time in days, despite her disappointment over Mark. In a few minutes he would leave, and she would probably never see him again. She'd get back to the life she'd started building since her divorce. Maybe she would even keep an eye open for someone *reasonable* to date.

When she turned back around, she caught him watching her and felt a tingling up and down her spine.

Okay, she conceded, so life wouldn't be simple . . . but she would manage. She had so far.

He looked away from her and picked up the floor lamp, passing it out over the couch. With his long reach he was able to get the lamp to stand up on the other side. "Do you want to climb out of here before I put out the desk lamp, too?"

"Yeah." She contemplated the side of the couch, remembering how he'd helped her climb over it the first time.

After a second of hesitation he held out his hand to her.

"That's okay," she said without meeting his gaze. "I can make it alone."

Chapter 7

GEOFF WATCHED HIS lovely Lara spurn his descendant's hand. He smirked to himself. When she'd let the fool kiss her, his heart had contracted, but now the lady was coming to her senses.

Admiring her pert nose and pouting lips, Geoff wished he could walk in Mark's shoes, if only for a day. He would show the dear girl the sort of man she deserved—a real lover, not a bumbling dilettante who retreated with anxiety after the merest kiss. Besides having no taste in poetry, the fellow lacked any savoir faire with women.

As Lara paused and looked around the room, Geoff's smile withered. He wished the living pair would stop this dallying and move into the library. Here in this room he sensed another spirit lurking, and the perception discomfited him. The intruder hovered just beyond Geoff's scope. He wondered if the other ghost could sense *him* any more clearly than he could it.

He frowned. The notion of an invisible Peeping Tom spying on him disturbed him—and the reminder of his own voyeurism embarrassed him. While he'd lived, he never would have resorted to such a shabby practice. Voyeurs, like critics of poetry, sank to their sordid pursuits because they lacked the capability to participate themselves.

He knew . . . only too well.

Ashamed and angry about his fate, he banished the other spirit from his mind and floated down closer to the mortals. In the dimly lit room, Lara shone like a diamond—though, admittedly, one "in the rough." If only she would dress in a manner befitting her beauty, she'd be a gem of unparalleled magnificence.

Entranced by her golden curls, he nuzzled up to her neck, trying in vain to detect the scent of her perfume with his useless ethereal nose.

"Oh!" She flinched and rubbed her upper arms, her blue eyes wide as she looked toward Mark. "Where is that horrible chill coming from?"

Horrible? Geoff balked, nearly as startled as she. For a moment he'd forgotten himself—forgotten what he was.

Shoulders sagging, he glided away from her. He only prayed that the other spirit skulking nearby hadn't seen what a spectacle he'd made of himself.

"I don't feel anything." Mark moved toward her but stopped short, passing up a perfect opportunity to provide comfort. Any real lover knew where that led.

"The feeling's fading now." She gave her head a quick shake. "That was really creepy."

"Come on. Let's get out of here." Mark took her by the shoulders and turned her toward the door.

Creepy, Geoff echoed in his mind, disgusted with himself. He had sunken to such a level! Geoffrey Vereker, poet extraordinaire, formerly known as the "Don Juan of the New World," could no longer get within a yard of a lady without making her shudder.

Not that her reaction had necessarily been all his fault. The macabre air of the room may well have affected her sensibilities. He looked around at the four walls. Though he could see no evidence, he still sensed another party's presence. When his gaze skimmed the fireplace, a feeling of familiarity struck him. He had been here before, sometime during his lifetime. Perhaps he'd once had a tryst in the little room. Indeed, he believed he had.

"Wait a minute." Lara froze in place, Mark's hands still on her shoulders. She stared toward one of the back corners. "There's something over there on the floor."

A folded paper lay where she indicated, tucked partially under the molding.

Letting go of her, Mark picked up one of those modern portable electric lamps. He aimed the beam into the corner. A red wax emblem stood out in the center of the document.

"Another letter." He raised his eyebrows. "Maybe this will answer some questions."

Lara bit her lip. "I'm not sure I want the answers."

Geoff tended to agree with her. He had a feeling of foreboding about the letter. As soon as he'd laid eyes on the slip of paper, something heavy had pressed down on him, an unexplained weight of despair. While he'd lived he had managed to avoid such unpleasant emotions, but after a century of virtual solitude he was no longer a stranger to hopelessness.

Mark stepped forward and picked up the paper, flipping it over to the other side. "It just says 'G' on the front. There's no street address."

Geoff swallowed, feeling strange. Had he been alive, he would have called the sensation dizziness. The addressee on the note had the same first initial as he. He couldn't help viewing the coincidence as an ill sign.

His descendant walked back to Lara and held out the letter. "Would you like to do the honors?"

She hesitated, looking at the paper with fear-filled eyes. Eventually she took it from him, though for another moment she only stared at the outside. At last she lifted the seal and unfolded the sheet. She glanced from Mark to the letter and moistened her lips.

"'Dear G,'" she read, "'Yes, I still call you dear, despite learning how slight your esteem is for me.'"

"Uh-oh, a jilted lover." Mark made a face. "This is bound to get melodramatic."

She fired a frown at him but continued reading. "'I know you returned from Baltimore a good week ago, and I have waited each night for you to come.'"

Peculiar, the ghost thought. Not only did this poor chap share his first initial, he too had been to Baltimore. Geoff had passed many happy visits in the city with a cohort who had moved there from Philadelphia.

"'But tonight when I saw you ride by with Miss Sullivan, I finally realized you would never keep your promise.'"

Geoff started. A Miss Sullivan—*Molly* Sullivan— had been a favorite consort of his at one time, until she'd left Falls Borough to "move up" to the demi-monde of New York City. Indeed, he had driven down this very street with the little trollop on many occasions. In fact—

His heart caught in his throat. Could this house be where—yes, it was!

He'd avoided the place for so long he hadn't recognized it, but now he realized that a lover of his had once lived here.

"Mariah," he whispered. He'd spent years trying to forget about the girl, but to this day there were times when she popped into his mind. She was a farmer's daughter, an innocent little creature, rather too naive for his tastes. But during one dull summer he had spent several evenings in her arms . . .

Damnation. He whirled around, taking in the room again. He *had* enjoyed a tryst in here—with Mariah.

And the letter was written to him.

"Did you feel a draft just then?" Lara asked. Without turning her head she flicked her gaze from side to side.

The sight of the fireplace primed Geoff's memory. They had made love in front of the hearth. Mariah had been beautiful—though not his usual ilk, for he'd typically preferred full-figured, experienced women. She'd been a wisp of a thing and completely new to the arts of love. Surprisingly, she had caught on quickly. Hot images of their lovemaking seared him with longing for the days when he could fulfill his passions.

"It's just the storm," Mark said. "Read on."

"I can't." Lara let her arm drop to her side, holding the letter against her thigh. "This is too scary. She goes on to say he'll be happy about her being 'gone.' She must have committed suicide."

Suicide? Geoff recoiled. The notion appalled him so much he nearly felt a physical sensation of cold.

"You don't know that. Maybe she ran away." Mark held out his hand, palm up. "Here. Let me read the rest."

Thunder reverberated outside.

Lara clapped her hand over her breastbone. "All right, but if the letter gets too upsetting, don't read it out loud to me. If the woman killed herself here in this room, I don't think I want to know."

Geoff shuddered. Surely not Mariah, not that ingenuous young girl. He looked at the fireplace and imagined the spot as it had been, filled with leaping flames and radiant warmth from glowing embers. Suddenly Mariah's face appeared in the empty hearth, not peach-tinged as it had been when he'd known her but gaunt and bloodless, like that of a corpse.

She fixed her gaze on him, her focus relentless, her irises black and hard like coal. He recalled that in life she'd had golden eyes, the color of topaz. Her lips wavered, as if she were trying to speak.

He froze, scarcely able to believe what he saw. Had he finally, after a hundred years, encountered another soul who wanted to communicate with him?

After the longest pause he'd ever endured, Mariah croaked, "Geoffrey . . . I carried . . . your child."

He gaped, speechless.

The phantom faded, and the hearth once again stood empty and dark. He glanced at the mortals to see if they had witnessed the apparition. The two of them stood as they had before, clearly undisturbed.

He gulped. His hands trembled at his sides. He had never before seen a ghost, and being one himself didn't make the experience one whit less frightening.

Having a tortured soul tell you she had carried your child added another upsetting dimension to the episode. He'd had no idea he'd gotten the chit with child. To his knowledge, the only progeny he had ever produced were the disappointing pair of lummoxes his wife Deborah had presented to him.

"'Those beautiful verses you write are nothing but empty words, aren't they, my love?'" Mark laughed and looked up from the letter. "So the guy was a poet, like my late, great forefather. From what this letter implies, he was probably full of the same sound and fury, too."

Geoff bristled. Speaking of his descendants, the line ended with this blathering fool. This was what one got for yielding to the wishes of one's family and marrying where one's parents recommended. Deborah, whom his mother and father had extolled for her fine stock, had given him the heirs they wanted: two talentless dullards who'd wasted their lives on nothing more interesting than overseeing fields and livestock. Neither had a single iota of poetry in his being.

"Maybe it is your ancestor," Lara said. "The man's first initial is G. Did Geoffrey Vereker live in this area?"

Mark snorted. "I'm sure that in the last century or so there have been plenty of local residents with the initial G who dabbled in poetry."

"But I found that volume of his verses that I have here in this house." She put her hand over her mouth. "Maybe it belonged to the woman who wrote that letter."

"Is the book inscribed to anyone?"

"No, I'm sure I would have noticed that. I don't think there's a bookplate inside the cover either. I'll have to take a better look, in case I've missed something."

He shook his head. "I really doubt there's any connection between my ancestor and this letter."

The ghost turned away, dismayed by the fellow's lack of insight. To own up to the truth, insight was not a dominant trait among his descendants. Some of the others had shown they took after Geoff in *other* areas—but with Lara at stake, he supposed he was lucky Mark was no lady's man.

Looking back at the fireplace, he wondered how the child Mariah had carried might have turned out. She'd said "carried," not "bore," so he guessed the babe must not have come to term. If he had chosen another path in life—perhaps married for a reason other than convenience—he might have taken a greater interest in his children.

A rumble of thunder broke him from this fanciful line of thought. In truth, what other reason than convenience was there to marry? He didn't really believe in love—not the sort people married for, in any case. When he had spoken of love in his poetry, he'd meant something more like passion, an emotion overpowering but fleeting. He suffered no delusion that desire of that order could last a lifetime.

"Listen to this." Mark grinned. "She's written him a poem. She says 'Be assured the sentiment is genuine.'"

"Oh, Mark." Lara shifted from one foot to the other. "I don't know if you should read any further, especially if you're going to make fun of what she wrote. That poor woman's heart was torn apart. There's nothing funny about her pain."

He pressed his lips together. "I know. I know. I'm only trying to help you keep a healthy perspective about this. Her story is sad, but it happened generations ago. By now, everyone involved must be dead. All of their pain is over."

Geoff felt a muscle in his cheek twitch. *Fool,* he admonished himself.

"I suppose so." Lara looked down at the floor.

"Then do you want me to read on?"

She hesitated, then shook her head. "No, not now."

He raised an eyebrow. "Okay. I'll just skim through the rest myself. There's not much of it left."

Geoff felt nearly as reluctant as Lara to learn what else his late lover had to say, but he thought he owed it to Mariah. Floating over behind the mortal, he read over his shoulder:

As you read these lines coming from the grave . . .

Damnation, he thought. She did kill herself—or did she? Her remains weren't here with the letter.

Despair of your own eternal rest to save.

His heart leapt into his throat. What was this about his eternal rest? Did Mariah know something about his ultimate fate?

Leaning closer to Mark, he read on:

Until you advance a love to stand in place,
Of the love you once had but chose to debase.

At that point the letter ended with several lines of prose, but the words before Geoff's eyes blurred. While his descendant finished reading in silence, the truth seeped into the ghost's consciousness like a slow poison. The pounding of rain against the house grew louder as he began to comprehend the implications. When they hit him full force, he felt as though he had been coldcocked.

She cursed me, he thought.

Great God, Mariah was the *cause* of all of this! The little witch had sentenced him to this purgatory.

Lara gasped. "The chill is back."

But Geoff swore that he felt heat. Though normally he no longer experienced bodily sensations, hot fury rose at the nape of his neck, slowly swelling to his ears. The burning spread around, up and down his being, filling him with rage like he'd never known before. This hell, this unending abyss of nothingness, was all that woman's doing.

"Mark." Lara's eyes were huge, her face white. She hugged her body, her teeth chattering.

Mark stepped up to her and put his free arm around her, the letter still in his other hand. His jaw taut, he darted looks around the room. His gaze cut blindly through Geoff.

Crazed with impotent wrath, the ghost let his head fall back. He felt as if he could explode. The ceiling mocked him, like a barrier between him and the heavens. But though he might have been obstructed from eternal rest by fate, he knew he had no material barriers.

He glared at the plaster and rocketed into the ceiling, blasting through the house's three other levels. His form soared up into the rain and pierced the black and swirling thunderclouds. Electricity crackled and sparked all around him.

The pure, unchecked energy suited his mood. He slowed his ascent and slashed his arms out through the dancing ions. Brilliant lightning flared with a deafening crash that roared in all directions around him.

"Mariah!" he howled.

Heartless wench! How could she have done this to him?

Chapter 8

THUNDER EXPLODED OUTSIDE, and Mark tightened his hold around Lara's shoulders, the letter still in his free hand. The lamps flickered and died, and the room went black. She yelped and buried her face against his chest, clinging to his waist.

After the initial fright, she loosened her hold but still didn't let go. Her body felt small and pliant, her breasts warm and soft against his abdomen.

"Just what we needed," she said, her breath coming quickly.

"The flashlight's on the floor, not far from our feet." In a clumsy attempt to soothe her without getting too familiar, he patted her back. His own heart was probably pounding in her ear, but at least that terrifying coldness had tapered off. He'd never felt a draft like that before—though, of course, there must have been some rational explanation for it. The violence of the storm had played tricks on their minds. "Let me stoop down and I'll get it."

A glint of lightning streaked through the opening to the studio. He glimpsed her face, completely white in the thin, cold light. The flash extinguished with a clap of thunder. He couldn't see her anymore, but her expression of fright stayed sharp in his mind.

"That wasn't as close as the last one," he said with more certainty than he felt.

As she moved apart from him, cool air fanned his chest. With the dark concealing her, he felt hyperaware of the rift between them. Grasping her hand, he asked, "Can you take the letter from me? I don't want to risk damaging the paper by stuffing it into a pocket."

Her body went still. After a pause she said, "Just throw it back on the floor."

"I'd really like to look at it again."

"Then put it in your pocket. I don't want to take it."

He couldn't really blame her for her uneasiness. The note had been disturbing, and the way the storm had surged as he'd finished reading added drama to the words. With lightning crashing around them and that nasty cold draft, who wouldn't have been freaked out?

Refolding the paper as carefully as possible with one hand, he slid it into the back pocket of his jeans. He squatted and fumbled around the dusty floorboards. His hand struck something warm and soft—alive!

"Oh!" Lara yanked her bare foot out from under his hold.

"Oops." A short laugh slipped out of him. If she weren't so frightened, the scene really would have been comical.

Another bolt of lightning gave him a glimpse of the flashlight. As darkness flooded the floor again, he lunged for the hand grip, inadvertently pulling on her arm.

"Ow!" Regardless of her apparent pain, she kept a firm hold on his fingers.

His free hand landed on the flashlight. "I've got it. Sorry about that."

"Never mind. Just turn on the light."

He flicked on the switch and pointed the beam toward the couch stuffed into the exit. "Come on. Let's get out of here. You can go first."

"Okay, but whatever you do, don't let go of my hand." She clambered over the side of the couch, somewhat awkwardly with only one arm free to support herself. Kneeling on the cushions, she waited for him to join her, unable to move farther without letting go of him.

Between her clutching his one hand and the flashlight in his other, he wasn't sure he could make it out of the room at all. After studying the problem for a moment he sat on the arm of the couch, swinging one leg over, then the other.

A crack of thunder made Lara jump and yank on him unexpectedly. He lost his balance and slid down the back cushions, flailing to try to grab the bookcase. The flashlight fell out of his hand, and he dropped on top of her.

Luckily the light landed beside them on the couch, still on.

"Are you all right?" he asked. They had settled into a surprisingly cozy position, side-by-side along the length of the cushions. Her body felt warm and slender against his. He felt an urge to pull her into his arms—ridiculous, when she was so wrong for him. He'd been stupid enough to kiss her tonight; he wouldn't repeat the mistake.

"Yeah." Only inches away from him, she looked into his eyes. "Sorry for jumping like that. The lightning scared me."

Their nearness felt inescapably intimate. He glanced at her lips, longing to taste them again—but he resisted. Lara and he could never make a relationship work. Their outlooks clashed on too many important issues.

He forced himself to look into her eyes. "That's understandable."

His words sounded formal and detached to his own ears. She watched him, as if she expected something more. He felt sure she could tell he wanted her, the same way he knew she returned the feeling. But to give in to temptation would only make it more difficult to part later—something they'd inevitably have to do.

Cutting off their shared stare, he clenched his jaw and reached for the flashlight. He never should have kissed her. The kiss had already complicated things between them. At the moment, he'd succumbed to the craving hoping to get it out of his system—but having a taste of her mouth had only made him want her more.

"Ouch. There's a spring digging into my hip." She shifted slightly and her pelvis pressed into him. His groin tightened in an instant.

He jerked away and pulled himself up on his knees, hoping he'd moved before she had time to notice his arousal. Holding on to the back of the couch so only the lower half of their legs touched, he said, "Let's move into the studio."

"I thought *I* was the timid one," she muttered. She untangled her legs from his and pulled away. Snatching the flashlight from him, she climbed over the far end of the couch. "I've got some candles around here somewhere. I'll go look for them."

She vanished around the bookcase, taking the light with her.

Left alone in the dark, he dropped back down on the cushions. If her views weren't so different from his, he knew he would have fallen for her hard and fast. What was wrong with him? Why did he always seem to want the exact woman he shouldn't? His attraction to Lara was the strongest he'd felt in as long as he could remember. Even the awareness of lying on her couch made him want to linger there.

He spread his arm out over the spot she'd vacated. The cushions still felt warm from her body. As he rolled onto his side, a flash of lightning gave him a glimpse into the secret room. From his position he could see only half of the fireplace, but the flickering conjured up images of how the hearth would have looked lit up with flames.

The glare died, but in his mind he pictured the room as it once may have been—cozy, intimate, the perfect spot for trysting lovers. He wondered if "M" and "G" had used it for that purpose. Maybe that was why "M" had chosen to leave the letter there.

The letter. He patted his back pocket and felt the edge of the paper sticking out. Funny . . . he'd almost expected it to have disappeared, the whole experience to have been imagined.

"Mark?" Lara's voice sounded shaky and far away.

As he looked back into the studio, a flickering light appeared in the library.

"One second." Snapping out of his lapse into speculation, he scrambled to turn around and climb over the arm of the couch. When he stepped past the bookcase, he saw her bending over the end table, lighting the last of three fat candles that sat on the scratched surface. "What is it?"

"I wondered what had happened to you." Waving out her match, she straightened up and looked at him.

The candlelight restored the natural warmth of her face. Her cheeks glowed and her eyes glittered. Golden flecks lit up her hair and changing shadows played on her lips, detailing their fullness. Her mouth had felt lush against his when he'd kissed her . . . without considering the consequences.

She picked up one of the candles and stepped forward. "Why don't we go into the parlor? I want to put some distance between that room and us."

"I really should get home."

"Now?"

The stunned look on her face pierced him with guilt, but he'd already done one thing he regretted tonight and didn't want to give himself the chance to make things worse. Listening to the pattering on the windows, he said, "The storm seems to be dying down."

"Don't go yet." She tilted her head to one side. "Please, Mark. I don't want to be here alone."

"Really? I got the impression you usually guard your independence pretty closely." He knew that under the circumstances his statement was absurd—more evidence of how idiotic he could be around her.

"Not after an experience like that." She looked away from him, gazing into the candle she held.

Watching her, he couldn't seem to look away. The candlelight drew long shadows out from her lashes.

Even with such dramatic shading, her nose looked pert and perfect. He could have spent the whole night just staring at her—or better yet, making love to her on the big red couch.

"I don't know if I can stand being alone right now." She twisted her mouth. The rain beat out a tranquil rhythm in the stillness. "'Solitude is a quiet and undisturbed state, But in the grave it is one's eternal fate . . . '"

The words brought goose bumps to his skin. "What is *that*?"

"Oh." She blinked and looked up to meet his gaze. "Something your ancestor wrote."

"Old Geoff wrote that?" The information astonished him. "I didn't know he ever reflected on serious subjects. In the poems I've read, he's usually trying to talk some poor woman into sleeping with him."

Two dimples crimped her cheeks. "He was in this case, too."

He couldn't help but laugh, releasing some of his nervous energy. "It figures."

She leaned over the table and picked up a second candle. Carrying one in each hand, she started toward the front of the house. "Your ancestor may have had a penchant for seduction, but there are a lot of deeper sentiments woven into his poetry, too."

"Hmm." Mark suspected she had read too much into the old boy's verses, but he decided to give her the benefit of the doubt. He grabbed the last candle and followed her to the parlor. "I'll have to reread some of his poems. Maybe you can recommend a few of the better ones."

"I'd be happy to." In the large, sparsely furnished room her voice sounded hollow. Stooping next to the fireplace, she set one candle on each side of the hearth.

As she knelt to arrange a pile of logs already stacked on the irons, she asked without looking up, "Does this mean you'll stay a little longer?"

He wanted to. The more time he spent with her, the more his curiosity about her grew. She was such a paradox: a woman who refused to acknowledge any concerns for her house that didn't fit in with her plans, yet could also give life to a piece of canvas with a paintbrush—and lend meaning to nonsensical poetry with the earnestness of her tone. He had to know more about her, to find out who she really was.

"I guess I don't have to leave right away. Let me make sure you get a good fire going."

"Thank you." She glanced up at him with a somber expression. Grabbing a section of newspaper from a holder near the hearth, she began crumpling up pages and stuffing them under the wood. "While I'm doing this, would you mind bringing in some cushions from the couch in the studio? We'll need something to sit on."

"No problem." He took his candle to the other room and set it back down on the end table.

The couch held six oversized cushions. When he returned with two of them, Lara was still working on lighting the fire. Since he had time to spare, he went back to the studio and got the rest.

Spread out on the floor and bathed in firelight, the makeshift seating looked like something out of a love den. With the idea of making love to her on the couch still fresh in his mind, he wondered if subconscious desires had led him to bring in all those pillows. In any case, he couldn't very well take some of them back now. He sat on the edge of one, trying to look casual but feeling totally awkward.

When the fire began to catch, Lara moved back onto the cushions and sat cross-legged. She didn't give the seating arrangements or him a second glance. Staring into the flames, she asked, "So . . . do you think the secret room is haunted?"

The question surprised him—so far separated from his own train of thought. Though the storm and the darkness had unnerved him at the time, he didn't believe in ghosts. "Of course not."

"Not even with the cold drafts and the lightning and—" She stopped and shook her head, still not meeting his gaze.

"And what?" He wondered if she'd heard the whispery hiss he'd caught that had sounded like a man's voice. Of course, the noise could easily be attributed to the wind. Not wanting to put ideas in her head, he didn't mention the incident.

"Never mind." She got up and went to the table. Lifting the pitcher she kept there, she asked, "Would you like some water? I know something stronger would be better right now, but last night before I went to bed I drank the only wine I had in the house."

"Water will be fine." As she set out two plastic cups and poured he said, "You know, lightning and cold drafts aren't exclusive to this house. I'm sure everyone in the area experienced both during that storm."

She raised an eyebrow and handed him one of the cups. Sitting down beside him, she took a sip of hers but didn't respond.

Searching for another topic of conversation, he looked around the room. Though the space held no real furniture, the walls all displayed works of art. When he'd been inspecting the architecture, he hadn't paid attention to them, but now he wondered if Lara had done the paintings herself.

A large canvas above the mantel caught his eye. The work, classic in style, depicted a bedroom scene. The decor of the room and the clothing lying around appeared to be Victorian. A woman lolled on a huge canopied bed, her nude body freed of the sheets down to her hips. Near the foot of the bed, a nude man stood facing her, his well-sculpted buttocks exposed to the onlooker. Both of them had an air of relaxed contentment. He got the sense they had just made love.

"Did you do that?" He gestured toward the painting, hoping the question wasn't stupid.

"Yeah." She sounded shy—unusual for her.

"Wow." Knowing the artist personally made the work even more intriguing. "The scene is so . . . serene. The muted colors, the easy poses, the deep shadows in the folds of the bedclothes. You've created such an air of contentment and warmth that I wish I could walk into the painting." Embarrassed by what his words seemed to imply, he tried to cover it up. "I didn't realize you had any interest in the Victorian period."

She gave him a small smile and picked up the poker, leaning forward to play with the fire. "Actually, that painting was inspired by a poem Geoffrey Vereker wrote."

"You're kidding." He looked back up at it. "What one?"

" 'A Maiden Unmade.' "

He searched his mind and shrugged. "Doesn't ring a bell. Apparently I have some reading to catch up on. You seem to be really familiar with Geoff's work. You must be a bigger fan of his than I realized."

"I guess I am—I mean, even bigger than *I* realized." She set down the poker and looked up at her painting. "It's funny. In school I never had the patience for poetry. The language always seemed too hard to interpret. But I found that little leather volume in the other room not long after I moved here, and something about the verses got to me. I felt like the words took me to another place."

Following the line of her gaze, Mark felt the same way about her painting. The ambience of the work penetrated his mood. The soft sensuality she'd captured seemed to radiate and blend with the atmosphere in the room. He looked down at Lara, and his desire for her flared. Quietly, he said, "I know what you mean."

She met his gaze, and this time he couldn't look away from her. They stared at each other, eyes intent. It felt as though they shared some unique insight—some brilliant spark of mutual understanding. He got an overwhelming urge to connect physically with her.

All at once a coolness swept the back of his neck. He felt the little hairs prick up on end.

Lara broke their stare and darted looks around the room. "Did you feel that?"

"What?" he asked, trying to ignore the goose bumps rising on his arms.

Geoff's venture into the storm had expended most of his fury, but he scowled at his descendant's feigned ignorance. The ghost had been drawn back into the house when the mortals mentioned his name, only to find them looking rather more cozy than when he had left. The effects of his rage, it seemed, had inadvertently drawn them together. What a fool he was.

"Another draft." Lara looked toward the window. "These sudden chills may have to do with the changing weather, but I sure wish I'd stop feeling them."

"A cold front has probably moved in," Mark said. "That's normal after a storm."

Geoff watched with misgivings as Mark nudged closer to her on the bed of cushions they'd constructed while he was gone. He would have liked to give the young jackanapes a true taste of haunting, but for the lady's sake he floated upwards until his back lay flush against the ceiling.

Mark put his arm around Lara and rubbed her shoulders. *That knave,* the ghost thought. *I underestimated him. He truly is going to try to take her from me.*

"How's that?" the mortal asked her, his voice husky. "Shall we move the cushions closer to the fire?"

"No, I'm feeling warmer already."

Geoff was in no mood to stand back and let this fiasco go further. The idea infuriated him that his worthless descendant, of all living men, should be paired with that lovely woman—while he, Geoff, a true master with the ladies, would never have a lover again.

A distant flash of lightning caught his attention, and he realized what he had to do. He had to get the lights back on and hope that the action would put a damper on Mark's advances. Electricity had fascinated him since the advent of its common usage, and he'd taught himself some of its workings.

Moving through the nearest wall, he floated back outside. If he couldn't have Lara himself, he'd be damned if his descendant would.

He *was* damned, he reminded himself and grimaced as he made for the power lines that ran from the house.

Though he perceived no rain, the air felt thick with

moisture, and the sky held no stars. He followed the wires down the block and found a cable with one end ripped from its connection to a metal tower. A large fallen branch lying on the ground revealed what had happened.

His state of high emotion gave him more physical control than he normally possessed. After several efforts and a great deal of concentration, he finally lifted the cable and restored the connection. It helped not to have to worry about being electrocuted, though the buzzing ions and flying sparks around him still proved distracting.

When the neighborhood lights ignited again, he flew back into Lara's house. Since he'd gone she and Mark had laid back on the cushions, but the sudden brightness had startled them. Now they propped themselves up on their elbows, blinking against the chandelier that hung above their heads.

Mark in particular looked bothered. Frowning, he sat up and let Lara's hand slide from his arm. He ran his hands through his hair. "I'm sorry. I don't think we should be doing this."

She frowned up at him. Her eyes darkened to the hue of stormy seas. "Doing what?"

"I mean, I shouldn't be lingering here, now that your electricity's back on. I really should get back to my place and see how the apartment has weathered the storm. One of the windows in my living room tends to leak."

Geoff smirked to himself. How he wished he could have served as a living rival to this fool. If he'd been in Mark's place, he would have stayed the night with Lara. Couldn't he see that the lady was ripe for the picking?

She looked down at her fingernails, rubbing her thumb against them. "Right. Of course."

Mark stood and brushed off his jeans. "I hope you'll be okay. You should keep the candles lit and the fire going, in case you have any more problems."

Her face paled. "Don't even mention the possibility."

He had shame enough to cast his gaze to the floor. "Don't worry. You're not likely to run into trouble now. The storm's well past. And if the lights do go out again, you can always give me a call."

"Assuming the phone lines aren't dead, too."

He just stood there hanging his head, and Geoff felt disgusted by him. He decided *he* would stay himself and watch out for Lara. If she had any further difficulties, he would simply fix the electricity again.

His mortal counterpart walked into the adjoining library. When he returned he held the portable lamp he'd carried earlier. "Here. Keep my flashlight. The batteries are fresh, so it's definitely reliable. I'm sorry I can't do more."

She let out a sigh but took the light. Rising, she said, "Don't worry about it. I'll check the forecast now. If there's even a hint of another storm in the area, I'm sure I can go to my friend Diane's house for the night."

He nodded, then paused, as if reluctant to leave. Geoff found his indecision even more annoying than his chastity.

Lara pursed her lips, apparently impatient with him, too. "I'll walk you out."

She went to the foyer, her back stiff.

Mark trailed behind her. When she opened the front door, he stopped and patted his back pocket. "I'd better give you the letter back."

"Keep it."

He frowned. "It really belongs in this house."

She shook her head. "I don't think a letter like that belongs anywhere."

Still he hesitated, while the damp night air drifted into her house. A moth fluttered through the doorway. He swatted at it, but the creature escaped into the parlor.

Lara shut the door again. She moistened her lips. "Mark, I was wondering, since you seem so interested in the letter, would you like to come back sometime and help me look through my attic? There are dozens of boxes up there full of old letters."

He looked down at the one he held. "I don't know. I have a lot going on at the moment. Maybe for now I'll just borrow this. When you feel ready to take it back, call me and I'll return it immediately."

She nodded and stood back as he reopened the door.

This time he stepped out onto the porch. "I'll see you."

"Good-bye." She closed the door and stood watching while he walked to his motorized carriage. Bolting the lock, she murmured, "I know exactly what you have 'going on'—that willowy redhead, Karen."

The ghost raised an eyebrow. Evidently his descendant had a betrothed, if not a wife. Geoff had seen him in the company of that short-haired redhead several times but hadn't detected any close connection between them. If Mark were engaged to the woman, he seemed to be even colder toward her than he was to Lara. Perhaps the arrangement was one of convenience. Unfortunate for him, if that was the case, but the ghost wasn't entirely convinced his descendant merited his sympathy.

Posture wilted, Lara drifted back to the cushions. She sat before the fire and stared into the flames. A veil of sadness dulled her blue eyes.

Geoff felt an uncharacteristic stab of compassion. She truly seemed to care for his descendant. Though her taste might have been questionable, he still felt sorry for her.

He longed to approach and try to comfort her, but any attempt he made would only frighten her. Hanging near the ceiling, he reflected that the lady and he had both had a difficult night.

The image of Mariah's face in the hearth returned to him, emaciated and pitiful. Her expression had been much like the one Lara wore now.

Exhausted by the evening, he couldn't muster up the fury he'd felt on first learning of his late lover's treachery.

Mariah had looked so miserable.

Had *he* truly brought about her pain?

Chapter 9

AFTER MARK LEFT, Lara had no further problems with the electricity. Over the next twenty-four hours, she experienced no strange drafts, either. She avoided going near the secret room and had trouble getting to sleep, but most of her worries centered around her feelings for Mark. He might have been moody and unpredictable, but she found him *interesting* . . . and she had really liked kissing him.

So now what was she going to do?

During her second night in a row of tossing and turning, she thought she would burst if she couldn't talk to someone about the situation. She hadn't spoken to Di since lunch on Tuesday, because she'd had too much to hide from her. Now she thought it might be time to lay everything out in the open.

When she got up the next morning, she showered

and dressed quickly. Too anxious to wait till lunchtime, she set off to visit the store where her friend worked.

"Wow, what a story," Di said, after Lara had spilled the tale to her between customers at the register. "I can't believe so much has happened since I last saw you. Now aren't you glad I told you to take the manuscript to his place?"

"Glad?" Lara gaped at her. "*Overwhelmed* is more what I feel. Have you heard half of what I said?"

"Yes. You found out that Mark is getting over an ex-girlfriend, which confirms that he's single. He stopped by your place and helped you check out the room, so now you don't have that hanging over your head. And, best of all, he kissed you, so you know he's interested—which is great, because you seem to like him, too."

Lara shook her head in disbelief. "First of all, I was convinced there was a *ghost* in that room the other night, so my problems there aren't exactly settled."

Coming out from behind the counter, Di stooped to pick up a blouse that a customer had knocked to the floor. "All that lightning and thunder probably just confused you. That was one nasty storm."

"As for the kiss," Lara said, ignoring her, "Mark *apologized* for it and told me he couldn't believe he'd done it . . . so where does that leave me with him?"

"You need to encourage him." Her friend brushed off the slinky fabric and hung it back on the rack. "Don't push him too hard while he's still feeling wary of women, but don't let him completely slip away from you."

She frowned. "I don't know if he's really wary of me or only wants his ex. He's obviously not over her."

"So, help him *get* over her. He can't keep pining over his ex-girlfriend forever, unless he's such a loser that he's not worth having, anyway—and I don't think that's the case with Mark Vereker."

"You haven't met this Karen person." Lara thought about the woman's sleek image. "She's a flashy dresser, sophisticated, poised—in short, everything I'm not."

"Maybe a few new outfits would make you feel better." Di smiled. "I can get you my discount here. As for sophistication, I'll bet you're ten times as cultured as she is. Do you think *she* has a master's degree in fine art?"

Lara smirked. "Does that make me cultured?"

"I like to think that my degree in lit makes *me* a woman of the world—which explains why I spend my days selling clothes like this." She held up a dress with a particularly loud print. They both laughed. "Seriously, are you judging this woman by her Sarah-Jessica-Parker wardrobe, or did she really show some sign of intelligence? What exactly did she have to say?"

"Not much. Maybe you have a point. But she definitely acted jealous when I showed up at Mark's, so it seems like they both have feelings left over for each other."

"If they felt very much, they'd be together."

Lara took a moment to think about that. "If you were in my place, what would you do—call him?"

"I don't know." Di pulled a size-thirteen skirt out of the size-three section. "Maybe you can run into him another way . . . get involved with the historical society or something."

"Yeah, right." She made a face. "He's probably told

them all about my evil plan to knock out a wall and destroy a perfectly good Victorian house. They're not likely to welcome *the enemy* with open arms."

"But you've had second thoughts about that wall, haven't you?"

She shrugged. "Maybe. But Mark doesn't know that, so neither do they."

"You can fix that easily enough."

A customer called Di back to the register, and Lara decided she should let her friend work in peace. She waited for her to complete the transaction, then said good-bye.

"Are you sure you don't want to drive down to Cape Hatteras with Jerry and me this weekend?" Di asked as they walked to the front of the store. "If nothing else, the trip will give you a break from your ghost."

"Thanks, but I don't like the idea of being chased away from my home. If there's a ghost hanging around, I want to find out why. Rather than be scared out of my wits, I'm going to do some research and see if I can figure out who might be haunting me. Of course, nothing strange has happened in the last couple of days, so it's easy to be brave about it now."

"Well, maybe things will stay quiet and you can forget about the whole thing."

"I wouldn't count on it."

When she left the shop, Lara walked several blocks to the Falls Borough Public Library. She hoped the local history books would offer her some information about previous occupants of her house—particularly an occupant with the initials "M.A.S." If the woman had come to a tragic end, that might make her a likely candidate to be haunting the place. The idea of ghosts still seemed a little crazy, but the sensations she'd felt during the electrical storm had brought her damned close to declaring herself a firm believer.

Two hours later she sat in the archive room with a stack of leatherbound volumes scattered on the table in front of her. So far the page of notes she'd been taking looked pretty sparse. She'd found no specific mention of her property other than on a map that labeled the block of land "Sulley." The diagram dated from 1868. Ron's family had lived in her house for well over a century.

Leaning back in her chair, she wondered again if the mysterious "M" was on the premises. The flashes of cold she'd felt on several occasions were creepy enough, but she'd experienced other strange sensations, too. Anyone could sense when a pair of eyes was fixed on him or her. She sometimes got that feeling . . . when nobody was around.

The memory of the incidents made her shudder again. She sat up straight and tried to concentrate on the book in front of her.

After fifteen minutes of skimming through the remaining pages, she shut the cover and frowned. She'd scanned four old volumes published to commemorate town anniversaries and hadn't even come across a Sulley family tree.

Ron must have one, she thought—but the realization wasn't enough to tempt her to contact her ex. She preferred to try to find some birth records among the papers he had left behind in the house.

Gathering up her reference books, she took them back to the section they'd come from and reshelved them. During her studies she'd also come across a biography of Geoffrey Vereker, and she decided to check that out.

As she stood in line at the front desk, she thought about the poet's descendant again. Now that she was trying to learn the identity of the ghost, she wondered if she should have kept the letter she and Mark had found in the secret room. Maybe she could just have him make a photocopy for her in case she needed it for reference. She tried hard to convince herself she wasn't just inventing a reason to call him.

She finished checking out and debated the idea during the short drive home. By the time she walked into the house, she'd made up her mind. Locating his business card, she dialed the number before she could chicken out.

"Hello?" he answered after only one ring.

"Hi, Mark. It's Lara."

"Oh, hi." He sounded surprised—not particularly overjoyed to hear from her, but at least not annoyed.

She swallowed her nervousness. "I'm sorry to bother you, but I've been thinking about the letter we found the other night. Is there any chance you could make a photocopy of it for me?"

"Of course. I mean, you can have the original back, like I said. Do you want me to drop it off today?"

The chance to see him again tempted her, but she didn't really want the original. "Thanks, but I still feel kind of creepy about the letter. A copy will be fine— and there's no hurry. You can just mail it to me."

"Okay . . . if you're sure."

"Definitely. I'm not even eager to look at it again, but there may come a time when I want to. I've been trying to learn more about the history of the house."

"Really?" His tone perked up immediately. "How's it coming along?"

She cleared her throat, embarrassed to talk to him—

an expert in the field—about her lame attempts at research. "So far I haven't had much luck. Today at the library I looked through some town-anniversary annals, but they mostly focused on politicians and prominent people in society. I get the feeling that the Sulleys never had a very high profile."

"I wonder if *I* could find you any information. I have a pretty good collection of local-history books here. What sort of facts are you looking for—mainly details about the family or anything about the property?"

"Mostly about the family, I guess." She let out a short, nervous laugh, then decided not to try to hide her reason for her research from him. What did she care if he thought she was crazy? "To be honest, I hope to gain some insight into who my ghost might be."

For a moment, he didn't say anything. Then he asked quietly, "You really think your house is haunted?"

"Well, *something* strange is going on. The 'drafts' I've been feeling are too cold to come from outside, and the timing of that storm the other night was awfully coincidental. My suspicion is that "M" might be hanging around. I had never noticed anything strange before you found the love letter to her in the parlor. And the other main source of eerie drafts is the hidden room, where she left the other note."

"But drafts are an everyday occurrence, Lara. I feel them here all the time."

"Hmm." A sudden thought occurred to her, and she frowned. "The coffee cup incidents happened at your place, too."

"As far as I'm concerned, that only proves that this is all coincidence. You have to admit it's not likely both of our places would be haunted."

"Maybe the ghost is following me."

He laughed. "There's no ghost following you any more than there's one following *me*."

Though she knew he meant to reassure her, his words had a different effect. She wondered if maybe the ghost wanted something from *both* of them. Strange things had happened at his apartment as well as her house, and her eerie feelings had started the day she'd met him.

"Did you ever experience anything like this before you met me?" she asked.

"Like what? Drafts? Of course, I did. It's going to take more than a little chill to persuade me something supernatural is going on. Listen, Lara, in my business, I've traipsed through a lot of old houses, and I've never come across any solid evidence for the existence of ghosts."

Though her intuition about this felt strong, she didn't have any "solid evidence," either. "Well . . . I can only hope that you're right."

The conversation lagged for a moment, then he asked, "Run across anything else of interest during your research?"

"A few things." Realizing he wanted to change the subject, she figured it was just as well. "I learned some intriguing tidbits about your ancestor, the poet. He's mentioned fairly often in the town annals."

"Is he?" His tone became scornful. "More for his poetry or for his womanizing?"

"A bit of both, to tell the truth—but he was also known for his cynical wit. I've run across half a dozen wonderfully barbed quotes of his about local politicians and socialites."

"Really?"

She smiled to herself. "Apparently he had as little tolerance for hypocrisy as he did for morality. How can you help but be intrigued by such a character? Frankly, I'd like to learn more about his torrid affairs. These old books I skimmed through today only hinted at what was going on."

"The family legends are like that, too." He spoke slowly, evidently considering her observations. "I think his fellow Victorians did their best to cover up how he led his life. The story is that after he died— fairly young, from what I remember—his wife burned all of his journals. She was supposedly a respectable type, though Geoff was better known for consorting with women of inferior reputation."

"His wife *burned* his journals? That's disgusting! They must have been fascinating. I would have loved to read them. The library had a biography of him and I checked it out, but I doubt it includes much in the way of juicy details." She pulled a small volume out of her purse and opened it to the copyright page. "It was written in the nineteen-thirties."

"Who's the author?"

She flipped back to the front cover. "Ernest Jamison."

"I think I have a copy of that one somewhere around here, too, but I've never read it. Maybe I should. I wouldn't mind hearing more about that 'barbed wit' you described. That might hold my interest more than his poetry."

The discussion reached another lull, and she decided to cut the call short. Though Di had told her to encourage Mark, Lara hadn't gotten over her feelings of rejection from the other night. She preferred to be the one to propose hanging up, rather than let him have the pleasure.

"Well, I've got to go. I'm having lunch with a friend." She didn't really have a lunch date, but if he asked her for details, she could always say she was meeting Di. "Thank you in advance for making me a copy of that letter."

"Oh. Okay. Um, I just want to say that I'm glad you're doing the research you are, even if your reason for it is a little misguided."

She stiffened. "That's a bit of a backhanded compliment, isn't it?"

"No, no," he said quickly. "I only meant that I don't buy into the idea that you're being haunted. What I should have said is that I'm glad you're exploring local history—and I have to add that I enjoyed your insights into my ancestor. Your views of his character have made me curious about him. I'm even beginning to wonder if there was more to the old boy than I've always thought."

"Maybe you should make an effort to learn more about him," she said, her feathers still ruffled.

"I'm going to. You made me realize I never gave him much of a chance."

"And you say *I'm* apathetic about the past." As soon as the remark had slipped out, she bit her lower lip. Here he was trying to see her view about something, and she had to bring up an old point of contention. With Mark and her actually getting along for once, she really should have kept her mouth shut. "I'm sorry. I shouldn't have said that."

"No, you're right." His voice sounded grim. "Geoff was my great, great grandfather, you know. I should be telling *you* all about him, rather than the other way around. I'm the one who owes you an apology—or several. It was stupid of me to accuse you of indifference to the past. The research you're doing now proves I didn't know what I was talking about."

She breathed a sigh, glad to have escaped another argument. "Either that, or it proves I'm a big chicken—maybe both. Anyway, I'd better go before one of us says something else to set the other off."

"Wait. While I have you on the phone, there's one more thing I've been wanting to talk to you about. I've been thinking a lot about those letters in your attic. That's another matter I should have taken more interest in. If your offer still stands, I'd really like to help you look through them."

Her surprise nearly made her speechless. "You've changed your mind?"

"Yeah. Have you had a chance to get started on them?"

"No." Excitement began to permeate her, but she tried to tamp it down. He hadn't asked her for a *date,* for heaven's sake. Trying to sound nonchalant, she said, "There's no question that I could use some help going through all of that stuff. In fact, you may even need to give me a pep talk so I can work up the nerve to go up there."

"I will if I have to. How about we do it tomorrow? Are you busy in the morning?"

"No, tomorrow morning will be fine," she squeaked out. "Shall we say around ten o'clock? I can have some sort of breakfast on hand."

"Sounds great. I'll bring you a copy of the letter we found the other night."

After a few more pleasantries, they said good-bye, then she hung up the phone and took a deep breath. He was coming over, after all. She wasn't sure if it meant he was interested in her, but at least he wasn't avoiding her. As long as they stayed on good terms with each other, there was always a chance something could happen.

Mark's hand shook as he set down the receiver. Asking Lara if they could get together had made him absurdly nervous. His mouth was dry, and he felt inordinately happy that she'd agreed to his proposal. Anyone would have thought he had a hot date lined up.

He sat back on the couch for a moment, surprised by his reaction. Though he told himself he should focus only on the chance to explore her attic, the conversation had given him reason to hope for so much else.

Getting up off the couch, he went into the kitchen to get a drink. As he took a glass out of the cupboard, he reflected on her decision to study the history of her house. This unexpected development gave him new hope that she might still change her mind about the wall. She'd taken a first step toward grasping what a unique place her house held in local history.

Of course, her reason for the research was silly, he thought as he filled the glass with water, but to a certain extent he could understand her worries. Their experience during the electrical storm had been pretty scary. Other women in her place might have moved out of the house by now. He had no doubt she'd come to see that the ghost was a figment of her imagination.

Sipping the water, he recalled her observations about his ancestor. Lara's fascination with ol' Geoff had actually spurred a touch of pride in him today, the first he'd ever felt about the poet. She had opened him up to a part of his life he'd always missed out on before. If he hadn't met her, he might never have come to question his own prejudice.

He shook his head to himself. After this phone call, he felt like he was just starting to get to know her. She wasn't the careless woman he'd initially thought she was, and the more he learned about her, the more he liked.

Carrying his glass back into the living room, he wondered what he could do to encourage her in her research. With his experience, he should have been able to make suggestions about resources she might not have considered.

Deed records, he thought. He could pop in Town Hall and look up the former owners of her house for her. Even if the property had only passed from father to son all these years, the names and dates would make a good point of reference.

Setting his water down on the coffee table, he grabbed his car keys and hurried out of the apartment. *Nothing like being eager to please,* he mocked himself—but he had no intention of putting off the errand. Lara's unexpected new interest in her house had reinforced his attraction to her, but his feelings hadn't exactly been dormant. Over the last two days, he'd spent far too much time fantasizing about kissing her, touching her, making love to her . . .

As he turned onto Main Street, he could hardly believe that only two nights ago he'd told himself he could never have an intelligent conversation with her. Now he saw how presumptuous he'd been. He had so many things he wanted to discuss with her.

After parking at a municipal lot, he entered the town hall and took the stairs to the second floor. He'd done similar searches on occasion in the past, so he knew which office to try.

"Hi, Mark," the woman behind the desk said when he stepped inside. Her use of his name surprised him. Taking in her bobbed brown hair and dark-rimmed glasses, he thought she looked familiar, but he couldn't recall how he knew her.

Apparently she noticed his hesitation and added, "I'm Paula Nesbitt—Karen's friend."

"Oh, right. I'm sorry. It's been a while."

"Yes, I believe the last time we saw each other was at Pam Drucker's Christmas party. Anyway, how can I help you today?"

Suddenly he realized that this was the woman who had warned Karen about Lara's so-called gold digging. He didn't want to create a lead-in for the subject now. Scouring his mind for an alternative reason to be there, he said, "I wanted to find out when the next zoning board meeting is scheduled. Do you happen to know?"

She glanced at a bulletin board on the wall beside her. "Next Tuesday, in the meeting room downstairs. Is there a special case you're interested in?"

"No, I just thought that in my business I should learn something about zoning laws."

"I guess there *are* details you'd need to know." She pushed her glasses up her nose and looked at him more closely. "Karen mentioned that you're consulting with Lara Peale on her house. I can't believe that woman's trying to build an art studio in a residential neighborhood—on a historical street, too! You must be pretty disgusted about her tearing down an exterior wall."

He clenched his jaw, wishing that he'd made a better effort to guide her away from the topic. "I don't know much about it. Ms. Peale is withdrawing her application for a grant from the historical society."

She lifted one eyebrow. "So you're not working with her anymore?"

"No."

"Really? Karen told me Lara was at your apartment the other day, so I assumed you must still be on the case. I thought maybe you'd talk the woman out of knocking down that wall, but so far she hasn't been in to change her permit application."

"I'm afraid I don't have any influence with her. Now, if you'll excuse me, I have an appointment to keep." He turned toward the door.

"Oh, sure," the woman called after him. "I'll tell Karen you said hello."

He didn't acknowledge that "favor," scowling to himself as he left. Was it his imagination, or had Paula Nesbitt been fishing for information about his relationship with Lara? He found it hard to believe that the clerk concerned herself so much with *every* zoning question in the town.

Worst of all, her mention of Lara's permit had put a damper on his mood, reminding him that there was still a great chasm between them.

He'd really had enough of Karen and her nosy friends interfering in his life.

Chapter 10

LARA GOT UP extra early, allowing herself plenty of time to get ready for Mark's visit. Of course, she knew it wasn't a date and, given her own circumstances, moving slowly was probably the best thing. She would, however, follow Di's advice—to a certain extent—and try to "encourage" him today by putting her best foot forward.

After a long shower she spent fifteen minutes subduing her curls and ended up pretty happy with the result. Though she didn't like to wear a lot of makeup—especially in the morning—she dabbed on a bit of lipstick and face powder. Then she dressed in a cute new short set that she'd bought late yesterday during a second trip to Di's store. The attic would be dusty, but for once in her life she would start out looking crisp and clean. She had purposely chosen a soft khaki fabric to camouflage specks of dirt.

In the dining room she laid out a healthy array of breakfast goodies. The night before she'd baked blueberry muffins from scratch and cut up melons and strawberries for fruit salad. Along with these she put out yogurt and a carafe of hot Kenyan coffee, the most heavenly blend she knew of.

When she'd finished arranging the plates, napkins, and utensils, she checked the clock. It was five of nine—perfect. Thinking it would be fun to "unveil" her efforts later, she closed the dining room doors. She grabbed a sweater and the newspaper and headed out to sit on the porch and wait for Mark's arrival.

She stepped outside into a perfect summer morning. Not a cloud interrupted the deep-blue sky. Dewdrops glittered in the grass, and a soft breeze carried the scent of budding flowers to her nose. A pair of squirrels were scampering in the big maple in her yard, while the local birds provided a musical score for the scene. The mood was so tranquil that she decided to abandon the paper in favor of taking in nature's beauty.

Within five minutes Mark pulled up and parked his car along the side of the road. He got out and nodded to her.

She grinned and waved, admiring his form as he came up the walk. When he got closer, though, she could see that the smile he gave her didn't extend to his eyes.

Damn it, she thought. For some reason he had put up his guard again. She'd have to accept his detachment . . . for the moment, anyway.

They exchanged quiet greetings, and she led him into the house.

"Shall we grab some food and take it out on the porch to eat?" she suggested as they walked through the main hall. "I hope you like blueberry muffins. I didn't make anything hot this morning."

"Oh, I like anything," he said in a polite tone, "but, if you don't mind, let's skip sitting on the porch. I'd rather get right to the letters."

"Sure." Swallowing her disappointment, she opened the doors to the dining room.

Despite his coolness, Mark's eyes widened at the sight of the food. "Lara, this looks great—but you really shouldn't have gone to so much trouble."

"It was no trouble." She reached for the carafe and poured coffee into the mugs she'd set out. "If you're really eager to get to work, we can bring this stuff up to the attic and eat there. Unfortunately, that will mean carrying everything up three flights of stairs."

"No, that's okay. Let's eat here and just take our coffee with us."

They sat down for a ten-minute breakfast, making small talk about his writing and her painting. Both of them noted that they hadn't accomplished much in the past week, but neither tried to explain why not.

Afterward Mark helped her clear the table. Though thoughtful, the gesture made her feel a bit rushed.

"Do you have other things to do later?" she asked him. He'd seemed so enthusiastic about this plan the day before that she'd figured he was completely free. Now she'd begun to wonder.

"Only some writing this afternoon. My deadline's still a couple of months off, but I have a lot left to complete, so I have to keep to my schedule."

"Of course."

As they made the climb to the attic, she briefly showed him the other floors of the house. Most of the rooms held no furniture and therefore weren't much to see.

When they got to her bedroom he peeked through the doorway but stood noticeably outside the threshold. She thought he lingered a moment longer than at the other rooms—probably just because this one was actually furnished.

"I saw that you have Geoff's biography on your nightstand," he said as they climbed the next flight of stairs. "Have you started it yet?"

"Yeah, I read the first chapter or so." The opening to the book had focused mainly on the poet's work. Knowing that in the past Mark had derided her for admiring his ancestor's poetry, she was reluctant to comment on the subject. "Have you looked at your copy yet?"

"No. I hunted around for the book last night but couldn't find it anywhere. It may be at my parents' house. My apartment doesn't have much space, so I have a few boxes of books and papers stored in their spare room."

"Yeah . . . well, I don't have that problem here."

He didn't ask for her impressions of what she'd read, and the conversation died.

Their last leg of climbing involved a steep staircase built into the back room on the third floor. Mark offered to go up ahead of her, and she gladly agreed to let him—even though she'd visited the attic for a few minutes the previous day without incident. Pushing two lit lamps and a plugged-in extension cord up ahead of her, she'd had the place positively bright before she entered. When she did go up, she hadn't found the area as scary as she'd expected. There were mostly just crates up there, but she'd found two wooden chairs and dusted them thoroughly in preparation for today. Then she'd zipped back downstairs, not wanting to give the ghost a chance to catch up with her.

While Mark made his way up now, she paused to take off her sweater and leave it downstairs.

"I can't believe how much space you have in this house," he called down to her. "This attic practically qualifies as a fourth story. In the middle I can stand up straight with no danger of bumping my head."

She climbed up herself, noting that he continued to survey his surroundings instead of offering her a hand.

Chicken, she silently accused him.

She'd only been in the attic momentarily the day before, so she took a good look around, too. The space felt almost comfortable. She'd left a pair of small windows open all night, one with a fan pumping the stuffy air outside, while fresh air and sunlight poured in the other. Dust particles lit up in the streaks of sun.

"I know I saw letters up here years ago." She walked to the back wall and stooped down in front of a trunk. "I wish I could remember exactly where."

The latch gave her a fight, but eventually she pulled it open with a jerk that sent her falling back on her rear end. *So much for my neat appearance,* she thought, brushing off her shorts as inconspicuously as possible.

When she opened the lid she found that the trunk held furs rather than papers.

"Not in this one," she said, disappointed.

Mark started searching, too—well across the room from her, she noted. In the first crate he tried, he came up with some documents dating from the nineteen-forties. Too recent for M.A.S., they both agreed.

After checking two more trunks without any luck Lara finally hit pay dirt, opening a smaller chest filled with old letters. She picked up the one lying on top and gasped.

"This one is addressed to a Miss Mariah Sulley: an 'M.S.' She could be our spurned lover! Here's another. They all belong to the same woman."

"How old are they?" Mark hurried over to join her, kneeling on the other side of the chest.

She opened the first letter. "December twelfth, eighteen ninety-eight."

Checking several others, she found they all dated from around the turn of the nineteenth century.

"Let's look for one with a return address that lists someone with the initial 'G.'" He started sifting through the yellowed papers, and she followed suit.

Half an hour later they had pulled out all of the letters without finding a single one from a "G."

"Maybe it's not the same woman after all," he said.

"Or maybe she kept his letters separate from all her other ones—hidden away somewhere special, where she could reach them whenever she wanted to reread them."

"If so, we have no idea where."

She looked back down at the pile of mail. A strong hunch told her they'd found the right person, though she had nothing to substantiate it. The letters had all been written *to* Mariah; none of them included the woman's own handwriting. "I'm going to read through some of these and try to find other clues."

"Okay. Meanwhile, I'll look around and see if I

come across a smaller stash from 'G.'" He stood up and went back to his side of the room.

Naturally, he couldn't hunt closer to her. With an exasperated glance toward heaven, she looked back down and started reading.

The correspondence originated from quite a few of Mariah's acquaintances, but most of the letters had come from a few key relatives and friends. Lara weeded through page after page telling of births, weddings, illnesses, and deaths before she found any reference to Mariah's personal life. At last a paragraph caught her eye.

"Here's something," she said to Mark. She read aloud from the letter:

> *My dear cousin,*
>
> *The news of your pitiful state deeply pains me. To answer your question, yes, you must indeed approach the man responsible. Knowing him myself, however, I'm afraid that you're unlikely to fare well. He may have the appearance of a caring and sensible man, but there are stories about him that never reach the ears of a young woman like you. If, as I believe, he has only wicked intentions toward you, know that you may come to me in your time of need. An unmarried female in the family way is truly at the mercy of others, but here, where you are unknown, we can tell the neighbors that you are a widow.*

"God, Mark, she was pregnant." Lara paused, distracted by a wisp of cold air—the ghost of Mariah? She glanced around, but the feeling faded. "Maybe she died in childbirth. No wonder she can't find eternal rest."

He shook his head. "It still makes no sense that she would be haunting *you*. What do you have to do with the abuse she encountered in life?"

"I don't know—but what does it matter?" A wave of dejection lapped over Lara. "Imagine how she must have felt after reading this."

He shrugged his shoulders. "Judging by what we know from the letter you found in the secret room, she continued to hope that 'G' would return to her. Apparently she waited for him until she saw him out driving with the other woman."

"And we know what *that* did to her." She pictured the scene in her mind: A pregnant Mariah standing at the front window downstairs, excited to recognize a certain carriage approaching. Maybe the poor woman had even run out onto the front porch to greet her lover. Then, as the carriage drew closer, she would have spotted that bimbo next to him . . .

Lara felt a stab of pain. In her imagination Miss Sullivan had short-cropped red hair and a willowy figure. She looked a lot like Karen.

She refolded the letter. "I think I've had enough of this for one day. I'm starting to get depressed."

"You shouldn't let this stuff get to you." Mark sat back on the floor, cross-legged. "Remember, it happened a century ago. These people are all dead and buried."

"Yeah, but I'm not," she muttered.

"What?"

"Never mind." She gathered up the correspondence she had skimmed so far and put the pile back into the chest. While Mark pried open one last crate, she began sorting the rest into stacks according to who had sent them.

"Here are some more letters," he said, "though none of the ones on top are addressed to Mariah Sulley." He looked at his watch. "I guess you have a point about quitting. We've been up here for over two hours."

Despite her gloominess about the day's findings, she decided to take a shot at inviting him over again— very casually. She meant to encourage him without pushing him. If she got him to spend enough time with her, he had to loosen up eventually. "If you want to, we can get together again tomorrow and pick up where we left off today."

"I don't know," he said without meeting her gaze. "I have quite a bit of work to do."

His lack of interest didn't help her mood. She got up and smoothed down her shorts. "Well, I'm done for now. I'll meet you downstairs whenever you're ready."

Mark watched her disappear down the staircase. He knew he'd built up a wall between them again. All day he'd wanted to ask her about her plans for the art studio, but he dreaded starting another argument. Instead he'd clammed up and alienated her, erasing all the progress they'd made the day before. The only thing he'd done was create a state of limbo between them, while he wondered whether or not she was capable of seeing reason.

Frustrated, he refastened the lids on the crates and trunks they had opened. For a few minutes he lingered in the attic, not knowing what to do to alleviate the tension between Lara and him. Finally, he gave up and made a slow descent through the house to the first floor.

He found her in the kitchen.

Looking up from a sink full of dishes, she asked, "Would you like another cup of coffee?"

Noting that she didn't smile when she issued the invitation, he shook his head. "I think I'd better get going. Got to stick to that writing schedule."

"Right."

"Maybe we can go through more of the letters another time, once we've had time to digest what we found today."

She nodded, again not smiling.

They said good-bye without ceremony, then she turned back to the dishes. He walked out to the front door on his own. With each time he came over, he observed, she showed less reluctance to see him go.

As he stepped out onto the porch, a car pulled into the driveway. A woman got out of the passenger side. From the driver's side, a man emerged. Both had brown hair, fit bodies, and looked about Mark's age.

The couple came up the walk and reached the porch steps at the same time he did, so he stood back, waiting for them to pass. When the woman looked up, noticing him for the first time, he realized that he knew her from somewhere.

"Mark Vereker, right?" She gave him a wide smile. "You and I went to school together. I'm Diane Golden."

"Oh, right." His memory flooded back. She'd been a few pounds heavier in high school, he thought—otherwise, he would have known her immediately. He remembered she'd been a friendly, funny girl. "Of course, Diane . . . from Ms. Hendricks's ninth-grade English class."

"Exactly." She motioned toward the man beside her. "This is my husband, Jerry Lyons."

The two men shook hands and exchanged greetings.

"Lara and I are good friends," Diane went on. "We work together at the high school. She mentioned she had met you."

"Really?"

She gave him a small smile, almost a sly one, and nodded. "Yeah, I noticed your book on her table the other day, so she explained how she happened to have it."

"Di and I are on our way down to Cape Hatteras on vacation," her husband cut in, giving her a pointed look.

"We sure are—in just a minute." She laughed and looked back at Mark. "This morning I remembered I'd lent Lara my raincoat, and I may need it during the week. Hurricane season is starting."

"The forecast is perfectly clear," her husband said, shaking his head. "But this gives you one last chance to try to talk Lara into coming along."

"That, too," she admitted.

"Well, don't spend too much time doing it. I want to get out on the road as soon as possible. We should have left early this morning."

"Then I'd better get inside. If you'll excuse me, Mark." She slipped past him. As she opened the door and let herself in, she added, "Nice seeing you again."

"You, too."

"So," her husband said, before Mark could make his own excuses and get away, "I hear you're helping Lara with her house. You're with the historical society?"

"Yeah, I was. I mean, I am, but today I came by more as a friend."

Diane's husband looked at him a little more closely, but if he didn't take the comment at face value, he pretended he had. "Have you two come up with any new ideas for her studio?"

The question surprised him. He wondered why the man would expect them to. "We didn't get a chance to talk about it."

"That's funny. Whenever I've been around her for the last six months, the studio is about *all* she's talked about. I guess she's holding off work on it since you made her think twice about knocking out that wall."

"What?" The remark practically knocked him over. Chatting with this guy suddenly seemed a lot more interesting. "I had no idea she'd changed her mind."

"She didn't tell you?" He hesitated. "I hope I wasn't supposed to keep my mouth shut . . . but I can't imagine why I would be. I know she's having a hard time coming up with an alternative plan. Maybe she hasn't said anything to you because she doesn't know what she's going to do yet."

"Probably." Mark was too excited to carry on a decent conversation. This news changed everything. Lara really had listened to what he had to say. She'd understood his feelings and taken them to heart. "I'll have to try to come up with some suggestions."

The thought, he knew, was a bit premature. She wouldn't want advice from *him* after the pompous way he'd presented his ideas in the past. In fact, their clashes of opinion might be the reason she hadn't told him she'd changed her mind. Getting her to open up to him again would probably take some work. Now he really wished he hadn't been so remote today.

"You may have all week to do it," Jerry Lyons said.

"If Di gets her way, Lara will be coming to Cape Hatteras with us."

"Oh." His bubble deflated somewhat. Now that he knew he had gotten through to Lara, he didn't want to wait a week to see her again—especially after he'd made such a mess of today. He frowned. "She isn't likely to go at the last minute like this, is she?"

The man smiled slightly, probably amused by the wistful note in his tone. "Lara can be pretty spontaneous. And Di says that lately she's been uncomfortable alone in the house. If you ask me, a week with nothing to do but lie on the beach would be the perfect thing to relax her."

Remembering how scared she'd been the night of the storm, Mark could see her accepting the invitation. He pictured her on a beach in North Carolina, looking great in a bikini. What if she met someone she liked down there? By the time she got back home, he might have lost his only chance with her.

"It's been nice meeting you." Jerry held out his hand.

He tried to think of a way to keep the conversation going or an excuse to go back into the house and prevent Lara from leaving on vacation. Nothing came to him, so he gave in and shook the man's hand. "You, too."

Jerry strode into the house as if he owned the place.

Envious, Mark walked slowly out to his car. He dawdled beside the door, fiddling with his keys, hoping to see the couple come back out and leave without Lara.

He killed another five minutes pretending to look for something in the trunk. The longer the others stayed inside, the more it looked like she had decided to go and was getting ready. No one came out, and he felt more and more foolish with each passing minute.

Finally he got behind the wheel and started up the engine. He took his time pulling out into the street, continually glancing back toward the porch.

When he drove away and the house passed out of sight, the situation felt hopeless. Lara had more than one reason to go with her friends. If her fear of ghosts didn't drive her out of the house, his behavior today might well have convinced her she needed a break from *him*.

All the way home he stewed to himself. If he'd known earlier this morning that she had second thoughts about the wall, he wasn't sure he would have brought up the topic, but he certainly would have behaved differently. Instead of confirming her view of him as sulky, he might have shown her a more appealing side of his personality. He might even have experienced the carefree day he'd dreamed of before Paula Nesbitt's reminders had soured his expectations.

Damn Karen and her nosy friends! And damn himself for paying the least bit of attention to what they had to say.

To think that now he might not have contact with Lara for another week frustrated him—and not knowing for sure was even worse. By the time he reached his apartment building, he knew he had to come up with some reason to call her as soon as possible. He needed to know whether she was leaving town or not.

An idea came to him immediately, based on her interest in his ancestor. He felt sure that with a little effort he could dig up some juicy family story about the poet.

Starting the engine up again, he pulled back out of

the parking lot. He would pick up his copy of Geoffrey Vereker's biography at his parents' house and pump them for information. His father usually had some good family stories. As soon as he got back, he would give Lara a call.

The only problem with the plan lay there, he acknowledged with a frown. If she wasn't home when he called, he didn't know what he would do.

Too bad he didn't have a good reason to show up in Cape Hatteras.

Chapter 11

DIANE LEANED OUT of the kitchen into the main hall, peering toward the front of the house.

"Here comes Jerry now," she said over her shoulder to Lara. She turned back around and slumped against the door jamb. "Damn. He doesn't have Mark with him."

Lara pursed her lips. Looking away from her friend, she picked up a plate to dry. "I told you that Mark was acting standoffish again today. I knew that he wouldn't come back inside. Jerry may be a personable guy, but he can't work miracles."

"Hello, ladies," the man in question greeted them as he stepped around his wife. He looked at her and then to Lara. "So, what's your final decision, kiddo? Are you coming along with us?"

"Sorry, but I can't." She forced a smile. After the

morning she'd had, she was tempted to grab a bag and run away—but she didn't think the company of two happy couples would bring her much consolation. She would only be reminded twenty-four hours a day of her own failures in love. "I appreciate the offer, but I really have too much to do around here."

"Are you sure?" He gave her a concerned look. "Di tells me that lately you've been uneasy here on your own. She says you've even been dreaming up ideas about having a ghost. A houseful of friends might be just the thing for you."

But not a houseful of couples, she thought. "I'll be okay. I need to work out this ghost thing for myself."

Di nudged closer to her husband, gazing up at him with a shrewd smile. "Now let's get to the really important point, honey. You were out on the porch with Mark Vereker for ten minutes. What were you two talking about?"

"Not much." He glanced at Lara, then looked away from both women, clearly uncomfortable with the role of go-between. "Mostly his work with the historical society."

"Never mind," Lara said. She finished drying her plate and stowed it in a cabinet above the sink. "We aren't in high school anymore. I wasn't expecting you to try to find out whether or not the guy likes me."

"*I* was," her friend objected. "Did he say anything at all about her?"

Jerry avoided his wife's gaze. "Nothing significant."

"As if you would know what's significant and what isn't!" She swatted his arm with a dish towel. "You men have no insight when it comes to matters of the heart. Tell me every word that passed between you, and let me decide for myself."

"Look, Diane," he said, his eyebrows crunching together, "you may like matchmaking, but please leave me out of this. If I run into that guy again, I don't want to feel like I've been plotting behind his back—and I don't want to have to worry about what I can and can't say to him."

"I never asked you to go to any great lengths—"

"But you make me feel like a spy," he interrupted. "You get carried away with this stuff. Now, I'm going out and checking the tire pressure on the car. When you're ready to go, meet me out front."

Giving his wife a final stern look, he left the kitchen.

Di turned to Lara and rolled her eyes. "Men! I don't know what the big deal is."

She shrugged, privately eager to change the subject. Wiping her hands dry, she hung up the towel. "I'd better run upstairs and find that raincoat for you."

"Thanks. I'll run outside and tell Jerry I'll be ready in a minute—before he finds another reason to be annoyed with me." She exited the room into the hall.

Climbing up the back stairs, Lara shook her head to herself. Thank goodness Jerry refused to go along with his wife's schemes. The one thing worse than having no love life was having everyone around trying to arrange one for you.

She had just located the raincoat in her bedroom closet when she heard footsteps coming up the stairs.

"It's just me—not a ghost," her friend called from the hallway. She walked in and sat down at the foot of the bed. "Oh, good, you found it."

"No problem." Lara folded the jacket carefully to make packing it easier for Di.

"Jerry's better now. I promised him that in the future

I wouldn't prompt him with any questions to ask Mark or tell him anything confidential about your feelings."

"Sounds good to me."

Di lay back flat on the bed. "I also managed to wheedle an encouraging scrap of information from him, though. He said that while he was talking to Mark, he happened to mention that you might be coming to Cape Hatteras with us. According to him, the news seemed to make your boy a little anxious. Jerry says Mark pressed him for reassurance that you weren't likely to go at a minute's notice. When Jerry told him what a spontaneous person you are, he didn't look very happy."

The third-hand intelligence didn't strike Lara as very reliable. Besides, Mark hadn't looked happy all morning—including when she'd invited him to come over again. She held out the folded jacket to her friend. "Wonderful, but what good does it do me to have him think I'm out of town for a week? Now if he actually gets the urge to call me, he'll figure I can't be reached."

"The point is that he seemed disappointed that you wouldn't be around. He *wants* to see you." Di got up, tucking her package under one arm. "Besides, you don't have to wait around for him to call. Come up with a reason to contact *him*."

Lara shut the closet door. "I'll keep it in mind, but I'm not eager for another dose of the cold shoulder."

"Oh, come on, you're exaggerating. He's shown a lot of interest in you—and if you're subtle enough, you can pursue him without him even realizing it. I still say you should get involved with the historical society. They could probably use an artist on their team."

She shook her head, leading the way out of the bedroom. "No offense, but if *I* showed up at a meeting of the historical society, I think it would be pretty obvious I'm chasing him. With my luck, he probably wouldn't even be there. I learned back in high school that preplanned 'chance encounters' always seem to backfire."

"They worked for me with Jerry in college. When I saw him behind the counter in the music shop, I suddenly became a regular customer. After I'd come in a couple of times asking for his *expert* opinions, he started lending me tapes from his own collection. I showed up one Saturday night right before closing time and it ended up being our first date."

"I remember the story." Lara wasn't convinced but knew if she said so her friend would only treat her to more successful case histories.

When they came down into the kitchen again, Di let out a yelp of surprise. She hurried over to one corner of the counter by the sink and picked up a man's watch. "Hey, this isn't yours, is it?"

Butterflies stirred in Lara's stomach. Mark must have taken it off when he'd helped her clear the dishes. "It must be his."

"Perfect! You can take it over to his place tonight or tomorrow."

"No way." She grabbed the watch and put it back on the countertop. "Now stop nagging me. How does Jerry get you to promise to drop these uncomfortable subjects? I think I could learn a lesson from him."

Di said nothing further, but as they walked out of the kitchen she glanced at the watch again, then gave Lara a meaningful smile.

Lara just turned away.

After the married couple had at last set out on the

road, she looked around the house and wondered what job to begin with. The overload of tasks on her list of things to do made it hard to get moving on anything. Worst of all, she didn't seem to have any creative energy. Though sunlight streamed in the windows, making the house look cheery and ghost-free, the empty rooms left her feeling lonely. She was used to seeing or speaking to Di almost every day. With her best friend a twelve-hour drive away, the week ahead would be a long one.

Not in the mood to paint, she occupied herself for a while straightening and cleaning the downstairs rooms. While dusting the parlor, she noticed the original love letter Mark had found, still lying on the window seat. Since that day she had been afraid to touch it, but in broad daylight the piece of paper looked harmless.

She set down her dust rag and tentatively picked up the note. Luckily, she didn't feel any strange rush of cold. Unfolding the paper, she skimmed through the contents. The words that had charmed her the first time around sounded empty now that she knew how the story ended.

"Mark was right from the start," she said to herself. "'G.' was a snake."

A soft sound pricked up her ears. She thought she heard a man's voice whisper, "I didn't know . . ." The phenomenon happened so quickly she couldn't tell whether it was real or a figment of her imagination. Goose bumps rose on her arms, but she didn't feel the chill she'd associated with the ghost before.

"Didn't know what?" she asked the air, her voice cracking.

She stood still, listening carefully, but silence filled

the room. The voice had to have been in her head. She remembered hearing a similar sound in the secret room the night of the storm, but she hadn't been able to identify it as a voice. This time she had a definite impression of a man speaking. Not Mariah, she noted, surprised.

Thinking of that night, she realized she'd forgotten all about the poem in Mariah's letter to "G." What had it been about? At the time, she'd had enough emotional trauma for one night and hadn't even wanted to hear the rest of the letter. Now she wondered if it could be significant.

She went to the kitchen, where she'd left the photocopy Mark had brought her. Skipping down the page, she reached the poem:

As you read these lines coming from the grave,
Despair of your own eternal rest to save.
Until you advance a love to stand in place,
Of the love you once had but chose to debase.

By the time she'd finished, her hands were shaking. *Good God,* she thought. Mariah had cursed her lover to roam eternally.

As the full implications came to her, the photocopy fluttered from her fingers to the floor.

"*G.*" was the ghost, not Mariah.

She froze in place, half expecting some sort of supernatural onslaught to herald her revelation—another thunderstorm or maybe even an apparition. Nothing in the room moved. Sunlight continued to stream through the windows, the lighthearted chirping of birds drifting into the house along with it.

Scanning her surroundings for anything unusual,

she took an uncertain step toward the hallway. Nothing happened. In the stark daylight her fear seemed ridiculous even to her, but she couldn't shake it.

Slowly she worked up the nerve to fetch her purse from upstairs, moving a few steps at a time. She got to her bedroom and back to the kitchen without incident. Snatching up Mark's watch from the counter, she buckled it onto her wrist and dashed out the back door to her car.

She drove straight to his apartment building and parked in the first empty spot she found in the crowded lot. Nervous energy spurred her to jump out of the car and start running across the asphalt. The heat of the blacktop radiated through the soles of her sandals.

About twenty yards ahead of her a redheaded woman got out of an SUV. *Karen,* she realized.

Lara stopped abruptly and ducked behind a van, praying she wouldn't be seen. In her current harried state, she didn't feel up to facing the woman's cool stares and insinuating remarks. What was Mark's ex doing here again anyway?

The woman leaned back into her vehicle. Wearing a short pink scooter skirt and a white scoop-necked top, she looked as fresh as a daisy. Still puffing from her sprint, Lara wiped a streak of perspiration from her cheek. She glanced down at her own short set, now smeared with dirt from the attic. Suddenly khaki seemed a dull choice of color. Why hadn't she bought something brighter? Compared to Karen, she felt *so* dowdy.

When she looked up again, the woman had straightened up. She now held a navy-blue button-down shirt, which she flung over one shoulder. Lara recalled that at their last meeting Karen had mentioned she needed to return a shirt of Mark's. She felt a pang of jealousy.

I have his watch, she thought with a sense of possessiveness about him.

What she saw next made her feel even worse: In Karen's other arm she cradled a casserole dish. Apparently she and Mark were having dinner together. Had they patched things up? It seemed unlikely that estranged lovers would share a home-cooked meal. No wonder he had been distant earlier.

Lara watched through the windows of the van until the other woman had gone inside the building. When she felt sure she wouldn't be spotted, she rushed back to her car and sped out of the parking lot as quickly as she could.

Driving home she felt almost nauseous. Her unannounced trip to Mark's had been pathetic. She was so naive, so stupid. What if she'd arrived ten minutes later and walked in on him and Karen embracing, or even simply smiling and joking together? The thought of being their third wheel made her cringe. She felt like such a fool she could hardly stand her own company. Now that it looked like they were a couple again, she realized how much she'd wanted a chance with him.

Searching for something to take her mind off the pair, she considered stopping at the mall or her mother's house—but she felt too dirty and hot. She didn't want anyone to see her like this. Since she still had full daylight to "protect" her from the ghost, she headed home instead.

Thankfully, the house still had a normal feel. When she first let herself in she moved cautiously, but she felt no cold drafts or sensations of being watched. The rooms were empty. She was utterly alone.

Tired and depressed, she microwaved a frozen dinner and ate in the dining room. The pieced-together "slices" of turkey fell apart on her fork and tasted dry. Meanwhile Mark and Karen would be eating homemade casserole, probably some specialty of hers. No doubt it contained *real* meat.

God, she felt lonely. She longed to tell Mark her theory about the ghost being "G." Who else could she discuss such a weird concept with? Her mother would probably freak out over any mention of a ghost. Di was on the road and hadn't left a phone number where she could be reached in Cape Hatteras. Any of her other acquaintances would be sure to think she was crazy if she brought up the subject.

She wondered if Ron knew anything about a packet of old love letters belonging to Mariah Sulley. If they'd been stored in a special way, they might be considered a family legacy. Maybe he'd taken them with him when he moved out.

Glancing across the hall into the kitchen, she spotted her cordless phone on the counter. She rose and retrieved it, along with her address book from the phone stand in the hall. Flipping through to the page listing Ron, she punched his new number into the pad.

His answering machine picked up. "Hello, this is Ron . . ." Hearing his voice after all these months seemed surreal—so familiar yet unfamiliar. She got flustered and didn't even catch most of his message. Before she knew it the machine beeped. She had no idea what to say.

"Uh, hi, Ron, this is Lara. Sorry to bother you. I, um, had a question about the Sulley family. I'm just wondering about some letters you may have. Nothing important, though. There's no real need to call me back. Thanks anyway."

She hung up, immediately regretting the call. Once she'd started speaking it had been too late to retreat. She could only hope he wouldn't get back to her.

The phone rang and she jumped. Her heart pounded in her chest. It had to be Ron; he must have just missed her call. The ringer sang out a second time. She didn't know whether or not to answer—but she couldn't very well pretend she hadn't called a moment ago.

She picked up the receiver and pressed the "On" button. "Hello?"

"Lara, it's Mark." His voice sounded excited.

"Oh—hi." Her first thought was that he must have seen her outside his apartment and wanted to know what she'd been doing there, but that had been hours ago. He had certainly taken his time about calling. Had he waited for Karen to go home first? But it couldn't be late enough for a date to be ending.

Remembering that she still had his watch on, she glanced at her wrist: seven-thirty. Maybe the woman was still with him.

"I hope I'm not interrupting anything," he said, "but I think I have a really interesting lead on 'G.' Do you still have that letter he wrote—the first one we found?"

She wondered if he had also deduced that "G." was the ghost—but, no, Mark denied that the ghost existed. "Yeah, I was just looking at it today."

"I need to see it again so I can compare the handwriting to some other samples I've found. Can I come over?"

"Now?" She looked down at her crumpled clothes. The image of Karen's crisp pastels flashed in her mind, and she hoped fervently that the woman had gone home.

"Yeah, if that's okay," he said. "If not, I'd like to do it as soon as possible."

"Are you alone?"

He hesitated briefly. "Yeah, why?"

"Never mind. But I can't do it right this second." If she was going to see him, she definitely needed to shower and change. "Can you give me an hour or so? I can come over there, if that'll be easier."

"Actually, that *would* be better. That'll give me time to do some more research. I have some other things here that I'm eager to look through."

"What sort of things?" she asked. "Books?"

"I'll show you when you get here. But hurry—and don't forget to bring the letter. I think you'll be as excited as I am. See you in a bit."

"I'll see you," she murmured.

He hung up.

Still stunned, she stared at the phone for another moment before she pressed the "Off" button. Then she remembered she only had an hour to make herself presentable. The effort might be futile, but she would try. She put down the phone and raced upstairs.

The fact that Karen had left so early seemed a promising sign, she told herself as she stripped off her dusty clothes. Maybe the reunion hadn't gone well— but if not, wouldn't Mark have sounded depressed instead of excited? Their dinner could have ended early for any number of reasons. Karen might have had a meeting to attend or a plane to catch. Lara had no idea what the woman did for a living.

Getting into the shower, she wondered if she could work up the nerve to ask Mark directly about his relationship with his ex. She might not like the answer she got, but it was the only way to find out if she stood the smallest chance with him.

She decided she would see if the apartment showed any evidence of a romantic evening. If so, she would come right out and ask what the story was.

Chapter 12

WHEN LARA GOT into her car to go to Mark's she was still wrestling with mixed feelings. Why on earth had she agreed to meet him without knowing whether or not he was back with Karen? If the couple had made up, she would be better off dropping his friendship than hanging around him feeling rejected. She had never been the type to compete for a man's affections. If the situation came down to that, she would concede defeat.

As she backed out of the driveway, she clung to her one token of hope: Karen's early departure tonight. Because of that detail she had tried to look her best for this visit, digging out a form-fitting sundress she hadn't worn in years. She doubted that the dress could still pass for stylish, but she knew that the pale yellow color flattered her. She looked far more cheerful than she felt.

During the short drive to the other side of Falls Borough, another problem bothered her. Mark had told her that he had a lead on "G.," but after the revelation she'd had about "G." being the ghost, she wasn't positive that she wanted to know more about him. Since she'd found out how much he'd hurt Mariah, she had come to dislike the man—and she certainly didn't want to deal with him herself. If the spirit wanted something from her, she saw no reason why she should help him.

She parked outside the schoolhouse apartments and walked into the entrance hall. Clearing her throat, she pressed the intercom button.

"Hello?" Mark answered the buzzer.

"It's me," she said simply.

"Lara!" His voice still sounded excited. "You're finally here. Come on up."

If his dinner with Karen had gone wrong, he would be in a bad mood, she thought again, remembering the first time she'd visited his place. That time seeing his ex had left him sulky and short-tempered.

She trudged up the single flight of stairs, bracing herself for what she might learn tonight.

"Hey!" He waited for her outside his apartment door, his face beaming. He had changed into clean jeans and a T-shirt, which he'd left untucked—unusual for him. His posture looked more relaxed than normal, too.

She had never seen him looking so carefree before. All morning—with *her*—he had acted like a zombie. *He and Karen must have made up.*

"Do you have the letter with you?" he asked as she got closer.

"Yep." She patted her purse.

"You look great." Giving her dress a quick once-over, he ushered her into the wide foyer that also served as the dining area. For an instant his smile wavered. "You're not going out later, are you?"

She was still recovering from his compliment—though the praise probably had more to do with his good mood than her looks. It was as if he were a whole different person tonight. "No, I just wanted to get out of those dusty clothes that I wore in the attic this morning."

"Good, I'm glad you don't have any other plans. I want to be able to savor this occasion." He gave her a mischievous grin and urged her ahead with a hand on the small of her back. "Come on through to the living room."

Her curiosity stirred, but his light touch preoccupied her more. Spine tingling, she worried about his relationship with Karen. As they walked past the kitchen, she looked for signs of their dinner. The stove top was empty, and there were no dishes in the sink. She couldn't even detect the aroma of food—but she noticed that all the windows stood open.

"What's all this about?" she asked. As they entered the living room, she took in her surroundings. The contemporary furniture surprised her, more evidence of Mark's varied tastes. Several impressionist prints—two Monets and a Van Gogh—decorated the tall walls. The hardwood floor gleamed with a new finish, set off by a thick, oval rug. A staircase on the inner wall led to an upper level.

"Before I tell you, can I see that letter again?" he

asked. "I want to make sure I know what I'm talking about. Please have a seat, by the way."

"Thanks." She dug out the paper and handed it to him, then chose a plush love seat to settle down on. *Very comfortable,* she noted, leaning back into the cushions.

"It's him, all right," he said, looking at the letter. Bending down next to the coffee table, he slid a large cardboard box out from under it and pulled out some yellowed documents. Sitting down next to her, he held out one of the sheets alongside the letter from "G." "Take a look."

The paper he'd found was filled with handwriting that matched that on the letter perfectly. She stared at the sheet in amazement—and with some trepidation. "Where in the world did you get that?"

"My parents' house." Eyes sparkling, he paused, as if for dramatic effect. "It's the original draft of an essay Geoffrey Vereker wrote."

"Geoffrey Vereker?" She let her jaw drop. Her favorite poet was the ghost?

Of course he is, she realized immediately. She remembered that the first letter had seemed familiar to her—because she'd recognized his style of writing, she now saw. Thinking about how often she'd had the urge to read the Victorian's poetry lately, she shuddered. Did the ghost have some sort of influence over her? Had she sensed his identity subconsciously?

A horrible sense of personal invasion engulfed her. Could she get away from him at all?

"I can't believe you actually guessed his identity the other night." Mark grinned at her. "Remember—when we learned from Mariah Sulley's letter that 'G.' was a poet, and you wondered if he might be Geoff? I have to apologize now for laughing at your suggestion at the time. I still can't imagine how you figured it out. Maybe there's something to be said for women's intuition."

She put her hand up to her mouth, staring into space.

"Why do you look so shocked?" He set both papers down on the coffee table. "Aren't you going to gloat about your insight?"

"I don't dare." She met his gaze, her lower lip trembling. "The creepy thing is that earlier today, after you left, I worked out that 'G.' was the ghost. That means your ancestor is the one who's been haunting us."

His smile disintegrated into a grimace. "I've told you there's no ghost."

"But the pieces are all coming together now—why the strange happenings started when you and I met, why he's been at both of our places. Geoffrey Vereker is your ancestor, and he has a connection with my house."

He shook his head. "There are a couple of coincidences, but stranger things have happened."

"No kidding. Stranger things have happened to *us*. Why, for example, did I get the urge to read his poetry the night before I met you?" As more thoughts bombarded her mind, she looked at him with wide eyes. "He's the one who knocked his own book of poetry on your head—and led us to the secret room. He wants something from us."

For a moment he studied her, his expression blank. He leaned back on the love seat. If she hadn't been in such a state of shock, his proximity would have unnerved her.

"I'm not saying you've convinced me," he said,

"but I have to admit you have some interesting points."

"'Interesting' is not the word I'd choose. 'Horrifying' is more like it."

"Now don't let this upset you unnecessarily." He looked at her intently, his eyes full of concern. "You have to stop thinking like that."

She swallowed. "I don't like the idea of letting him get to me—especially when I know what he did to Mariah. But I'm not sure I *can* think of this experience as anything but horrifying."

"Try to consider it an adventure. Ghost or no ghost, you and I are getting a fascinating glimpse into the past." He motioned toward the box on the floor. "These papers all belonged to Geoff. Do you think you're up for helping me take a look through some of them tonight?"

"I don't know." The idea scared the wits out of her, but did she really have a choice? If she didn't try to find out what the poet wanted, he might not leave her alone.

Mark stood up. "I'll get us a couple of drinks to relax us. Would you like some red wine?"

"Please." She thought she might need a whole bottle. While he ducked into the kitchen, she sank back into the love seat. At least she wasn't in this on her own. Mark had to figure prominently in the reason why all this was happening. She'd lived in her house for five years and before meeting him there had never been any otherworldly incidents.

In a minute he came back with a bottle of merlot and two goblets. He poured with a steady hand, she noticed. Accepting a glass from him, she wondered whether he was really as fearless as he appeared. Did he truly still believe the ghost could be explained away, or was he just trying to keep her from getting hysterical?

She sipped the lush red wine and tried to emulate his calm demeanor. Letting the liquid loll on her tongue, she took in the smooth, dry taste. "This is good."

"Thanks. The brand is nothing fancy, but it's a favorite of mine." He set his glass down on the table and dragged the box of papers out farther into the open. "I'll say one thing for Geoff, he was prolific. His wife may have burnt his journals, but look at all the stuff that's left behind."

Leaning forward, she scanned the mound of ledgers, envelopes, and loose papers. "Is all of that his writing?"

"No, there are also letters here written to him from other people." He sat back down next to her and bent over the box, flipping though the contents.

His knee brushed hers, reminding her how close he was to her. What a difference from this morning when he'd kept to the opposite side of the attic. Apparently after Karen's visit he'd gone beyond thinking of *her* as a temptation.

He selected a leatherbound ledger from the pile and placed it in his lap. "My dad thinks we may find something juicy among all of this. He says that one of Geoff's sons hid a lot of his father's effects from his mother and didn't return them to the family archives until after her death."

"Can I look through the letters *to* him?" she asked. "Maybe if I don't rummage through his personal writing, he'll allow me some privacy, too."

He smirked but didn't argue with her, handing her a stack of correspondence.

As she read through the letters, she soon found that

they proved far more absorbing than the ones from
Mariah Sulley's chest. Many of them were from fans
of the poet, including females making barely dis-
guised—and sometimes boldfaced—propositions to
him. Lara wondered if Geoffrey had ever responded to
the women, or even met some of them. If he hadn't
gotten some kind of kick out of these letters, she
doubted he would have kept them.

She finished her glass of merlot and Mark poured
her another. The wine soothed her and, though she
couldn't exactly enjoy the research, their findings intrigued her. Whenever she or Mark came across an interesting passage, they read aloud to each other. At
first he chose most of his excerpts for a chance to
make fun of his ancestor's romantic phrasing, but after
a while the examples of "barbed wit" that he quoted
outnumbered the ones he mocked.

Lara pulled a particularly well-preserved letter out
of her stack. Her heart sank when she spotted a familiar *M* on the wax seal. Turning it over, she saw that it
was addressed to "G." She stared at it, reluctant to un-
fold the paper. "Here's one from Mariah Sulley."

Mark met her gaze, his features solemn. "Well, if
there was any doubt left, that confirms the lovers'
identities. Should we read it?"

"I don't know. I'd say no, but maybe we're meant
to. Can you do it?"

"Sure." He took the letter and read out loud:

My dearest G.,
    *Your pain is contagious. I suffer every pang
along with you, and I can no longer endure this
anguish. Pray meet me at midnight tonight at the
kitchen door to my house. I have the perfect re-*

treat for us. You are likely unaware that prior to the Civil War my ancestors aided with the Underground Railroad. They built a secret room into our house, and it still remains. My sisters and I played there as children, but for years the room has lain undisturbed. After the rest of the household has retired, this haven will serve us well.

Your own tormented M.

For a long moment neither Lara nor Mark spoke.

At last he refolded the paper and set it on the coffee table. "Well, now we know that the secret room didn't have a diabolic origin."

"That doesn't mean something terrible didn't happen there later." She looked away from him.

"I doubt Mariah committed suicide in the room, if that's what you're thinking." Shifting on the love seat to face her more squarely, he lifted her chin to meet his gaze, his touch warm and tender. "If she had, someone would have found her note when the body was discovered. In that setting, the death would have looked suspicious enough that they would have scoured the premises."

"I guess." The reflection didn't bring her much comfort. Reading Mariah's letter had renewed her sympathy for the woman. She needed a break from probing into the past. "Can I use your bathroom?"

"Of course. You don't have to ask." He pointed her in the right direction.

Passing the bistro table, she dismissed the Victorian couple from her mind by reverting to her fears about Mark and Karen. In the bathroom she checked for evidence of a woman's touch. The sparse decor seemed appropriate for a man's apartment. The room gleamed with cleanliness, but she felt safe attributing that to Mark. She didn't stoop to peeking in the medicine cabinet but noted that the sink and shower area held no feminine toiletry products. So far she saw no indication that Karen kept any of her things here. Of course, that didn't mean that they weren't dating again.

When she returned to the living room, Mark was reading a different letter. He looked up at her with a funny expression. "I've found another one of ol' Geoff's brilliant love letters. This one addresses a woman with the initial *R.*, but the words sure sound familiar."

Despite getting a bad feeling, she took the paper from him and skimmed the meticulous handwriting. She glimpsed the phrases "exotic flower," "a rose on the morn it blooms," and "our love will flourish fully."

"Oh, my God." She thrust the letter back at Mark. "How disgusting. He wrote the exact same things to Mariah."

As the paper exchanged hands, chilly air skimmed the back of her neck, making her shudder.

Her gaze shot to Mark's, but he looked down at the letter—so quickly that she suspected he too had felt the draft but didn't want to admit it.

"It's unfinished," he said. "See? He didn't sign it. He never sent it."

"Big deal." She took a step away from the love seat, then paced back toward him again. "He probably signed and sent out a hundred others like it. You were right all along, Mark. He was a real snake. I'm so disappointed. His poetry will never be the same for me."

He stood up as if he meant to come to her, then stopped. To her it seemed like he had remembered

Karen and had thought twice about making physical contact with another woman. "I'm sorry this has ruined something that you loved. I wish I hadn't shown you the letter."

"Oh, I was getting the picture anyway." She heard her voice reach a higher pitch. His hesitation to touch her revived her frustration over him and added to her annoyance. "You said it yourself: Women have intuition."

He blinked. "I don't know if that applies in this case. You thought the first letter was beautiful when you read it initially."

"That's only because I didn't know Geoffrey Vereker personally . . . and Mariah's problem was that she was so naive. A woman with experience knows when a man is toying with her. In fact, even she may have known but refused to accept the truth—like you said this morning. Why else would she have waited for his return from Baltimore when her cousin had warned her about him? Sometimes it's easier to cling to little signs of hope than to admit defeat."

"Maybe the matter wasn't black and white for Geoff either." Mark put down his ancestor's letter and grabbed the one from Mariah. "He saved this letter that she wrote. She must have meant something to him, or he wouldn't have kept this till the day he died."

"He also saved fifty letters from unfamiliar fans making him propositions." She pointed to the stack she'd read. "I'll bet they all meant about as much to him as Mariah did."

He shook his head. "I think I have as much intuition as you, and I suspect she meant more."

"Why?" It occurred to her that Geoff's presence in her house might indicate he was trying to resolve the rift between him and Mariah. She waited to see if Mark would confess to thinking along the same lines.

He looked down and set the letter from Mariah on the coffee table. "I don't know. Intuition can't be explained, can it?"

"You'll have to do better than that, Mr. I-Need-Solid-Evidence. Intuition is grounded in observation." The thought flashed in her mind that some observations contradicted others, like the fact that she'd seen Karen walk up to the apartment building with a casserole, but a couple of hours later both the woman and the dinner had disappeared without a trace. "I find it easier to believe in the existence of ghosts than in Geoffrey Vereker's loyalty."

"I'm not saying he was loyal to her." He met her gaze again, his brown eyes round and his focus direct. "We know that he was involved with other women, but we don't know the nature of his feelings for any of them. He may have cared a lot about Mariah Sulley."

She stared at him. Suddenly he'd become awfully protective about the ancestor he had always scorned. Was he talking about Geoffrey Vereker or really referring to himself? What was he trying to tell her—that despite his involvement with Karen, he might be interested in her, too? Well, sharing a lover was the last thing she intended to do.

"Sorry, but I think an adult man should realize he can't have his cake and eat it, too. Someone always gets hurt in the end." She bent down and picked up her purse from beside the love seat. "It's getting late. I think I'd better go."

"No, Lara, don't leave like this." He followed her as she brushed past the bistro table. "I don't understand. Why are you so upset?"

"Use your intuition to figure it out."

He grabbed his keys from the table and trailed her out into the hall, pulling the front door shut behind them. "Are you sure that you're all right to drive? Remember—you've had a couple of glasses of wine."

"I'm fine." She marched downstairs with him still at her heels. "Thanks for having me over."

When she paused to unlock the door to her car, he caught up with her and stood beside her. "I really am sorry you're disappointed. I know Geoff's poetry meant a lot to you. Maybe at some point you'll find that you can separate the man from his art and enjoy the poems again."

She shook her head to herself as she got behind the wheel and buckled her seat belt, yanking the strap tight across her lap. He totally didn't see what was bothering her—but maybe that was just as well. At least he didn't realize how hung up on him she'd become.

"Good night, Mark." She started up the engine and put the car into reverse. He had no choice but to step away and let her back out of the parking spot.

"Good night," he called after her.

As she pulled out of the lot, she saw him in the rearview mirror, watching her drive off. She stepped on the gas, still stewing over how clueless he was.

When she reached home and pulled into her driveway, she looked up at the house. Though she'd left the lights on in several rooms, most of the large building loomed dark. Shadows in the nooks and crannies looked ominous. Was that a bat fluttering past the roof or just a falling leaf?

Getting out of the car, she slammed the door. Her emotions were running high and her patience low. She'd had such a long day that she didn't have any strength left to waste on being afraid of her own house—not to mention that she was fed up with Geoffrey Vereker. If anything ghostly happened tonight, she refused to let it scare her. She wouldn't give that two-faced jerk the pleasure.

She unlocked the front door and stepped into the foyer, flicking on the switch that lit up the main hallway. The area looked mundane, and the house stood quiet.

Nevertheless, as she started down the hall, she did get a feeling that someone was watching her. *Intuition is based on observation,* she reminded herself, trying to dismiss the sensation.

As she passed the door to the studio, a thud from inside the room made her jump. Frowning, she poked her head through the doorway and turned on a lamp. Immediately she spotted the volume of Geoffrey's poetry lying open on the floor near one of the back bookcases.

She suspected that if she looked more closely, she'd find that the poem on that page held some sort of significance—but she refused to humor the ghost.

Taking a deep breath, she turned the light back out and continued through the kitchen to the back staircase.

As she climbed to the second floor she swore that she could feel his presence behind her. For once her anger outstripped her fear, and she stopped and spun around.

The stairwell appeared empty.

"Leave me alone," she said to the air. "I've had my fill of game playing. If you want company, go to Mark's."

Chapter 13

MARK WATCHED LARA'S car until it pulled out of his view. Down the street the engine revved, and he frowned to himself. He hoped that she wouldn't drive recklessly. She'd only had about a glass and a half of wine, but she had been really upset. He wished he'd told her to call when she got home to let him know she had arrived—though in her mood she might have ignored the request anyway.

As he started back toward the building his keys jingled in his pocket. He could follow her to reassure himself, he realized. Running over to his car, he jumped inside and took off in the direction she'd taken.

She had too much of a lead for him to know exactly which way she'd gone, so he took his usual route through town. He didn't see her during the drive.

When he got to her place, her car already stood in the driveway, empty. He let out a sigh of relief. Something under her hood crackled softly as the engine cooled. He looked toward the house and saw a light on the second floor come on. She'd definitely made it home safely.

Waiting a moment longer, he stared up at the window but saw no movement inside. He wished he had been able to calm her down back at his place, but the attempts he'd made had only irritated her more.

Beginning to feel like a Peeping Tom, he drove away.

As he retraced his path back to the apartment building he still felt surprised that Geoff's letter to "R." had disturbed her so much. He could understand her disillusion—even *he* had felt disappointed—but she'd really taken the blow personally. He supposed Geoff's poetry had once seemed heroic to her, making his artifice all the more painful.

A chilly breeze blew in the open car window, reminding him of her ghost speculations. Despite the creepy coincidences she had pointed out, he found it hard to believe that Geoff or any other spirit had visited them. He wished she wouldn't give those ideas any more thought. That sort of thinking only spurred the imagination. Since she'd started with that kind of talk, he himself had thought he'd heard a voice whispering something on a couple of occasions.

When he got home he locked up for the night and wandered to the living room. Spotting Lara's unfinished wine on the coffee table, he pressed his lips together. He'd hated to see her run out so quickly. If only he'd known how to talk some sense into her without coming across as overbearing . . .

Taking up her glass to finish the wine himself, he sat down by the box of his ancestor's effects. One positive result of this whole strange experience was that he'd gained an interest in the poet—only fitting, since the man *was* his great, great grandfather. Good and bad, Geoff was a part of him. Rejecting the connection hadn't taken that away.

He picked up a stack of the poet's letters and leaned back in the love seat to read.

Two hours later he could hardly keep his eyes open, but he couldn't seem to put the correspondence down. Reading the impressions Geoff's verses had made on some of his fans truly moved him. Many of the readers correlated significant events in their lives with passages in the poetry. Mark found himself wishing that his own work inspired such strong emotion. Maybe he needed to write something other than local history—something more grand in scope.

One more letter, he told himself, propping his elbow on a throw pillow, *then I'll go to bed.*

Pulling a random choice out of the stack on his lap, he unfolded the paper. When he saw the greeting he sat upright, at once alert. The note was addressed to "M."

He read the body eagerly:

My dearest M.,

I hardly know what to write—a rare predicament for me. Leaving for Baltimore this morning will be agony. I can scarcely bear to relinquish your precious love for a day, let alone several weeks. The coachman has been waiting outside for an hour, but I haven't had the will to set off. Though you and I said our good-byes last

*night, I am bursting with passion I wish I had
expressed.*

*These past few evenings with you have left me
in a state of awe. Your innocence is so refresh-
ing. You make me see the world in a different
light. Unveiling the mysteries of love to you has
rekindled an ardor in me that I haven't felt since
my youth. Your guileless enthusiasm quite erases
a decade or more of ennui.*

*I fear saying anything more. You threaten to
make an honest man of me . . .*

The letter cut off there, unsigned.

Staring at the paper, Mark whistled to himself. His
invulnerable ancestor had nearly fallen for the ingenuous Mariah Sulley! The knowledge made Geoff seem
considerably more human, despite the fact that he'd
clearly never sent the letter. The old dog had probably
turned tail and run away to Baltimore, putting Mariah
safely out of sight and out of mind.

Mark had to admit he could understand that type of
apprehension. How many times had he backed off
from Lara for fear of getting hurt the way he had with
Karen? He wondered if Geoff had ever had an experience with love that had left him scarred. The poet's reluctance to get involved with Mariah suggested so—in
Mark's eyes, anyway.

Folding the paper up again, he shook his head. By
leaving the letter unfinished Geoff may have given up
his one chance at happiness. From what Mark had
heard of his eventual marriage, it couldn't have been
satisfying. Family stories held that the poet's wife had
always derided his work. As a child, Mark had laughed
over that. Now he felt sorry for his ancestor.

He set the letter down on the coffee table and polished off the last of the wine. Finding the letter had done him good. Earlier in the evening he'd told Lara that matters weren't always black and white, yet until now he had painted his ancestor that way. Now he suspected that Geoff's passions ran as deep as anyone's. He himself had been the shallow one, clinging to his childhood impressions. With any luck, tonight's experience had helped him grow up.

As he carried the glasses into the kitchen, it occurred to him that this new letter might ease Lara's disappointment, too. Geoff's unsent vows would prove to her that Mariah Sulley had meant more to the poet than the miscellaneous fans whose letters he'd saved.

Deciding he would take the note to her in the morning, he went to bed feeling satisfied. As he drifted off to sleep, life seemed to make more sense than it had in a long time.

In contrast to his descendant, Geoff endured a restless night—a fitting end to a miserable day. Lara's reneging her admiration for him had been enough to make him feel dismal, but then she'd refused to read the poem he'd tried to place in front of her and, finally, actually demanded that he leave her house. Not wanting to deny a lady's wishes, he had gone back to Mark's—only to have his descendant find that mortifying letter he'd written to Mariah a century ago.

Geoff had hovered above, straining to read his own long-forgotten words. As the note came back to him, so did memories of the day he'd written it—perhaps one of the most distressing of his life. He recalled sitting in his study for some two or three hours, debating whether or not to go to Baltimore and leave Mariah behind. Even then he'd known that if he went he would never come back to her. He was too afraid. Once—as a mere stripling—he'd confessed his naive love to a woman. His older, married lover had laughed in his face.

That was why in the end he had gone to Baltimore, eager to break Mariah's spell over him.

Watching his worthless descendant pore over the letter had embarrassed Geoff. He'd never shared his feelings for Mariah with anyone, not even her. Whether Mark took his words seriously he couldn't tell, but the mortal's posture had shown that the note grabbed his attention. He wondered what the letter had meant to the fellow.

Now morning was here and Mark tucked the missive into his shirt pocket as he put the finishing touches on his toilette. He combed his hair and fetched his wallet from the dresser. Unquestionably he planned to take the letter somewhere. Geoff had a notion he meant to show it to Lara, though he didn't know why. He'd been surprised when his descendant had defended him last night. Could that possibly be his motive now?

Curious, he followed the mortal out into a flawless summer morning—sunny and temperate, with an occasional breeze to quicken the senses . . . assuming one had one's senses. Mark stopped briefly at a bakery, where he made a purchase, then drove on to Lara's house, as expected.

Perched above, Geoff watched him ascend the steps to the porch. Mark glanced at the empty swing where the lovely divorcée had been sitting the day before, then he looked toward the house. The storm door stood open beyond the wooden screen door. Somewhere in the back of the residence, music played softly. Lara was likely working in her studio.

Mark rapped on the door frame and peered through the screen, obviously eager to see her. After a moment he tried the door. The latch didn't budge.

He knocked again, harder, and called, "Lara, it's me."

"Just a minute," a faint answer sounded in the distance.

A moment later the lady appeared in the hall. She wore a dreadful rumpled shirt that could have served as a man's underclothing, along with tattered denim pantaloons, cut off at midthigh. Geoff frowned to himself. He wished she had a sense of how a woman ought to dress herself—in crisp, new satin and lace, not harsh and bedraggled fabrics.

Yet as she ran a hand through her unruly curls he had to admit that, even tousled, she looked adorable.

"Mark?" She shaded her eyes against the morning sun. "What are you doing here?"

His descendant grinned, ignoring the fact that her greeting had been less than enthusiastic. "I couldn't resist stopping by. Hope you don't mind. To try to make up for barging in I've brought doughnuts ... and something else that may interest you."

"Doughnuts?" The confusion on her face didn't lift, but she opened the door to admit him. "Well, I suppose I could use an accompaniment for my coffee."

As she led him toward the kitchen Geoff floated behind them, feeling a twinge of guilt for intruding where he wasn't wanted.

"Shall we sit out on the porch?" Mark asked.

She shot a surprised look at him over her shoulder. "You're not in such a hurry today?"

He shook his head, a sideways grin stealing to his lips. Their gazes locked for a moment, and something about his expression startled Geoff.

The inept puppy is entranced by her, he realized. Mark's detachment was all a hum. Geoff looked more closely into the man's eyes and saw a spark of fire in them. His descendant had lost his heart; he was certain of it. The knowledge alarmed him. For the first time since Mark had come upon the scene, Geoff saw him as a real threat to steal Lara away.

He watched with concern as the couple got coffee in the kitchen and carried their cups out to the porch. Mark's gaze followed Lara's every move, no matter how mundane her actions. Geoff couldn't understand why the fellow maintained such an aloof stance with her if he was well on his way to love. But perhaps he had answered his own question: The idea of love was a frightening prospect. Perhaps Mark would still be cowed by it.

"So what, besides the doughnuts, did you bring that's supposed to excite me so much?" Lara balanced her coffee in one hand and slid a small wicker table around to the front of the swing. She took a seat, steadying the swing with her foot.

Mark sat next to her and set down his cup and the bag of pastries. "Maybe I should show you now, before we get our hands sticky."

Geoff cringed as his descendant pulled the letter to Mariah out of his pocket. He hated having his private feelings bandied about. True, he'd occasionally let a thread of raw emotion slip into his verses, but he'd certainly never meant for this intimate letter to be seen by the public—or anyone. He had to wonder why he'd even kept it.

Mark gave the paper to Lara, along with a smitten grin. "Last night you seemed to take Geoff's treachery so personally that I felt terrible. Maybe this will help you see him in a different light."

Eyebrows raised, she took the letter. "Don't count on it."

She read the missive in silence, Geoff studying her face for a reaction. As her gaze skipped down the page, her expression gradually altered from one of curiosity to one of melancholy.

On finishing, she stared blindly at the letter. He saw her blink back tears.

Mark frowned. "What's wrong? I thought you'd be happy to find out he cared for her after all."

"It's just so sad. None of this had to happen—the pain Mariah suffered, her untimely death, the curse she put on Geoffrey—"

"Wait a minute. We still don't know how she died. And what curse are you talking about?"

"The one in that poem she wrote, telling Geoffrey to despair of eternal rest." She thrust the note back at him. "It was cruel of her but done in the heat of anger. Unfortunately, a curse probably can't just be taken back later."

"So you *have* read the rest of that letter." He took the paper and refolded it. "Well, the way I see it, melodrama was simply part of the belles lettres of the day. I strongly doubt that even *she* believed she was sentencing a man to purgatory."

Geoff winced. The mortal could go on fooling himself, but *he* knew the truth of the matter. He suspected Lara was right about the needless nature of his fate.

What if he had sent the unfinished letter to Mariah, if he'd stayed with her instead of going to Baltimore? How would his life have played out differently? Where would he be now, in death?

"Even without the curse," Lara said, "you must see what a shame their story is. Geoffrey might have been a lot happier with her than with that wife who burned his journals. What kind of widow does that? If he'd trusted in his feelings for Mariah, both of them might have lived longer and more meaningful lives."

The reference to Deborah particularly stung Geoff. During his life she'd never been a partner to him, let alone a mate. Nothing had ever hurt him so much as when she'd burned his journals. Those essays had contained his life's story, his legacy. As a ghost he was now immortal in a way, but the only immortality he'd wanted had gone up in smoke with those journals.

"Yes, I thought that, too," Mark said.

"You did?" Lara's gaze shot to meet his.

He nodded and set the letter on the table. "But it's all water under the bridge now."

She raised her eyebrows. "Maybe. Maybe not."

Geoff felt the most asinine he ever had, having his life analyzed and second-guessed—especially when the people examining his decisions seemed to see them more clearly than he had.

Mark twisted his mouth and sat in quiet reflection. After a moment he picked up the sack of baked goods and held the open end out toward Lara. "Would you like a doughnut?"

She looked into the bag and chose one iced with chocolate.

Shrugging off all the worries of the world is fine for some, Geoff thought with resentment. While the mortals ate their pastries he continued agonizing over his farce of a marriage, his dissatisfaction with his family, and his current struggle for peace. He acknowledged that the only matter for which he could condemn Mariah was his ghosthood; the blame for the remainder of the mess lay squarely at his feet. In fact, maybe all of the blame did. If he'd properly sorted out the rest of his life, Mariah might never have cursed him.

The sound of Lara's laugh drew his attention back to the mortals.

"You've got powdered sugar on your nose," she said to Mark.

"Where?" He swiped at his nose but only smeared more of the white dust on it.

She laughed again. "Now it's worse."

Leaning forward, she rubbed the powder off with her thumb. With their faces so close together, their gazes locked. As she stared into his eyes, her smile faded. She started to back away, but he caught her hand in his.

He bent closer and kissed her.

Geoff winced. The kiss was gentle and slow—not ardent but full of emotion nonetheless.

When Mark pulled away, Lara looked down at her doughnut. She cleared her throat. "There's something I need to ask you. It's important for me to know if we're going to keep . . . um, getting together like this."

"What's that?" he asked.

After a pause, she looked him in the eye. "Are you back together with your ex—that is, with Karen?"

As distraught as he was, Geoff found it hard to care about this turn in the conversation. Still, he noticed a flicker of a smile touch his descendant's lips before Mark schooled his features into blandness.

"Of course not. Why do you ask?"

She cast her gaze downward again. "I had a feeling you were."

"Your intuition fails you." His grin still threatened to break, and Geoff felt a twitch of annoyance with him. The fellow might well act tickled over the lady's interest in him. He didn't deserve her.

Studying him, she asked, "Did you have dinner with her last night?"

The shadow of a smile faded, replaced by a look of mild surprise. He shook his head. "I ate with my parents, at their house."

"Alone?"

"Yes." His air changed to one of consternation. "Is there something on your mind, Lara?"

She swallowed. "I actually should have asked you last night, but I felt kind of stupid—and then we got so caught up with the letters I never got around to it."

"To what?"

"To telling you that I almost stopped by your place yesterday afternoon. You left your watch here—oh, that reminds me." She rolled up her sleeve and undid the buckle on a thick leather strap. Taking the watch off, she gave it to him. "I'm sorry I forgot to give it to you last night."

"That's okay." He took it and wrapped the band around his wrist. "But what is it you really wanted to talk about?"

She moistened her lips. "Well, to pick up where I left off, I actually drove to your apartment yesterday. But when I got there I didn't think I should go in. I saw Karen walk into your building ahead of me carrying a casserole dish."

"Really?" He looked up at her, and a short burst of

laughter escaped him. "Well, I wasn't home all afternoon. If Karen planned a surprise dinner, *she* ended up with the surprise."

Lara watched him closely. "You *would* tell me if you were back together with her?"

"That's an 'if' that's never going to happen, so you don't have to worry about it." He smiled at her, and she held his gaze, apparently still in doubt of his word.

The scene had started to bore Geoff—then his descendant leaned forward and kissed her again. This time he met her mouth with more hunger, reaching up with his doughnut-free hand to cup her cheek. She let him part her lips with his tongue, and a soft moan escaped her.

Geoff's jealousy surged.

For an instant he debated dumping Mark's coffee on his lap to foil the mood—but suddenly that sort of prank seemed childish. Why should he care how these mortals conducted themselves? What did anything matter in comparison with the mess he'd made of his existence?

When Mark released Lara, she stood and seemed to have a hard time meeting his gaze. "I think I'll just top off my coffee. Can I get you anything?"

He shook his head and, with a wistful smile, watched her walk into the house.

Geoff hovered above feeling numb. For lack of anything better to do he decided to follow Lara inside. As she walked down the main hall she looked back over her shoulder toward the porch several times.

When she reached the kitchen, the telephone rang and she jumped.

Taking a deep breath, she picked up the receiver. "Hello? . . . Oh, Diane, am I glad to hear from you. . . .

No, no, nothing's wrong, not really. Did you make it to Cape Hatteras all right?"

She listened to the party on the other end, nodding and making sounds of understanding. "Good. . . . That sounds great. . . . No, it's really not that big of a deal—or shouldn't be, anyway."

Peering around the corner toward the front of the house, she shielded her mouth and whispered, "Mark's here now so I can't talk, but he just *kissed* me . . ."

Geoff raised his eyebrows. His descendant had certainly frazzled her. He supposed Mark must have a bit of the Vereker mystique in him somewhere.

"Well, I don't know what to think. It's a long story, but I'm still not completely convinced things are over with him and Karen."

She took another peek around the corner. "Yes, well, *you* would say that, wouldn't you? Listen, I know this is a weird question, but do you think womanizing runs in families?"

The ghost frowned to himself. Was that aspect of his personality the only one she'd judge him by from now on?

"No, I suppose not," she said. "Anyway, I'd better go. Is there a number where I can call you back later?"

Jotting down the information, she promised to phone that afternoon and said good-bye. She started back up the hallway but swung around and returned to the kitchen. Grabbing her cup, she slopped a few extra ounces of coffee into it and hurried back out to the porch.

"That was Di on the phone," she said breathlessly to Mark. "They made it safely to Cape Hatteras."

"I'm glad to hear it." His eyes held a question that

had nothing to do with Lara's friend. Geoff knew he must be wondering how soon to try kissing her again.

"I told her I'd call her later." Looking away from his gaze, she perched on the edge of the swing, leaving more space between them than before. "There's something else I need to talk to you about: the ghost. I know you don't buy the idea, but I really need your help. To me it's obvious that this problem affects both of us. For my sake, try to suspend your disbelief."

He studied her with a sober air. "What exactly do you have in mind?"

"Well, I've been telling myself I don't want anything to do with this, but I suspect we don't have a choice. If that's the case, we need a clearer picture of what's going on." She shifted slightly but kept her distance. "Did you ever take a closer look at the letter Mariah wrote—the one we found in the secret room?"

He frowned. "I've read it, but, as I've told you, I think that poem is nonsense."

"Well, I don't. I think the words may hold the key to finding rest for Geoffrey."

Geoff's ears perked up again. By Jove, could she be right? The curse had been written like a riddle. He couldn't remember exactly how the verse went, but if there were a remedy for his circumstances, he'd wager anything that the poem contained it. He needed to see the letter again.

Mark made a face.

"I think we should take another look at it," Lara said. "Please. Indulge me on this. What harm is there in it?"

He sighed. "I don't like encouraging you to believe you're being haunted—but if you really want to examine the letter, I'll help you. Do you have the copy I gave you?"

"It's in the studio. Shall we go and look at it now?"

"Might as well." He rose. "While we're in there, can I take another quick look at the secret room? Now that I know about the connection the place has to my ancestor, I'm curious to see it again."

She hesitated but got to her feet as well. "I guess so—as long as you don't expect me to join you. I mean, I'll wait in the studio in case you need me, but if something weird happens I can't guarantee I'll have the nerve to come in after you. I may resort to dialing nine-one-one."

He laughed. "In that case, I'll only ask for your help if I need an ambulance."

Geoff followed the pair into the house with as much trepidation as Lara—perhaps more. He dreaded re-entering that frightening room, but if exploring it might give him the slightest chance of altering his wretched existence, he damned well would go through with it.

They reached the library, and Lara stood back while Mark fiddled with the mechanism in the bookcase. After a moment the door ground across the floor. She flinched visibly, Geoff empathizing with her for every quiver in her muscles.

"I've still got your flashlight here," she said as Mark looked around the bookcase. She snatched up the portable electric torch from her drawing table and handed it to him.

"Thanks." He flicked on the switch and aimed the beam into the secret room. Wasting no time, he stepped through the entrance.

Geoff faltered, then floated in behind him.

Mark directed the ray around the small space, examining the barren walls. When the light came to rest on the fireplace, he paused and stared for no apparent reason.

An unusual sensation—what he would have called tingling during his lifetime—struck Geoff as he gazed at the hearth. Was Mariah in the room? He concentrated on perceiving her presence and could feel her just beyond his reach.

The beam of light wavered as his descendant shuddered.

She is here. Excitement coursed through Geoff like warm red blood in a living being. He knew that he was close to reaching his lost lover, and he found that he longed for the contact—even if her appearance upset him again. Real communication had eluded him for the last hundred years. Until now he hadn't quite realized how lonely he'd been.

Mark seemed to be frozen, pointing the flashlight into the fireplace. As Geoff stared at the scene, recollections of making love to Mariah flooded his mind. He could almost feel her in his arms, her body small and pliant. Her mind had been lithe too, he recalled. She had loved to listen to his poetry and offer her interpretations. In fact, she'd often given him insight into the workings of his own mind.

Some of the moments he'd spent with her had formed the times when he'd felt most like a legitimate poet—and most like a man. What he felt now, however, startled him—a heartrending yearning that he'd always managed to sidestep during his life.

"Mariah?" he asked aloud.

The only response was a glance over the shoulder from Mark.

Geoff ignored his descendant and scoured the room

for some sign of his lover. He couldn't see, hear, or feel her. Desperately, he said to the air, "I didn't know about the babe. I wish I had."

"Mark?" Lara called from the library. Her voice sounded sharp and alive, somehow disturbing to Geoff. "Is everything okay in there?"

The mortal scanned the four walls around him. "Yeah. I'll be right out."

He aimed the beam of light at the fireplace again. The hearth stood quiet and lifeless. Frowning, he directed the light toward the back of the bookcase/door and walked out of the room.

Geoff lingered behind in the darkness, but without Mark there he no longer got a sense of Mariah's presence.

"Mariah?" he whispered in spite of himself. The pain of desperation cut though his being.

The room remained still.

He waited a few more minutes, but somehow he sensed that she wouldn't come to him on his own. So far she had made her points to him via Mark and Lara. He had an idea that if he wanted to get through to her, he would need the mortals' help.

Chapter 14

AFTER TAKING A few minutes to pull himself together—and ensure that Mariah wouldn't come to him after all—Geoff drifted back into the library to see what the mortals were doing.

"It's here somewhere." Lara sifted through a mass of papers on her drawing table and pulled out a sheet. "Here we are."

She turned around and looked at Mark expectantly, but he just stood, gazing at her, expressionless.

"Everything all right?" she asked.

"Of course."

She studied him more closely. "Are you sure nothing happened while you were in the secret room?"

He shrugged. "There's just something creepy about the atmosphere in there, like you've said. Maybe it's the isolation from the rest of the house—and the world."

"So you still deny there's a ghost?"

"I don't profess to know *anything* about ghosts." Frowning, he glanced around the room. "I guess we'd better sit down and look at that damned letter, if we have to."

She lifted an eyebrow. "I think we do. Why don't we have a seat on the couch—unless that's too close to the room for you."

His mouth twisted. "That'll be fine."

Mark's obvious tension made it apparent to Geoff that he *did* have qualms about ghostly goings-on, but Lara didn't press him to admit to his fears.

She walked over to the large red sofa. Choosing a spot in the middle, she sat down.

He had no choice but to sit fairly close to her and, when he did, the pillows formed a semicocoon around them. The effect looked intimate. Geoff could see that his descendant's thigh was touching the lady's, though the two layers of denim their clothing formed between them likely made the touch less tender than it could have been.

Lara held the letter out to him, and he took it, looking down to read it. His eyes darted back and forth as he skimmed over the contents.

"I think the poem is the key area to study," she said.

"Yes." He cleared his throat and read the verse aloud with no sign of emotion:

> *As you read these lines coming from the grave,*
> *Despair of your own eternal rest to save.*
> *Until you advance a love to stand in place,*
> *Of the love you once had but chose to debase.*

On hearing the cruel words again, Geoff winced.

Mariah, he thought, shaking his head, *how I wish I had spoken to you instead of running away.*

"So she's telling Geoffrey there *is* something he can do to find peace," Lara said slowly. She looked off into space, clearly pondering the meaning of the words. "He has to 'advance a love' somehow—encourage a love. Between him and someone else? I doubt Mariah would have wanted *that*. Do you think she means he needs to bring two lovers together?"

She and Mark looked at each other and an idea struck Geoff. *Could they be the lovers I'm supposed to encourage?*

The mortals seemed to have the same thought. Their gazes locked. For an instant they stared at each other, then both looked away at once.

Mark folded up the letter. "Well, it's up to ol' Geoff to work that one out, isn't it?"

She turned away from him.

Clearly neither of them wanted to discuss the possibility, but Geoff was intrigued. He hated the idea of his descendant ending up with Lara—she was far too good for him—but if their union meant a chance for Geoff to find peace, wasn't it worth the sacrifice? The only question was what Mariah meant by telling him he must "advance" their love? How was he to advance someone else's love when he'd made such a muddle of love in his own life?

"Is that a speaker tube?" The sound of Mark's voice drew the ghost out of his reflections. The mortal gestured toward an iron device mounted on the wall. Getting up, he walked over to inspect it.

"Mmhmm." Lara remained sitting. She rubbed her forehead as if trying to clear her head. "The pipe connects to the third floor. If I had servants, I could call them down to wait on us."

He stood looking at the mouthpiece for a moment longer. "I see something new every time I come here."

Their casual observations had a hollow tone, but Lara continued. "I'm still learning about the house myself."

Mark wandered to the hearth. "I love the ornamentation around this fireplace. The work is so intricate."

"It is. There are even hidden drawers in the surround. They've always been a favorite feature of mine." Getting up, she walked over to where he stood and leaned down to pull out a compartment. "I have potpourri in here and matches in one of the others but couldn't think of anything to keep in the rest. How many matches can one nonsmoking person use?"

"Wow," he said. He knelt and took a moment to play with the drawer, testing to see how well the facade blended into the wood around it.

Watching him, she smiled. "You make me remember how fascinated I was with the details of this house when I first moved in. It really *is* an amazing place. The years of . . . well, let's just say *bad memories* made me forget how much I originally loved these rooms."

Mark's gaze roamed up to the top of the outside wall—the one she had planned to knock out for her addition. "Aren't the carved chrysanthemums and dogwood flowers in the millwork of the molding great? There's an oriental influence in some Victorian architecture."

"I don't think I've ever noticed those particular details before." She stared up at the exquisite design. "There are hundreds of the little buds! Looking at them, I can imagine myself in a wooden garden. . . . God, how many hours of skill and loving patience must have gone into that work?"

Mark watched her but didn't say anything. For a moment they both stood still.

She glanced at him, then looked downward. Without meeting his gaze she said softly, "I've decided against tearing down the wall."

Good for you, Geoff thought.

Mark stood without speaking or moving for a few more seconds. Finally, he asked, "Have you come up with an alternate plan?"

"No, but I will." She turned to face him. "The majority of my renovations may have to wait until next summer . . . but things don't always go as planned."

He stared at her, his expression almost sad. Geoff was surprised to see that he didn't gloat. His descendant had some breeding, after all.

"I'm glad you were able to look beyond my arrogant insistence and come to that decision yourself," he said.

She laughed, again looking away from his heavy gaze. "Well, I'm glad *you* helped me see past a few raw memories so I could take in the big picture. Preserving this for the future makes a lot more sense than destroying it to try to erase a painful period of my life."

He gave her a look so tender Geoff knew that barriers were breaking down between the couple. To his surprise, instead of feeling envious, he felt a bud of hope.

Kiss her, he thought. *Kiss her, for heaven's sake.*

Stepping toward her, Mark reached up and brushed her cheek with the backs of his fingers. "No one can erase his or her personal history, but I hope you'll find another way to get past the pain."

Geoff sucked in his breath. As the mood grew more tender, he began to feel ashamed of his voyeurism.

I'll leave them now, he thought. *I can check back in the morning and see if he's still here.*

He drifted out of the house, hopeful yet afraid to be so.

The earnestness of Mark's words moved Lara. No other man she knew had ever spoken to her with such sensitivity—certainly not her ex-husband. At times Mark may have had his moods but only because he felt life so *fully.* Now she wanted to share more of her life with him. She wanted to enrich her experiences with his perspective and to add to her own.

Her gaze dropped to his lips. Most of all, right now she wanted him to kiss her.

As if reading her mind, he bent and pressed his mouth to hers, the touch warm, the pressure tentative. She put her arms around him, taking in the broad strength of his shoulders. Closing her eyes, she tilted her head back and let her lips part. He deepened the kiss, his tongue playing at her mouth. She met it with hers, hungry to taste him.

His arms slid around her, and her body melted into his. She felt warm, safe, like nothing else mattered. His closeness, the clean scent of his skin, and the warmth of his body comforted her. Amid all of her recent fears of the supernatural and the unknown, he felt reassuringly physical, of this world.

Briefly he let go of her lips and looked into her eyes. They faced each other, inches away, with solemn expressions.

"Is this real?" she asked, even though the question sounded silly. "The ghost . . . he can't make us do whatever he wants, can he?"

He shook his head. "There's definitely nothing otherworldly about my feelings now—no mystery. I want you, Lara, because you're not only beautiful but full of insight and brimming with life."

She smiled softly. "Then we have more in common than I realized."

He grazed her lips with his. "Do *you* feel like you're being controlled from beyond?"

"No. But I hope your ancestor is discreet enough to give two people some privacy when they need it." The words popped out of her mouth before she thought about what they implied. Now she realized she'd practically come out and told Mark how much she wanted him.

She lowered her gaze—but she couldn't deny her feelings. She did need to be alone with him. Taking him by the hand, she led him over to the couch.

They collapsed onto the cushions in each other's arms. He pulled her close to him, kissing her more urgently now. She felt her heart pounding in her chest and heard his breath quicken.

He's going to make love to me. The thought made her dizzy with excitement. It had been a long time. For years Ron hadn't seemed to care much about whether or not they made love. After a while she had built up her own walls of defense and shied away from trying to entice him. Now she remembered what it felt like to *long* to become one with another person—and to know that he wanted you, too.

She kissed Mark like a woman starved for love and held him tightly, squeezing him against her. With one will, they slid down to stretch out on the couch, him on the outside, her inside. She felt the length of his body flush against hers, as she had experienced it for one short moment on the night of the storm—but now she could respond the way she couldn't then, the way she'd wanted to.

Pushing her hips into him, she reveled in the feel of his erection, hard and insistent. *He does want me,* she marveled. Until that instant she hadn't completely believed it.

"Oh, Lara." He buried his face in her hair. "You smell wonderful . . . and you feel fantastic."

He sank his fingers into the curls at the nape of her neck and kissed the sensitive skin beneath her earlobe. Tingles of excitement flickered along her spine.

She let her head fall back to allow him access to her throat. The baggy T-shirt she wore suddenly felt constraining. When he slipped his arm under the hem and palmed the exposed skin of her waist, she propped herself up on one elbow and pulled off her shirt with her other hand.

"You have a beautiful body," he breathed, his gaze encompassing her bare belly and wandering upwards.

Did she? The fire in his look made her believe him at this moment. But she was glad she'd worn one of her nicer bras, an ivory satin confection trimmed with lace.

Focusing on her eyes, he smiled and leaned down to meet her mouth again. The kiss built slowly, first tender and gradually more demanding. He reached around to her back and unclasped her bra. The release of tightness from around her chest felt like a magnificent gift of freedom.

He cupped one of her breasts, which she'd always considered a little deficient. All of her body was small.

"You're perfect," he murmured and lowered his mouth to her, circling his tongue around the rim of her nipple. Spirals of pleasure radiated from the hot trail he left. She arched her back, and bliss sparked through her, warming her, charging her with life.

She slid her hands under his shirt and felt the heat of his skin, the firm muscles of his abdomen. As if automatically, her hands drifted to his waistband, and she undid the top of his jeans.

He had a button fly, she realized as she felt several of the other fasteners loosen. The backs of her fingers grazed the single layer of cotton that covered his erection. She gasped—in unison with him.

"I want you, Lara," he whispered in her ear.

She wanted him, too. Closing her eyes, she touched him again, this time not by accident.

He pressed against her fingers, and she basked in the hard heat of him. She wanted to feel him inside of her.

Running his hand down to the waist of her shorts, he undid the button and pulled down her zipper. She felt his fingers slip under the denim, and she lifted her hips to let him push the fabric down past her thighs. Kicking off her sandals, she reached down to make the job easier for him, helping him pull off her shorts. While he took his jeans off, she wriggled out of her panties.

There was a stark yearning in his eyes when he looked down at her nakedness. He settled down on top of her, his body strong and warm.

She pulled him tightly to her, lifting her chin to meet his mouth with hers. As she reveled in the taste of him, he slid his hand down her torso and slipped his fingers between her legs. She sucked in her breath and writhed with ecstasy, astonished by her own response. If she'd ever wanted a man this much before, she couldn't remember. She certainly hadn't imagined she could feel this way *now*.

"Make love to me, Mark," she murmured, surprising herself.

He answered by kissing her more deeply, as if he wanted to consume her. His fingers still played at her body, and she felt herself growing close to climax already—but she wanted to reach it *with* him, not alone.

"Now," she urged him. "Please."

Pulling away from her mouth he met her gaze, his eyes intent, his expression serious. He shifted his hand from her body to guide himself. She felt the tip of him press at her—then push inside.

"Oh . . ." she moaned. He filled her, and euphoria flowed through her being, emanating from the point where they were connected.

Kissing her neck, he pushed again . . . and then again, each time elevating the degree of her pleasure.

"Oh, God," he said, breathless. "*God.* Lara, you feel amazing—too amazing."

She gasped as he thrust again.

Grasping his buttocks, she drove him deeper into her. They both moaned.

He pushed into her again, and the tension in her exploded. She shuddered with wave after wave of bliss.

"Oh!" He looked at her with wide eyes, then thrust once more and broke into his own climax.

She trembled again along with him, warmed with the knowledge that he was giving her his very essence. It occurred to her that they should have discussed "safeness," though she knew she wouldn't get pregnant, because she'd been taking the Pill to fend off menstrual cramps.

As their swells of pleasure tapered off, he leaned forward and dotted her mouth with baby kisses. "That was wonderful."

"It was."

He gently slid off her, taking the outside of the couch again, holding her close to him.

She rested her cheek against his chest and listened to his heart, still beating rapidly. His skin felt hot and moist. He smelled sexy, she thought.

They caught their breath in silence. Overwhelmed by this sudden development in their relationship, she didn't quite know what to say to him. She hadn't expected to make love with him today or at any time in the near future. Her thoughts hadn't even progressed to that point. She wasn't sorry about their intimacy—it had been too fantastic to regret—but she wished she had made the decision with her head about her instead of on the spur of the moment.

He stayed quiet, too, but he snuggled close to her. His nearness reassured her. She took it to mean that he didn't regret their actions either—at least, not yet. He may well have been having similar thoughts to hers. Given his unhealed wounds over his ex, he couldn't have seen this coming.

Her gaze wandered to the bookcase that housed the secret entrance, and she remembered the ghost. A flutter of uneasiness shivered through her.

"Are you cold?" Mark asked. "Maybe we need a blanket."

"No. I'm okay." She hesitated but decided to voice her concerns. "I was just thinking about the ghost again. All this between us happened so suddenly . . ."

"Not really. When you think about it, this has been building up for a while. It seems like a natural progression to me. Don't you think so?"

She reflected on how her feelings for him had evolved since they'd first met. Their conversations and his writing had influenced her changing views. The course of events *did* feel natural. She'd come to know him over the last week or so. That was all. "I guess so."

"I'll tell you what." He lifted her chin to tilt her face up toward his. "Why don't we go out somewhere tomorrow, away from both your place and mine? Then we can see how we feel about everything away from this charged atmosphere."

She nodded slowly, a sense of relief spreading through her. "I like that idea. Did you have something specific in mind?"

"How about a ride into the countryside—maybe up toward the mountains? I know a little historic village with some nice shops, including a candy store that sells homemade chocolates. There's a beautiful old inn that serves great tavern fare. We could have dinner there."

"Sounds perfect." She let her head drop back on his chest. Closing her eyes, she savored the magic of the moment. She couldn't remember the last time she had felt so much at peace. She *belonged* here in Mark's arms.

A tiny voice in the back of her mind reminded her she'd vowed to be cautious about this relationship. Mark may have spoken of tomorrow, but what would happen beyond that?

As happy as she felt, she tried to dismiss the thought. A person could always find time for worry and speculation, but moments like this didn't come often.

Chapter 15

MAKING LOVE TO Lara had blown Mark away. He couldn't remember ever feeling so in sync with a lover. In the aftermath he still felt strongly connected to her, as though she were a part of him.

He wanted her to stay that way.

She fell asleep in his arms, warm and trusting. Her soft, shallow breathing made her seem vulnerable. He felt an overpowering urge to protect her—not that she wasn't strong on her own, but her life must have been hard this past year, going through a divorce. Now he wanted to take care of her. He only hoped he could give her what she needed.

For a moment the idea scared him. What *did* she need? Support of her art and her ideas, he supposed—and that would come easily enough. Besides, he would learn more about her and find out what made her happy. There was nothing to be afraid of. In fact he couldn't wait to get started . . . though at the moment, sleep did seem a welcome second choice.

He drifted off not long after her.

Hours later he woke to find her stirring beside him. Dusk had fallen and the room had grown shadowy. Feeling chilly, the two of them cuddled up to each other. They had a belated discussion about contraception, and he was relieved to learn she'd been taking the Pill. Without grilling each other on their sexual histories, they also decided to go for HIV testing together soon. So settled, they eventually ended up making love again.

Later they ordered Chinese take-out for dinner and drank a bottle of wine between them. He didn't leave until three in the morning—and then only because both of them thought they wouldn't get anything productive done the next day if he stayed.

Despite having such a late night Mark woke up early. Thoughts of Lara flooded his mind like the morning sun streaming through his window. The events of the previous night felt almost like a dream. He couldn't wait to see her again and assure himself that it had all really happened. When they'd parted in the wee hours they'd thought it best to wait till afternoon to get together again, but now he regretted the delay.

Too wound up to go back to sleep, he got up and worked on his manuscript for the next few hours. Though his thoughts kept straying to the huge change in his life, at the same time his mind was alive and sparkling—capable of moving in several directions at once. Before he knew it he'd pounded out five typed pages. His inspiration seemed to be back.

The time finally came to leave his apartment. A little nervous but walking on air, he stepped outside into another perfect summer day and took a deep, satisfying breath. Only a few white puffy clouds floated overhead—just enough to make the sky interesting. He climbed into the car reflecting that they'd picked a great day for a ride into the country.

Anticipating the sight of Lara the whole way, he drove with the windows down and the radio playing. He prayed that she'd be as eager to see him as he was to see her.

When he pulled into her driveway and saw her sitting outside his heart thumped in his chest. She smiled and waved, and he breathed a sigh of relief. If last night had been a dream, it hadn't ended yet.

As he got out of the car, she stood and walked to the edge of the porch. In simple jeans and a baby-blue short-sleeved top she looked absolutely beautiful. He liked the way she didn't usually make a fuss over her clothing—of course she didn't need to. With her body she would have looked great in anything.

He hurried toward her, grinning. Not used to their new relationship, he felt sort of shy. Less than twelve hours ago something really special had happened between them, but would the magic still be there today?

"Hey," he said.

"Hi." She came down the steps to meet him, her face radiant and slightly flushed.

Is that glow really for me? he thought. He reached out and took both of her hands in his. Karen had never lit up like this for him.

He leaned down and kissed her softly. Her lips were warm and sweet—too sweet to give up after only a taste. He pulled her into his arms and he kissed her more soundly, hoping she didn't care what her neighbors thought.

"Mmm," she said as they drew back a little, still holding each other. "Did you sleep well?"

"You bet. And, for once, I actually got some work done this morning."

"Me, too. Would you believe I've been up since eight?" She slipped her hand into his as they turned to climb the steps. "Now I'm looking forward to seeing this village you mentioned. I'll just need to get my purse—and maybe a sweater, in case it cools down later in the day."

"That's a good idea."

While she ran upstairs he waited in the parlor, admiring the room one more time. The fragrance of roses drifted in the open front windows, adding to the pleasant atmosphere. If she ever got furniture, the room would be a great place to relax. He could picture himself spending many enjoyable hours in here with her in the future.

Maybe I'm jumping the gun, he thought. Until very recently he'd believed he needed a break from women. Now his feelings for Lara were snowballing by the minute. He cautioned himself to slow down and take the relationship one day at a time . . . for now.

To redirect his thoughts, he looked up at the painting over the hearth, the sultry bedroom scene that Lara had done. She was a very sensual woman, he noted with a private smile. But when he remembered that his ancestor's poetry had inspired the work, his amusement faded.

Was it really possible that Geoff had been responsible for the cold drafts and weird mishaps he and Lara had experienced? Mark wished she had never sug-

gested the idea. The world of the dead was one realm
he wasn't anxious to explore.

He heard her footsteps bounding down the main
staircase and turned around to see her enter the parlor.
Slightly out of breath, she carried a camera case and a
sweater.

"I'm ready when you are," she said, smiling.

"Great." He gladly dismissed the ghost from his
thoughts. "Let's get out of here."

The ride up to the foothills of the Pocono Mountains
flew by. While he drove she flipped through stations
on the radio, stopping whenever she came across a
song she liked. The day turned to be a good one for up-
beat oldies, and the songs fit his mood well. Before
long both of them were singing along with love songs
from the last three decades.

After passing two quick hours this way they reached
the little town he'd had in mind, a two-hundred-year-
old village called Durnford. Parking along the out-
skirts of the main road, they walked toward the center
of town. Along the way they stopped to take pictures
and browse through shops.

Halfway into the village they came across a gallery
and checked out the work of the local artists. The mer-
chandise ranged from handcrafted jewelry to large
sculptures and paintings. Lara raved over many of the
pieces, though personally he thought hers were far
more remarkable. After twenty minutes of looking
around she bought a pair of earrings made in a classi-
cal Greek style.

"I wish I could afford to get one of the paintings,"
she whispered to him as they headed for the door, "but
I'm at the very limit of my budget."

"Living alone isn't easy." He gave her a philosophical lift of his eyebrows.

"Tell me about it." They left the shop and she picked up the conversation in a normal tone, stuffing her purchase into her camera case. "My salary is barely covering the bills. If I hadn't gotten back a big tax return this year, I never would have made it this far. Eventually I'll probably have to get a housemate to help me out."

"With a house like yours, you'll have candidates knocking down the door." He resisted the urge to hint that he'd be first in line. "Frankly, I'm amazed your ex-husband gave the place up, especially since it was his family home."

She fixed her gaze on something—or, more likely, nothing—down at the end of the street. "Ron has a tendency to take the easiest course open to him."

"If it had been me I would have fought tooth and nail to hold on to my heritage."

She let out a humorless laugh and took his hand as they started walking again. "Well, you're not like Ron, thank goodness. He doesn't fight for much. Evidently heritage isn't particularly important to him."

He was glad to hear she didn't think he was like her ex, but he still wondered about the situation. He had no reason to believe Karen's suggestion that Lara was a gold digger, but what *had* happened in her divorce?

He hesitated but decided to go on. "Surely he didn't just hand the house over to you?"

"No, not exactly." She took a drawn out breath. "It's kind of a long story. When we got married we bought the house from my in-laws at a bargain price. Having always lived at home and having worked all through college, I had enough savings for a decent down payment, and his parents matched it with a gift. That kept the mortgage payments within our budget."

"Sounds like a good start."

"I thought so, too—until a few years later when Ron broke the news to me that he'd built up credit-card debts amounting to almost twenty-five thousand dollars. He wanted to take out a home-equity loan to pay them off."

He stopped in his tracks, turning to face her. "*Twenty-five thousand dollars?* How on earth did he spend so much money? Was he a gambler?" He remembered stories like that about Karen's ex-husband.

She shook her head, her expression bland. "No. He would call himself an 'entrepreneur.' His dream was to get rich on some household invention that he would patent and sell to manufacturers. Unfortunately he never hit on the magic formula, but he kept spending money on his workshop and materials. He was spoiled by his parents and never learned the value of money. Besides the stuff for inventing he bought a lot of electronic toys and always had a new car. He liked to eat out a lot—that sort of thing. But I think what caught up with him was that he only made minimum payments on his bills, and the interest kept growing and growing."

"Didn't you know about the bills?"

"No." She shook her head and looked away from him. "You must think I'm stupid. I knew he had his own credit cards, but I had mine, too, and I never suspected he had a problem. When we bought the house he told me his debts were almost paid off. We had no trouble getting the mortgage, so his credit report couldn't have been too bad. Looking back I realize that he was secretive about his finances, but at the time I never dreamed I might have to police him."

"I *don't* think you're stupid," he said firmly. "I know what it's like to trust in what a person tells you, then find out they haven't been open with you."

She gave him a look of concern. "Did something similar happen to you?"

"Nothing quite *that* crazy." He waved off her question, more interested in *her* story than in rehashing his own problems. "It must have been a shock believing you had a certain amount of assets and finding out he'd blown a huge chunk of them. How could a grown man with a wife be so irresponsible? You must have been worried sick about what he would do next."

"Not at first—not when he came to me crying and falling apart." She started walking again and he followed suit. "At that point I wanted to try to help him. I wouldn't agree to the home-equity loan, but I sold a fairly new car that I owned and lent him the proceeds. He had to sell his, too, of course, and he got his parents to pitch in with a loan."

"People like him always get bailed out by someone," he muttered, disgusted.

"Yes, that's how they learn the behavior in the first place." Her voice grew lower. "What really got me was that as soon as we had pulled him past the crisis he went back to his carefree ways, while *I* had lost all sense of security. I started worrying where I would end up in my old age. The possibility of having kids suddenly looked like a bad idea. I felt like the floor had fallen out from under me."

As he comprehended more of the repercussions, he felt an overwhelming surge of resentment toward her ex. "Was this what brought on the divorce?"

"One of the last straws, I guess. We had other problems, too. Our personalities clashed . . ." She trailed off for a moment but snapped back quickly. "Anyway, in the end when we divided up our assets he still owed me and his parents money. He felt he needed his share of equity in the house to live."

"So *he* actually proposed that you buy him out?"

She nodded. "This time *I* borrowed money from *my* parents. The weird thing is that I didn't do it because I was thinking about the house. It just seemed the quickest way to get everything settled and have Ron out of my life."

"I can understand that," he said under his breath, steaming more by the minute as he thought about what the idiot had put her through. The urge to protect her that he'd felt the night before returned with added strength.

"Actually, I shouldn't make it sound like he was such an awful person," she said. "He had his good moments, too—but at this point I don't bother dwelling much on them. It took me a long time to put everything into perspective. Ron and I even dated for two years before we got married, so I invested a huge portion of my life in him."

They walked along in silence for quite a while.

"Is that the chocolate shop you were telling me about?" she asked now. She pointed to a storefront on the opposite side of the road.

"Oh—yes, it is." He was surprised they had gone so far.

They crossed the street and walked through the open door. A mouthwatering mix of sweet, rich aromas filled the air. The place was even more tantalizing than he'd remembered. He'd only been there once before, on the way up to the mountains on a skiing trip with friends.

"It smells wonderful in here. You can tell they make good candy." Lara moved from display to display, excited over each one. She stopped in front of a bin of vibrant red treats. "Swedish fish! I haven't had these since I was a kid. . . . Wow, those pecan turtles look good."

In the end she settled on a quarter-pound of yogurt-covered raisins, telling him, "At least I can pretend these are somewhat good for me."

He smiled for the first time since she'd told him her story. "Yes, if you ignore all the sugar in them."

For himself he bought a bag of the Swedish fish, charmed by the image of Lara eating them as a little girl. He couldn't resist getting several dark chocolate pretzels, too, which he shared with her as they left the store.

Not far past the chocolate shop the town thinned out again. They came across a park and continued walking, following a paved bike trail into the woods. With dinnertime approaching, the area seemed to be deserted except for them.

Intermittent bird calls punctuated the rhythmic background noise of crickets. Being alone with Lara in such a peaceful setting helped restore Mark's mood. He put his arm around her waist and pulled her closer to him as they strolled among the trees, their only company an occasional squirrel.

The pavement came to an end too soon, splitting off into two dirt paths.

"Should we turn back?" he asked reluctantly.

She bit her lip. "My feet *are* starting to hurt a tiny bit, but I don't know if I'm ready to give all of this up.

Let's go a little further and see if there's a clearing where we can sit for a few minutes."

"Okay."

They lucked out. The path they took came out of the woods and continued along the edge of a cornfield. To their left stood an area cleared to store large farm equipment. They found a huge flat cart and climbed up on it to rest.

He chose a seat by a bale of hay, leaning back against it.

She brushed off a spot next to him and sat down. "We'll be covered with bits of straw after this. I hope the restaurant you have in mind for dinner isn't too fancy."

"Not at all. It's something along the lines of an English pub." Putting his arm around her shoulders, he snuggled up to her. Her body felt small and warm, and her hair smelled faintly floral. Holding her gave him a rush of pleasure. He felt like he didn't have a care in the world.

She looked up into his eyes, smiling.

He leaned down and kissed her. Warm and soft, her lips hinted faintly of chocolate. "You taste sweet."

She laughed.

He bent to her mouth again, his senses waking up. The sensations he'd experienced the night before were fresh in his mind, and all of those feelings flooded back to him. Aching for her, he parted her lips with his tongue. Heat began to spread through his body.

She stretched both of her arms around his shoulders and pulled him close to her. Sensing her hunger accelerated his. Wrapped in each other's arms, they sank to the wooden floor of the cart.

With her mouth and her body pressed against his,

his longing for her built quickly. Gasping for breath, he told her, "Lara, I want you . . . so much."

"I want *you*," she said with her mouth on his. Reaching down to his waistband, she undid the button.

He didn't hesitate to return the favor. Both of them glanced around to make sure they were still alone, then scrambled out of their jeans. They lay next to each other, face-to-face.

The wood beneath them was hard, and he didn't want to crush her against it. He rolled onto his back, pulling her on top of him, her slender legs straddling his.

After a brief look of surprise she fell back into sync with him. Taking his cue for her to lead, she sowed kisses down his throat, sparking pleasure in him at each point of contact. Instinct took over and he pushed up against her. She reached down between their bodies, guiding him to her.

They both groaned. She was so warm, so liquid—like heaven.

He let his head fall back and lost himself in the rhythm of her movements, a willing slave to the pleasure she was giving him. The sweet pressure within him grew and grew.

Little whimpers coming from her throat prompted him to open his eyes again.

She met his gaze, her eyes full of passion, and his own emotions soared. Cupping her beautiful bottom with his palms, he reveled in the tension building between them. Her whimpers came more and more frequently.

"Oh, Mark," she gasped—and he felt her body contract around him with a series of breaking waves.

The sensations set off his own orgasm. He fell into

shudders of almost unbearable pleasure. They reverberated through him, rocketing him to heights of ecstasy he could barely fathom.

"You're amazing," he said when she collapsed onto his chest. He kissed the top of her head, stroking her hair.

"Mmm." She gave his body a squeeze. "*We* are."

After they lay catching their breath for a moment, she lifted her head to look at him. "We'd better get dressed. I'd rather not wait till we hear someone come crackling through the woods."

"As much as I would love to stay here in your arms, I have to admit you have a point."

They scrambled back into their jeans and brushed hay from each other's clothes and hair. Neither of them said much while walking back through the park, commenting only on some of the trees and the wildlife.

The inn he'd chosen for dinner lived up to his memories. Somewhat off the beaten track, the restaurant appeared to be popular with the locals, but they didn't have to wait for a table. A waitress seated them by a bay window that looked out on a country road. Sipping imported ales, they both ordered English pub specialties.

Between hearty bites of shepherd's pie and lamb curry, they exchanged stories about their families and growing up. He learned that she had a brother who lived on the West Coast, and he told her how close he was to his sister. Besides both coming from families with two children, they found they had attended the same college but at different campuses.

"I had an idea earlier," he confessed as they lingered

over coffee and dessert, "but I'm not sure what you'll think."

"What sort of idea?" She met his gaze squarely, clearly open to listening. Their relationship certainly had turned around since they'd first met.

"I've always wanted to do a book about lost houses—ruined ones too far gone to be restored. My idea is to choose a collection of ruins, research them, and re-create an image of what they once were."

A soft smile pulled at her lips. "You'll do a wonderful job. I love the concept."

"Good—but that's not all I was thinking about. Originally I only planned to include photos of the ruins and descriptions of what they looked like when they were first built. Then today it occurred to me that the book would be a lot more powerful if *you* illustrated it."

She blinked at him. "Are you serious?"

"Of course. I can't think of any better way to show what these houses once were, short of actually rebuilding them. Since that will never happen, this is the closest possible thing to bringing them back."

"Do you realize that I don't have any experience in book illustration?"

He laughed. "I've seen enough of your work to convince me of your talents. Say you'll do it. Buildings like these are too intricate to capture completely with words. Most people reading my descriptions won't be able to conjure up the sort of image that you could give them with your paints."

She looked down into her coffee. "It's tempting—but there are a lot of considerations. Before I could even think about agreeing, we'd need to discuss the number of illustrations, what sort of medium to use, the time frame for the work . . . and probably a hundred other details I'm overlooking. Let me put some thought into the idea and try to come up with some suggestions, as well as some questions for you."

"Great." He grinned, more excited than he'd been about a project in years. The idea of spending time with her working on something so meaningful really appealed to him. "I couldn't ask for more."

He polished off his coffee in quiet satisfaction. Lara seemed reflective but happy, too.

During the drive back to Falls Borough they listened to music again but this time without much singing or talking. The abundance of activity and lack of sleep over the last twenty-four hours had finally caught up with him. Content just being in Lara's company, he concentrated on the road.

With so much to feel good about, the miles passed as quickly as they had that afternoon. The next thing he knew he was turning onto her street. Night had fallen, and her house loomed huge and dark. He felt a twinge of sadness at the prospect of leaving her. The clock on the dashboard read ten forty-five—getting late for a weeknight.

"I'm surprised you can stand being all alone in that big house," he said.

"Sometimes I can't." She let out a laugh that sounded more nervous than amused. "In fact, right now I'm hoping you'll come in and keep me company for a while. I know it's late, but maybe just for fifteen minutes . . ."

"I'd love to."

He parked the car, and they went inside, where she offered him a nightcap. Sitting beside her on the big red couch felt cozier than anything else he could imagine at the moment. The day had been a busy one and, after a glass of wine, he could barely keep his eyes open.

"Let's go to bed," she said, startling him out of a doze. Getting up, she took his hand in hers.

He gave her a groggy smile. The idea sounded perfect.

With her to help him, he made his way upstairs.

Chapter 16

WHEN LARA SAID good-bye to Mark the next morning, the weather had turned drizzly and dismal. As she watched him drive away, a wave of sadness washed over her. The time they'd spent together had been so wonderful she hated to see it end.

When the car disappeared from sight, she turned back into the house, telling herself not to be silly. They had plans to get together again that night.

But it just seemed hard to believe, after all the tension between them, that things were going so well now.

She went to the studio, hoping to get several hours of painting in before lunch, but she couldn't seem to shake off her mood. Her creative juices weren't flowing, and the lack of good natural light made working a chore.

After about an hour she put down her brush, deciding that her time could better be used doing something else.

As she cleaned up, she considered several errands she needed to run. To her, the most important was to revise her application for the building permit. Since she'd finally told Mark she'd changed her mind about the wall, she wanted to make it official.

She finished putting away her supplies, then got her purse and drove into town. Parking in the municipal lot, she crossed the street and climbed the steps in front of Town Hall.

"Lara Peale," a feminine voice addressed her from above.

She looked up to see Mark's old flame coming out of the entrance. Today she wore a brown pin-striped version of her trademark minisuit. Lara had no desire to speak to her, but the woman was pretty much blocking her way.

"Hello, Karen," she said, maneuvering around her.

"Hey, that's too bad about your building permit being turned down," the woman said behind her.

Lara turned around in confusion. "What?"

"Oh, didn't you know?" She lifted an eyebrow. "I guess you haven't received the notice yet. The zoning board rejected your application. They're barring your addition of a studio because of the commercial nature of the proposal."

"Commercial?" She frowned. "My studio's not commercial. It's strictly for personal use."

"The board seems to think that your plans indicate otherwise."

"Where did they get that idea?" Wondering what had happened, Lara looked away from her, thinking.

"Wait a minute. How did they even know that I use the room as a studio? I didn't mention it in my application."

"I guess you must have told *someone*."

"I haven't told anyone but . . ." She trailed off as her mind made the connections.

"Mark," the other woman finished for her. "Yes, he's very concerned about housing regulations. He's a bit of a stickler, don't you think?"

Lara met her gaze again. "Are you saying that *he* went to the board about my application?"

"Well, I'd hate to tell tales . . . but you did just say he was the only one you told, didn't you?"

The smug look on the woman's face made Lara want to slap her. Before temptation became too much, she brushed past her and ran back down the steps.

As she waited by the street for a break in traffic, she felt like her brain was caving in. Could Mark really have stooped so low—coming on to her while he sabotaged her plans behind her back? He wouldn't do something like that, would he?

But he must have, she thought, an ache rising in her throat. The only other people she'd ever told about her plans were her closest friends and immediate family. None of them had connections to the zoning board. Given Mark's involvement with the historical society, *he* probably did. Naturally, he would know who to go to about blocking her permit.

Traffic cleared, and she hurried across to the parking lot. She hoped Karen wasn't still watching her, but she refused to turn around and check. On top of Mark's betrayal, she couldn't bear to see that woman gloating.

As she got into the car, she thought back over the

past few weeks. Right from the start, Mark had made it clear how strongly he opposed her plans. At one time she'd even suspected that some of his "friendly" gestures amounted to bribes—but in the end she'd believed what she wanted to believe. She should have seen this coming all along.

She started the ignition and pulled out of the lot, blinking back tears. How could she have been such an idiot? Once again her attraction for a man had made her too blind to see him for what he really was. Things had been the same with Ron. When it came to the opposite sex, she had no sense of judgment.

Nevertheless, her anger outstripped her self-reproach. When she reached the house, she ran inside. Finding the cordless phone in the kitchen, she punched in Mark's number.

"Hello?" he answered after the first ring.

At the sound of his voice, she felt her eyes sting again. She managed to utter, "Hello."

"Hey! I was just thinking about you. What are you up to?"

She swallowed against the lump in her throat. "Listen, Mark, I know about your going to the zoning board." Her voice cracked with emotion.

"What do you mean?" He sounded truly confused. The man was a master of deceit.

"I heard that my permit's been rejected," she spat out, "because of the 'commercial nature of the proposal.' They don't want me building a studio—which I never mentioned on my application, by the way. *You* were the only one I told about the studio—other than my closest friends, of course."

For a long moment, he was silent.

"Lara . . ." he said finally, his voice now sounding

strained, which she took as confirmation of his guilt. "It didn't happen the way you think."

She shook her head to herself. "I can't believe this. While you were pretending to . . . to make peace with me, you went to them behind my back. You actually told them lies to make sure they'd turn down my application. In case you hadn't noticed, my studio is *not* a commercial venture."

He let out a heavy sigh. "Lara, I swear I didn't go to the board. I have to admit that my big mouth is at the root of this mess, but it was all an accident. I just let it slip about your studio in front of the wrong person."

The intensity of his tone made him sound sincere— but she knew he couldn't be.

She clenched her teeth. "And I'm supposed to believe that, knowing how you felt about the wall? You *accidentally* told someone on the zoning board that I was building a studio? And then you accidentally omitted the fact that it's strictly for personal use!"

"Let me explain how it happened—"

"Oh, I know exactly how it happened." She felt her lower lip quiver. "When you couldn't bully me into changing my plans, you decided to pull some strings with your friends at Town Hall. This trick was on top of all the little ways you tried to butter me up—giving me the autographed book, helping me with the kitchen, even suggesting that I illustrate your next manuscript."

"I never meant to—"

"Save it." She snapped. "That wall must mean a lot to you. I hate to think how far you'd go to save it. I'm afraid to ask how much of the last week has been inspired by *me* and how much by my house."

"Now you're being ridiculous. The way I feel about you has nothing to do with—"

"I don't want to talk about it, Mark." Suddenly, all she wanted to do was hide. She didn't want to let him see how much he'd mattered to her. Obviously she hadn't meant enough to *him* for him to be honest with her. "I don't ever want to talk to you again."

Pulling the cordless phone away from her ear, she pressed the "Off" button. She wished she'd used the regular phone so she could have slammed the receiver down.

A pathetic, childlike sob escaped her, and she finally let her tears flow. Her arms went limp, and she dropped the phone on the floor. She couldn't believe how stupid she'd been. In the last few days, she'd truly believed their relationship had grown. Now she wondered how much of his behavior had been designed merely to get on her good side. Did he feel anything *real* for her at all?

Slumping onto one of the dinette chairs, she cried until her watery nose forced her to get up for a tissue. In the bathroom mirror, a repulsive figure with a pink, puffy complexion stared back at her. Her head had started to ache.

Opening up the medicine chest, she swung the reflection out of her view. She grabbed a bottle of pain reliever and went back to the kitchen for a glass of water.

While she stood at the tap, the phone rang in the hallway. She jumped—then let the call go until the answering machine picked up.

"It's me, Lara." Mark's voice floated into the room, his tone anxious. "I realize you don't want to talk to me, and I can understand why. But I need to try to convince you that I wasn't the one who went to the zoning board, and I never intended for anything I said about you to get back to them. I wish I could have that day back and do it over again."

Still holding her glass, she wandered into the hall. Though she doubted that anything he said would make a difference, she couldn't resist listening to him.

"The day you applied for the permit, I ran into Karen outside of Town Hall."

She frowned. Just the mention of the woman's name turned her dejection into outrage.

"She asked me if I'd met you through the historical society," he went on.

Karen was asking questions about *her*? Lara shouldn't have been surprised, given the woman's nosiness in the office that day—and her interference today. Well, she'd had just about enough of Mark and his ex-girlfriend sticking their noses into her business.

"You may remember that she was the one who told me you'd applied for the permit. A friend of hers works in one of the town offices. Karen's also the person I told about your studio. It slipped out before I realized what I was saying."

He'd told *that woman* about the studio! She slammed her glass down on the table beside the answering machine, sloshing water over the rim. *Does he expect me to find that less offensive than his going to the board himself?* Why was he always with that woman anyway, if they weren't still involved?

She reached for the receiver, but suddenly another thought struck her: Were they really not involved anymore? Was it possible he'd lied when he denied having dinner with her the other night?

"I'm not trying to claim that this isn't my fault," he

said, "but not like you thought—not directly. Please try to see that I never set out to hurt you. Her questions took me off guard, and—"

She yanked the phone cord out of the wall, putting an end to the call. *Off guard, my foot,* she thought. He had *gone out* with the woman and he didn't know how nosy she was? Lara had known it after two minutes in her company. Besides, if he hadn't intended for his "slip of the tongue" to hurt *her*, why hadn't he at least warned her what had happened? She could have gone to the board herself and explained the true nature of her studio.

The cradle for the cordless phone stood next to the machine, and she unplugged that too, throwing the plug down on the floor. Now he couldn't bother her again tonight. Picking up her water, she gulped down two painkillers.

Going to her room she collapsed on the bed again, disgusted with herself. How could she have been so stupid? She had overlooked Mark's hot-and-cold treatment of her time and time again. She had even seen Karen walking into his house with a casserole dish. But all he had to do was deny that they were together and she'd bought it—hook, line, and sinker. He'd told her what she'd wanted to hear.

After another round of sobbing she had to get up for a tissue again. Trying to calm herself, she considered calling Di but remembered she had unplugged the phone. It didn't seem worthwhile to run downstairs again and plug in the cord, risking another call from Mark. Di couldn't help her anyway. Why interrupt her vacation?

She spent most of the day in bed, trying to read or watch TV but mostly thinking about Mark. When night came, she lay in the dark for what seemed like hours before she eventually fell asleep.

In the morning she woke up late and didn't feel like getting out of bed. Life felt like too much work. She was tired of trying so damned hard all the time, only to end up failing. Her marriage had failed, and she hadn't even learned from her mistakes.

She dozed off and woke a second time around eleven—later than she'd slept in years. Guilt radiated through her. Time was too valuable for her to waste it wallowing in self-pity. She had to pull herself together. Determined to get a few errands done, if nothing else, she dragged herself into the shower.

By the time she'd dressed and dabbed on some lipstick, she felt somewhat better. So she'd picked the wrong man again—what else was new? She reminded herself that she still had her art to fulfill her and her house to keep her busy. All in all, things could have been worse.

As she put on her sneakers she heard a knock downstairs at the back door. Her first thought was of Mark, but he always came to the front. *Strange,* she thought, hurrying to finish tying her laces. Could Di be home early? She wasn't due back for another day, and it seemed unlikely she'd rush over to Lara's the moment she arrived. But who else would come to the back of the house?

Just as she opened the door, she thought of one other person who had always used this entrance.

Sure enough, her ex-husband stood outside.

"So you *are* here," he said as if they'd spoken five minutes ago, instead of months before. "Yesterday I got home from a business trip and your message was waiting for me. I tried calling all last night and again this morning but couldn't get an answer. Isn't your machine working?"

"It works." Surprised by his appearance, she ran a nervous hand through her hair. *Damnit.* She'd completely forgotten that she'd called him. "I have the phone unplugged . . . too many telemarketers."

"You should plug it back in. Who knows how many calls you're missing?"

"Sorry. I've been so busy I forgot all about it."

A moment of awkward silence passed between them. Eventually he asked, "Well, aren't you going to invite me in?"

She didn't want to but couldn't see a way out of it without causing unnecessary friction between them. Having an ex-husband was uncomfortable enough; she didn't want to make him her enemy. "Oh, of course. Come on in. I'll make some coffee."

"Wow, what have you done in here?" he asked as he stepped inside. He took a turn around the room, taking in the newly exposed brickwork.

"This is the original floor." Expecting him to criticize her for the change, she kept her gaze fixed on the coffee carafe as she filled it with water.

He hesitated. "This was under the vinyl?"

"Yes—under several layers of it."

Another moment passed, and she couldn't resist asking, "So what do you think?"

"I don't know." His brow wrinkled as he looked around the rest of the room. "Didn't you have a table and chairs in here the last time I stopped by?"

"I moved them into the dining room."

He peered across the hall. "Oh. You *use* the dining room now?"

"Yeah, I have to, now that the table's in there." She

was grateful for his innocuous comments but not in the mood for small talk. Dumping a scoop of coffee into a filter, she turned around to face him. "I'm afraid that I have a lot of work to do this afternoon, Ron, so we can't make this a long visit."

"No problem. I'm on the way to a meeting in the city." He leaned against the counter. "So what's this question you have about my family?"

"Oh, right. I almost forgot." She flicked on the cof-feemaker, hardly able to believe she'd gone two days without thinking about the letters and the ghost. Now that Mark was out of her life, she wondered if Geof-frey would leave her alone or continue to visit her. "It's no big deal. I only wondered if you'd ever heard of an ancestor of yours named Mariah Sulley."

He shrugged. "Doesn't ring a bell. Should it?"

"Probably not." Reaching into the cupboard for two mugs, she realized she should have known he wouldn't have anything to tell her. He'd never shown much interest in his family history. She considered her remarks carefully, not wanting to tell him about the ghost and definitely not about the secret room. Even *he* might be curious about something so unusual and would probably want to see it. She didn't want to have him in the house any longer than necessary—espe-cially today. "I came across some letters of hers and wondered who she was."

"Anything interesting in the letters?"

"Not really. They're dated from the end of the nine-teenth century." She hesitated. "Would you like to have them?"

He looked down at his shoes. "I don't have much storage space in my apartment."

"Right. Why don't I just keep them here for now?"

To her surprise she felt relieved that he didn't want them. If she'd had any sense she'd have been eager to get rid of the letters, but somehow she felt attached to Mariah.

"Thanks," he said. "I'll take them off your hands when I get a bigger place."

"Okay." She knew he'd never ask for them. To forestall future visits from him, she thought she'd give him an opportunity now to request any other mementos he might want. "While you're here, is there anything else you left behind that you wish you'd taken? For instance, I know I have far more than my share of the Christmas decorations. I don't think you took *any* of the lights."

"In the apartment I really can't use much in the way of lights. Wait—" He rubbed his chin in thought. "Come to think of it, my mother did ask me to check with you about something she wanted. Do you remember the ceramic tree that Aunt Helen made—the one with the little plastic bulbs that light up?"

She nodded. "And I think I know right where it is, too. Let me run upstairs and take a look. Can you fix the coffee for us when it's ready?"

"Sure thing."

As he stepped up to the counter, she turned toward the back stairs. Wanting to end the visit as soon as possible, she hurried up to the spare bedroom where she kept the decorations. She was glad that she and Ron seemed to be getting along, but seeing him brought back all the disappointment of her failed marriage. After yesterday's fiasco, she didn't need any further reason to feel sad.

*   *   *

Mark hadn't slept much. He'd spent most of the night searching his brain for a way to make things right with Lara. He couldn't stand losing her now, when he'd finally come to realize how much she meant to him. Damn it, he really wanted to be with her. Why had he ever opened his mouth to Karen about the studio? He swore that from now on he'd never speak to that interfering bitch again.

In the morning he'd woken up feeling frantic rather than rested. If only he could convince Lara to give him a chance, he would find some way to make this up to her. In his state of mind, he wasn't sure how. All he knew was that he needed to talk with her and try to explain.

As soon as he got up he tried calling her house again, but the phone rang without any answer. When her line had gone dead the night before he'd had a feeling she'd pulled out the cord. Presumably she'd never plugged it back in.

Throughout the morning he dialed her number every fifteen minutes but had no better luck. He had only one choice: He would have to go back to her house and hope that she'd calmed down enough to see him today.

The three miles of road between their neighborhoods had never seemed so far a drive.

What if she won't talk to me when I get there? he worried. *What if she won't even answer the door?* Even if she did answer, he still wasn't sure what he would say to her.

He pulled up to the house and had to park along the street because the driveway was full. Besides her car, it held a second vehicle, an unfamiliar van.

Great, she had company. He considered turning

around but decided the circumstances might work in his favor. With someone else watching over her shoulder, she might not want to make a scene by chasing him away. Maybe she would take him aside and give him a few minutes of her time. A minute or two would be infinitely better than nothing.

Gulping down his nervousness, he parked along the road and got out of the car. He took his time walking up to the house, half expecting her to run outside and cut him off before he got to the porch. She didn't. He climbed the front steps and knocked at the door.

In a moment he heard the latch clicking open. His heartbeat quickened. For a split second he dared to feel hopeful—then the door swung open to reveal a man.

Mark stared at him in surprise. Probably in his early thirties, he stood about average height and had a stocky build.

"Can I help you?" the guy asked.

Mark wondered if he could be Lara's brother but saw no resemblance to her in the man's sandy hair and brown eyes. He cleared his throat. "Uh, yes. Is Lara home?"

Her visitor frowned. "Are you a friend of hers?"

He nodded. A feeling of possessiveness stung him and he threw back, "Are *you*?"

"I'm her ex-husband, Ron Sulley."

Her ex? The piece of information almost knocked him over. What was her ex doing here, answering the door as if he owned the place? From everything she'd said, she wanted nothing more to do with him.

His jealousy raged, along with a sickening feeling of déjà vu. Karen had gone back to her ex, despite all of their problems. Had Lara done the same? He would have liked to think not, but his experience with Karen left him worried. He remembered Lara insisting that her ex had his good points—the guy who'd run up all those bills behind her back!

"Who should I say is here?" Sulley asked, his mouth twisting in an unpleasant way. He didn't look as though he appreciated Mark's presence any more than Mark did his. Maybe Lara had told the jerk about their relationship.

"Never mind." He turned toward the steps, then thought twice and looked back over his shoulder. "If you cared anything about her, you'd keep your problems to yourself."

"What problems?" His rival gave him a look of confusion. "I don't know what you mean. I came over here because Lara called me."

So she'd called him—exactly as Mark had feared. Heat rose under his collar. He didn't know whether he was more angry at her or at himself. She might have been weak enough to run back to this idiot, but *he* had driven her to it . . . with one stupid mistake.

"I'll come back if she ever comes to her senses," he snapped and bolted down the steps.

As he hit the slate walk, he glanced back and saw Sulley step out onto the porch. The man still looked more baffled than mad, but Mark wasn't in the mood to have it out with him. What good would arguing with him do? The guy wasn't likely to change his ways—and he certainly wouldn't give up Lara.

Before Mark turned back toward the car something prompted him to look up at one of the upstairs windows.

Lara stood at the glass staring down at him, her eyebrows lifted in surprise. When he met her gaze they both froze for a split second, then she looked away. A second later she disappeared from view.

He watched the window for a moment longer—until Sulley shouted to him again.

"Hey, buddy! What the hell were you talking about? Who are you anyway?"

"Someone who has Lara's interests in mind—rather than just my own." He sounded like a self-righteous clown, but he was too wound up to be eloquent. Furious with himself, he stormed out to the car.

As he opened the door he heard the man let out a snort. "Well, I'll be sure to let her know that some fruitcake has her interests in mind. That should be a great comfort to her."

Mark climbed inside and slammed the door. Damn it if Sulley wasn't right. His declaration wouldn't mean a thing to Lara. Had he had her interests in mind when he let Karen go to the zoning board about her studio? He could have at least tried to find out if the studio really was commercial—or warn Lara about what was coming.

He started the engine and lunged out onto the road, spinning the wheels. Why had he said something so stupid to Sulley? He hoped the guy wouldn't actually repeat the statement to her. If she'd been there to hear it herself, she probably would have laughed in his face.

Imagining her and Sulley laughing together over him, he slapped his palms against the steering wheel. Losing Lara was bad enough without losing her to *him*.

He never should have gotten involved with another divorcée. Why hadn't he gone with his initial instinct and stayed away from her in the first place?

Because, he thought, *I didn't want to stay away from her then any more than I want to now.*

Chapter 17

GEOFF WATCHED HIS descendant speed away in the motorized carriage. A week ago Mark's bungling of the situation would have amused him. Now, since he'd taken note of the riddle in Mariah's poem, he suspected that his only chance for salvation might lay in the success of Mark and Lara's love. His descendant's failures had become a source of concern rather than one of laughter.

Floating in the cloud of dust the vehicle's tires had kicked up, the ghost frowned. If he meant to "advance" the mortals' love, he clearly needed to allay the current crisis. Unsure what steps to take, he decided to linger at Lara's. Since she was the party putting up resistance, he concluded that he must need to concentrate on her. He glided into her house with no idea what he would do.

As he passed through the foyer, he reflected on the events of the last few days. He'd been following the mortals' budding romance closely but hadn't understood how he could play a role in it. The two had fallen into each other's arms from practically the moment Lara introduced her theory about Mariah's curse. The change in their relationship seemed sudden to Geoff, but it suited his purposes—except for one important detail. They'd wound up together so quickly that until now he'd wondered if he would ever get a chance to help them.

Now trouble had arrived, and he had his opportunity. A nervous shiver billowed through him. He hadn't the faintest idea how to nurture love. His strong point had always been *avoiding* entanglements.

He heard voices coming from the kitchen and drifted in that direction. When he entered the room Lara stood before her former husband carrying a large cardboard box. She held the carton out to him. "Here's your aunt Helen's tree."

"Thanks." The fellow took the box. A slow grin spread across his face.

Geoff felt a wave of distaste toward him. The ghost had been present when he moved out, and he'd observed the man's gruff manner toward Lara. Plainly he was no gentleman. Learning that the boor was related to the demure Mariah had come as a surprise.

Sulley stooped down and placed the carton on the floor without bothering to look inside. Standing back up, he said in a sly manner, "By the way, while you were upstairs, you had a strange visitor."

Lara walked up to the counter, where two steaming mugs of coffee stood. "Which one of these is mine? And what do you mean by 'strange'?"

Geoff knew that she'd spotted his descendant from the window. She must have been too embarrassed by his behavior to admit she'd witnessed the scene. At least she wasn't encouraging her ex-husband's line of conversation. If she'd chimed in and called Mark a few choice epithets of her own, matters would have looked worse.

"The white mug." Sulley stepped up beside her and handed her the drink, taking the other one for himself. "Some guy came to the door asking for you, but he wouldn't give me his name. He ran off in a huff muttering something about having your interests in mind."

"Is *that* what he said?" A hint of disdain twitched her lips.

"Yeah." He looked at her more closely. "Does it sound like someone you know? He claimed to be a friend of yours."

Her expression went bland, and she looked away from him. "It must have been the guy from the historical society. He's been here a few times to talk about the house."

"This visit seemed to be about something else." Sulley continued to study her. "He acted very worked up about you. I got the impression that he had more at stake than a passing interest in the house."

"The man I'm talking about has a *great* interest in historic homes. He can be pretty fanatical about the subject."

His lips stretched into an unpleasant grin. "Well, this guy may well have been a fanatic of some sort, if not a flat-out lunatic."

Geoff scowled. It was one thing if he himself insulted Mark, but he didn't like having a stranger deride his family. In the time he'd spent with his descendant, he'd noticed how the mortal's attitude toward him had changed. Unlike Lara, Mark hadn't completely condemned the ghost for his mistakes. On the contrary, he seemed to be trying to understand Geoff. The mortal had spent hours with his nose buried in his ancestor's biography and his letters. He'd even taken up reading the poetry he'd once dismissed as "maudlin." Geoff had been pleased to find that Mark wasn't so devoid of discernment as he'd initially seemed.

"In any case, if he had something important to say, I'm sure he would have stuck around." Lara stared into her coffee. Her blue eyes looked huge and sorrowful. "Let's forget it. Why don't you tell me what you've been up to, Ron? Anything new going on in your life?"

"As a matter of fact, there is." His smirk broadened into a genuine smile. "I think I've finally sold one of my household appliance ideas to Lambro Corporation."

"Really?" Her gaze shot to his.

He nodded. "That's who I'm meeting with today. The deal's all but final. They've even given me reason to hope this will only be the first of many ideas they buy from me."

"That's great." She hesitated. "Are you getting the sort of money you were looking for?"

He shrugged. "What I actually make will depend on whether or not the product takes off—but if it does what we expect, I should be pretty well set."

Wonderful, Geoff thought. Her former husband had suddenly come into money. He worried that the development would make Sulley more attractive to her. Success meant a lot to women. His own love life had soared through the roof after he'd started publishing poems.

"You'd better make sure you're getting a fair percentage of the profits," she said, her brow furrowing.

She appeared more concerned than Geoff liked. Months ago, when he'd last seen these two together, he'd detected only contempt between them.

"I've read the contract and I'm happy with it. I only have a few minor questions before I sign it."

"Do you want me to take a look at it for you?" She set her mug down on the counter. "I'm no legal expert, but a second pair of eyes can't hurt."

The ghost frowned to himself. She was definitely softening toward the fellow.

"There's no need." Sulley flashed a smug look at her. "My brother has a friend who's almost finished law school. We had him review it. He even checked into other similar contracts and compared them."

"Good. It sounds like you're handling it the right way." She shook her head and gave him a small smile. "I have to say that I'm proud of you."

Her show of pleasure deepened Geoff's fears. He hoped she'd keep in mind that the fellow couldn't hold a candle to Mark. Sulley's inventions hadn't earned him anything yet, but Mark was a successful author. Over the past few days the ghost had read some of the mortal's work from over his shoulder and come to respect his talent. Having another decent writer in the family, after all these years, had been a welcome surprise.

"Wow." Sulley actually looked a little sheepish about her compliment. He glanced down at his watch. "Well, I'd better get moving, if I'm going to be there on time."

"Yeah, and I need to start working, too." She took

his mug from him and placed it on the drain board. "Good luck today—and in the coming months."

"Thanks. I'll let you know how it goes."

They said good-bye and she showed him to the door, watching as he walked to his motorized carriage.

When Sulley had driven away she went to the coffeemaker and poured another cup. Softly she said to herself, "Well, who would ever have imagined that?"

An ominous feeling descended on the ghost. Damn her ex-husband for showing up now, of all times. If Geoff didn't come up with a way to mend matters between her and Mark, he might miss his only chance to find peace. For a century he'd done his best to avoid thinking about his dismal future, but with the possibility of rest dangling before him he couldn't forget what the alternative was. What could he possibly do to bring the couple back together?

While he racked his brain, Lara took a box of breakfast grains out of the cupboard and poured a serving into a bowl. Retrieving a paper container from the ice box, she added milk to the granules. She carried her mug, bowl, and a spoon into the dining room.

Geoff watched her eat without any ideas. How could he influence this woman, who viewed him with disgust? Perhaps the first step was to try to regain her respect, to show her just how important Mariah had always been to him.

He thought of a poem he'd once written that hinted about his feelings. Unfortunately, the last time he'd tried to get Lara to read one of his poems, she'd ignored the open book he'd left on her library floor. Then again, he couldn't think of a better way to communicate to her. All he could do was try again. He had nothing to lose.

Floating across the hall to the library, he found his book back up on the shelf. Once more, he knocked it to the floor. Blowing to turn over the leaves, he found the poem he wanted.

He glided out into the hall to see if Lara was responding to the thud the volume had made.

She still sat at the dining room table, her back to him.

Frowning, he returned to the library and searched for a way to make a louder noise. His gaze fell on her easel, currently empty. Mustering up all his energy, he rushed at the wooden contraption. The legs folded together, and it fell to the parquet floor with a loud clap.

He heard Lara's chair screech across the floor in the other room. Almost instantly she appeared at the entrance, her hands upon her hips. Her gaze shot to the easel, then to the open book beside it.

"All right, already," she murmured. "If you're going to be insistent about it, I'll look."

Stooping, she picked up the volume and read the lines he'd written about Mariah:

Your love rides over me like the sea.
The danger ought to be clear to me,
But, cherished lady, sometimes I wonder
Whether to save myself or go under.

As much as the waters of your love soothe me,
As much as the attention you give me moves me,
As much as I love to hear your heart pounding,
How can a man submit to drowning?

As she finished, her lower lip began to quiver. She stared at the book a moment longer, then sniffed and closed the cover. Getting up, she returned to the dining room and picked up her dishes, taking them into the kitchen. To Geoff's consternation her sniffling continued, gradually increasing in frequency. By the time she'd rinsed out the bowl and mug, she had dissolved into tears.

Frustration ate away at him. Why was she crying— over his mistake with Mariah, over Mark's mistake with her, maybe even over Sulley? Geoff had never been one to abide tears, and his instinct was to flee.

He tried to float out of the house, but the stone wall blocked him. What was happening to him? Early in his ghosthood he'd learned that he faced some barriers, but normally he could go anywhere he'd been during his lifetime without worrying about passing through objects.

Lara picked up a napkin and blew her nose loudly. He knew she'd spent most of the previous night crying, too. The woman was a virtual watering pot. If she was so unhappy, why didn't she do something to improve her lot?

With growing aggravation he tried passing through the doorway leading to the hallway. To his shock he came up against an invisible barrier. He couldn't even get out of the room!

Glancing over his shoulder, he threw Lara a spiteful look. He didn't understand this muddle about building permits and zoning boards that had her upset with Mark. What did such matters have to do with love? How was he, a ghost, supposed to fix something that he couldn't even comprehend?

Desperate, he charged toward one of the inside walls. He passed through easily and found himself in the secret room. All at once a heavy weight pressed down on him—a devastating sense of heartbreak like he had never felt before. For the first time in his existence he knew what it was to long for something—someone—with all of one's heart.

Initially he thought that Lara's feelings had somehow come upon him. Good God, was she *that* lonely without Mark? Then a flicker of light in front of the fireplace caught the corner of his eye.

"Mariah?"

When he turned to look, the hearth stood empty.

"Mariah, is it *you* I'm feeling? Is that dreadful pain yours?" His voice broke under the stress of his emotions. Staring into the hearth, he looked for a sign of her presence but couldn't detect a trace. He tried to concentrate on the memories he'd recently recovered of making love to her here. Instead of the pleasurable sensations that he anticipated, yearning and despair cut through him.

The pain in the room was *his,* he realized with a shock. Mariah wasn't here. He was all alone.

To his horror, a tear squeezed out of his eye. He dropped to his knees in front of the fireplace and asked the empty air, "How can I bring you back to me?"

Naturally, he got no answer.

He let out a sob, reduced to the wretched state he'd scorned in Lara only moments before. Intently aware of his isolation, he couldn't bear staying in the room where he'd once been as one with Mariah. With no particular aim he floated upward and through the wall into the hallway.

He came across Lara in the dining room. Standing beside the table she slid Mark's book toward her. As she reread the inscription inside the cover, her eyes looked round and soft. Whatever Mark had written obviously eased her anger with him, if only temporarily.

There's the answer! Geoff saw suddenly. As a poet he should have thought of it before. Mark was a man of letters . . . and words could be a powerful thing.

A swell of inspiration rose inside him. All he had to do was convey the information to his descendant, to show Mark how he could reach Lara. For the first time in as long as he could remember, he felt that he had a purpose.

Plunging through the dining room wall, he passed through to the outdoors without effort. His freedom of movement seemed to confirm that he'd taken the right path, and the conviction exhilarated him.

Immediately he warned himself to temper his elation. Though he appeared to be on the right course he didn't want to speculate how far it might lead him. Hope had eluded him for so long he didn't dare try to grasp on to it now.

Mark stared at the computer monitor on his desk without seeing the words on the screen. He'd been sitting at the keyboard for over an hour but hadn't written a single sentence. Since he'd come home from Lara's house, all he could think about was her—what he should have done differently throughout their acquaintance . . . how it was too late to do anything now. Why hadn't he tried to reason with her in the beginning, instead of insisting that his way was the only way? If he'd acted sensibly, she wouldn't have applied for her building permit until they'd developed workable plans *together*.

That would never happen now.

The screen saver came on for the fourth or fifth time

since he'd sat down. This time he didn't bother to turn it off.

Getting up from his chair, he paced away from the desk. So much for the burst of productivity he'd enjoyed two days before. Feeling the way he did now, he doubted he would ever manage to finish his manuscript.

He went to the window and looked out at the parking lot. His apartment may have been laid out in an interesting way, but the view left much to be desired. Currently under a cloudy sky, the stretch of asphalt below looked even more gray than usual. Even the cars present seemed to be the dullest ones in the lot. The lack of color suited his mood.

The scene in front of him blurred as his thoughts lapsed back to the crisis in his life. How could Lara have called that jerk, Sulley, and asked him to come back to her? Didn't she realize she'd be sorry? People didn't change, not really. Judging by Karen's recent behavior, *she* already regretted making up with her ex . . . but he supposed Lara wouldn't appreciate that example. Trying to explain Karen's involvement in the zoning problem to her had probably been a big mistake. He would have been better off simply taking the blame himself. After all, he *had* been the one who'd let the information slip in the first place.

The morning continued to pass with agonizing slowness as he alternated from the desk to the window to the bookcase, pacing back and forth, mentally kicking himself. He checked his watch and found the time finally approached noon. His stomach rumbled, and he remembered that he'd never eaten breakfast.

Dragging himself to the kitchen, he rummaged up some leftover pasta from the fridge and microwaved it. The food turned out dry, and washing it down with a bottle of beer he didn't like only made it less appetizing.

Afterward he went to the living room. He sat down in front of the TV but didn't even turn it on. Nothing interested him now that he'd ruined things with Lara.

As he sat in gloomy silence, a glimpse of movement from the corner of his eye drew his attention to the shelves under the stairs. His gaze shot to the neat rows of books and CDs he kept in the built-in case. Everything looked to be in place, and he hadn't heard anything fall. The idea of being haunted occurred to him, but he refused to get caught up in that kind of thinking. His state of mind was already bad enough. Outside the clouds had grown dark, and in the dusky lighting his eyes must have been playing tricks on him.

Forcing himself to get up off the couch, he turned on a floor lamp that stood beside the stairs. He glanced over at the shelves again and noticed one of his ancestor's volumes of poetry among the books. Lately he'd found himself caught up in Geoff's verses—a world Lara had opened up to him.

Hoping the words might offer him something now, he reached for the book and pulled it out.

He returned to his seat and opened the cover. To his surprise, a folded piece of paper slipped out and fluttered to the floor. Though he'd skimmed through the book within the last few days, he didn't remember seeing the sheet before. He leaned down and picked it up.

White and unfrayed, the paper looked new—but when he unfolded it he saw that elaborate old-fashioned writing filled one side, taking the form of poetry. He recognized his ancestor's hand. If Geoff had written the words, the paper must have been older

than it looked—a good, acid-free pulp that held up to
time.

Curiosity piqued, he read the lines:

The past is a heavy and clinging matter.
We carry its burden, beaten and battered.
But if we could dare enough to break free,
A whole new future might be there to see.

Two lovers I know found a moment of bliss,
Duly entranced in one another's kiss,
But, weighted down by their worldly affairs,
They lost sight of how they had come to care.

Dear Lovers, forget the problems you bear,
Remember the blessings you have to share.
When happiness calls, don't close the door.
If you lose this chance, you may have no more.

Your fears of change may now seem sound,
But if you linger on separate ground,
Time will teach you how much you missed,
The day you renounced each other's kiss.

As Mark finished reading, a chill shivered through
him. As much as he kept trying to deny the existence
of ghosts, he couldn't help wondering if his great,
great grandfather had spoken to him through the
poem. The words seemed conspicuously applicable to
him and Lara—and the paper looked perfectly new.
Was it possible that the lines were actually written *for*
them?

The thought made him gulp. He wasn't about to try
asking the ghost for clarification—but he thought that

the poem made sense. If Lara wouldn't see him, maybe she would read a letter from him, especially if he enclosed Geoff's poem with it. Instead of sitting here passively while she made up with her ex, he would make sure she knew how he felt about her.

Taking his ancestor's poem to his desk, he sat down and grabbed a piece of paper and a pen.

"Dear Lara," he wrote . . . then stared at the empty space beneath the words. What did he really have to offer her? How could he get her attention enough to make her care how he felt about her? In her point of view, he'd tried to block her plans for her house. How could he make that up to her?

The beginnings of an idea came to him. Earlier he'd been sorry that he'd missed out on the chance to work with her on an alternate plan for her house. What if he could come up with a great concept now and present it to her? With all of his experience with old houses, he had to be able to think of something.

The scheme excited him. It was the one way he might be able to offset some of his past mistakes.

Tapping his pen on the desk, he contemplated the studio, visualizing its beautiful architecture. Of course, tampering with the original layout of the house was out of the question—so what could they do?

All at once, an idea clicked in his mind. He'd have to confirm a few details if Lara ever let him in her house again, but he felt almost sure he had the perfect solution.

As he put his pen to paper again, Geoff's poem caught his eye, and he silently thanked his ancestor for his help—coincidental or intentional. The verses had inspired him, and he had a feeling they might influence Lara, too. She had once loved the old boy, and, whether or not she approved of his exploits, she believed she had a connection to his ghost. Mark thought that if she wouldn't listen to *him*, she might pay attention to Geoff . . . but he couldn't depend on it. Right now, more than ever, he had to make his own words count.

Leaning over the paper, he started writing the most important letter of his life.

Chapter 18

LARA STOOD AT the stove cooking an omelet when she heard a knock at her back door. *Ron,* she thought, *here for the second day in a row.* This time he'd playfully tapped out the "shave and a haircut" beat—kind of a lighthearted thing for him to do. He must have been in a good mood. She guessed he'd come back to brag some more about his manufacturing deal.

Frowning, she set down her flipper and turned down the burner. She may have been glad to hear about his good fortune the day before, but if he planned to make a habit of dropping by, she'd have to put an end to it now.

Instead of answering the door right away, she peeked out of a window to its side.

Di stood on the back step. She spotted Lara and waved, a grin spreading across her face.

The tension drained from Lara's body. Nothing could have been a more welcome sight. She threw open the dead bolt and stepped outside to greet her friend with a hug. "God, it's good to see you. You don't know how much I've missed you."

"I've missed you, too." Di looked tanned and relaxed after her week at the beach. She thrust a box of saltwater taffy toward Lara. "I like my sister-in-law well enough, but she and I don't have a lot in common. We ran out of things to talk about days ago."

"Thank you," Lara said as she took the candy. Glancing down at the box, she hoped it contained a lot of chocolate ones. She could use the comfort of chocolate. "I didn't think you'd be home till tonight, and I never expected to hear from you today."

"The forecast sounded shaky, so we left a day early. I don't know if it made the news here, but they were expecting a big storm along the coast. We didn't want to get caught in a lot of rain driving home."

Lara shook her head. "No, I hadn't heard, but I'm glad you took precautions. I hope you had better luck with the weather the rest of the week."

"Oh, we did." Di dropped her keys into her purse. "Most of the time it was beautiful, barely a cloud in sight."

"Good. Can you come in for a minute now, or do you have too much to do?"

"Of course I can come in."

Lara stepped back and held the door open for her.

As Di entered the kitchen, she sniffed at the air. "What smells so good?"

"I was just making breakfast." She went to the stove

to turn the eggs over. "Do you want some of this omelet? As usual, I've made enough to feed an army."

"No, thanks, I've already eaten—though I wouldn't say no to a cup of coffee." Her friend set her purse down on one corner of the counter. "Go ahead and fix your omelet. I can get the coffee myself."

"So, tell me all about your vacation," Lara urged her, glad to have something besides Mark to focus on.

While Lara finished cooking and dished out her food, Di described the highlights of her time in Cape Hatteras. The house they'd rented sounded great, but there hadn't been much else besides beach in the area. If Lara had come along, the isolated location definitely would have left her stranded with the two couples.

Of course, considering her devastation at home, she probably would have been better off.

"Enough about my boring trip," Di said as they carried the hot drinks and food into the dining room. "I'm dying to know what's been going on here with you and Mark."

"Not what you would hope, I'm afraid." Lara looked away from her. Between bites of egg, she summarized the past week's events. She tried not to show how depressed her falling out with Mark had made her, but when she got to the end of the story she couldn't keep her voice from cracking.

"How awful." Di blinked in shock. She reached across the table to give her friend's hand a squeeze. "I can't believe Mark Vereker would act like such a jerk—especially when you two were getting along so wonderfully. I always thought he was such a nice guy. Did he offer some sort of explanation for talking to the zoning board? Maybe he didn't *mean* to screw things up for you."

Lara leaned back in her chair, swirling the last bit of coffee in her mug. "Well, that's what *he* claims—that it was all a mistake—but I don't believe him for a second."

"Why not?"

She pursed her lips. "You know what a hard time he gave me about the wall when we first met. When a guy feels that strongly about an issue, he doesn't just turn around and forget about it. I knew something was funny when he suddenly started paying me all kinds of attention. Now I wish I'd listened to my instincts about him."

Her friend frowned. "I hope you're not suggesting he's been faking an interest in you."

"That's exactly what I'm suggesting." Her anger growing, she gulped down the rest of her coffee. "All along he's been running hot and cold with me, and his supposed ex-girlfriend is always hanging around him. I don't think they ever got over each other. Maybe they never really even broke up. Who knows? That might have been a story formulated solely for my benefit—just so he could get in tight with me and try to keep me from knocking down the studio wall."

Di wrinkled her nose. "I can understand why you're upset, but aren't you getting a little carried away? I went to school with him for years, and I never got the impression he was a devious person. If he *is* a bit obsessive about preserving houses, wouldn't intervening with the zoning board have been enough to foil your plans?"

"I don't know. To be honest with you, nothing is clear to me anymore." With her wounds still open, Lara wasn't in the mood to go easy on Mark. "Maybe he wasn't sure whether the board would listen to him and didn't want to leave anything up to chance."

Her friend rested her elbows on the table and leaned her chin on her palms, her expression pensive. "But if he were only pretending to be interested in you all of this time, wouldn't he keep up a constant act instead of having all those mood swings? To me, his volatility makes it seem more likely his feelings for you are genuine."

"Then how do you explain why he's still in touch with Karen so frequently?"

She shrugged. "She might be pursuing *him*. You said she acted jealous the first time you ran into her at his apartment. Have you tried coming out and asking him directly what's going on with them?"

"I did earlier in the week, and he claimed he doesn't want anything more to do with her, but yesterday he admitted she was his connection with the zoning board—the one he told about the studio." Glancing over at his book, still on the table, she frowned. "He tried to blame the whole thing on her, saying she's the one who went to the officials—as if that makes a difference."

Di sat up straight and gave her a look of disbelief. "Of course it makes a difference! Why didn't you tell me that before? I'll bet I know exactly what happened. Karen is jealous of your relationship with Mark and tried to ruin your plans out of resentment. He probably had no idea she was going to the board about them."

Lara shook her head. "I'm sure he knew. He *told* me about it, remember? You're just trying to find excuses for him, because you want so much for me to have someone. Your intentions may be good, but you're going to have to realize that Mark simply isn't the one for me."

Di started to say something but stopped herself. After a moment she sighed. "Won't you even give him the benefit of the doubt?"

"Why should I?" Lara stood up, holding her empty mug. "I've had enough of his wavering back and forth. Every time I start thinking I'm interested, he does something to make me doubt I know him at all. Well, this time I'm getting off the roller coaster."

Before Di had a chance to come up with another argument, Lara picked up her mug, too. Stepping toward the kitchen, she threw over her shoulder, "Do you want any more coffee?"

"No, thanks," was the quiet answer.

As she crossed the hall, a loud boom startled her—the front door knocker slamming down on the wooden panels. She juggled the mugs but managed not to drop them.

Catching her breath, she wondered who could be there now. Was it possible Mark would come by again? Her heartbeat quickened.

She backtracked into the dining room and whispered, "I don't want to get that, in case it's him."

Di rolled her eyes and got up out of her chair, marching toward the hallway.

"What are you doing? He might see you."

"He can see our cars in the driveway, anyway, so he knows we're here." She turned into the hall toward the front of the house and hissed, "I'm going to answer the door. If it's him I'll tell him you're in the shower and ask if I can take a message."

Lara wanted to drag her back into the room, but Di was already halfway up the hall. Desperate to avoid

Mark, she ducked around the corner and hid from view.

She heard the hinges of the front door creak and her friend say something she couldn't make out. A man's voice answered . . . yes, it sounded like Mark. Despite herself, she held her breath. If he kept coming over to try to see her like this, was it possible he really did care?

Not enough to have been honest with me, she remembered.

Still, she couldn't resist trying to hear the discussion going on at the front of the house. Unfortunately, she couldn't quite grasp any of the words.

After what seemed like ages the door creaked shut again. She stood still, afraid Di might have let him in.

Luckily, she didn't hear them talking anymore.

At last her friend walked back into the dining room, alone. She gave Lara a somber look. "I think you're crazy for not seeing him. He's a perfectly nice guy. I don't believe he cares more about this house than you. Why would he keep coming back here if he didn't have feelings for you?"

A spark of something frighteningly like hope weakened Lara. She bit her lip. "What did he say?"

"That he really needs to see you. He wanted me to try to get through to you. If I can't talk you into meeting with him, he wants me to at least try to get you to read this." She held out an envelope.

Lara stared at the piece of paper. The thought popped into her mind that it might be another one of Geoffrey Vereker's letters—but lately Mark had acted like he wanted to avoid dealing with the ghost. Why would he change his mind now? "What is it?"

"I think it's a letter but, of course, I haven't looked inside. Why don't you open it and see?"

Unsure whether or not she would look at the contents, she took the envelope and read the front. Written across the face, in Mark's handwriting, was her name.

She sighed, relieved to find it wasn't a letter of Geoffrey's. In her state of mind, she didn't feel prepared to deal with the ghost. But was she ready to read what Mark had to say?

"Well, aren't you going to look at it?" Di asked.

If she'd known what was good for her, she probably would have thrown it out unread—but she found that she didn't quite have the will.

Tearing open the seal, she pulled out several sheets of paper and read the top page to herself:

Dear Lara,

I know you don't want to hear excuses from me, and I understand why, so I'll spare you. The bottom line is that the debacle with the zoning board was my fault. There's no way of getting around it.

Given that, I've been pondering how I can make amends. The only way is to see that you get the studio you want and deserve. I've racked my mind, and I think I've come up with a solution that may satisfy everyone, but I'll need to confirm a few details about your house. Please consider letting me stop by soon . . . for this reason and because I need to see you.

If you won't meet with me, I have no right to complain. I'll outline my ideas and send them to you anyway—but please try to find it in your heart to give me this chance to prove that I'm not all bad.

Before closing, I also wanted to tell you that I've found another poem of Geoff's, one I don't believe was ever published. Thanks to the insight you've given me into him, I'm finally able to appreciate him for what he was. The poem particularly inspired me, and I'm enclosing it in hope that the verses will mean something to you, too. Reading them gave me the courage to try contacting you again.

Please keep the poem. I realize that Geoff and I both rate low with you these days, but try to remember how much you used to love his work. Whether or not you can forgive me, I hope that someday you'll be able to overlook his faults and love his poetry the way you used to.

I have so much more to say to you—too much to try to put into writing. I really need to talk to you. Please call me as soon as possible.

Nothing in the world would mean more to me.

Love,
Mark

The word "love" stood out like a beacon to Lara—or maybe a flash of warning. Did he *love* her?

Before their falling out, she'd realized that her feelings for him had been growing warmer and more powerful—but even then she'd avoided thinking about love. Now she felt completely confused. Too much had happened in the last week. She didn't know what to think.

Feeling numb, she folded up both sheets of paper

and put them back in the envelope. She wasn't interested in reading Geoffrey's poetry.

"What does he say?" Di asked her.

Covering her mouth with one hand, she held out the
letter. "Here, read it for yourself, if you want."

Her friend took the envelope and sat down at the
table. While she pulled out the sheets and flattened
them, Lara turned to look out a window, not even seeing the scene outside.

"You've got to see him after this," Di said from behind her, following up the statement with the soft
swish of a page turning over. "Does the poem by his
great-great-grandfather say anything relevant, or
should I skip it?"

"I don't know," Lara murmured. "I didn't look at
it."

Her friend lapsed back into silence, apparently reading on. A few moments passed, then she said quietly,
"My God. This is *too* weird."

Caught up in her own thoughts, Lara didn't pay attention to her.

"*Mark* must have written it," Di said after another
minute. "Lara, you've got to see this."

She doubted she could possibly find it interesting,
but she turned around. "What?"

"This poem—it's got to be a joke . . . or something.
It's about two lovers, and they sound an awful lot like
you and Mark." Di met her gaze, her forehead crin-
kling. "I guess it's possible that Geoffrey Vereker
could have written about a couple with a similar
story a hundred years ago, but it seems like a hell of a
coincidence."

A hard lump jelled inside of Lara's stomach. Lately
she'd had too many weird experiences to write much

off as coincidence—especially where Geoffrey was concerned.

Her friend glanced back down at the poem. "This paper doesn't even look old. Mark must have faked this old-fashioned handwriting, trying to get your attention. That's pretty creepy of him! I guess you're right about his being devious. I never would have imagined he'd do something like this."

Despite Lara's doubts about Mark, she believed that the ghost was the more devious of the two Verekers. Though the poem Geoffrey had shown her the day before had softened her anger toward him, she still didn't want much to do with him. Unfortunately, she had a feeling that the ghost wasn't going to let her go that easily.

Di got up and held the sheet out in front of her. "Look—no yellowing, no musty smell. This stationery could have come out of the box yesterday."

Lara stared down at the poet's familiar handwriting, knowing that Mark hadn't forged the elaborate curlicues. What would be the point? She frowned. "Maybe it did . . . but Mark wasn't the one who wrote it."

"What do you mean—" Di cut herself off, her eyes opening wide. The page fell from her hand and drifted to the floor. "Oh. You think the ghost wrote it."

Seeing her poor friend's look of horror, Lara suddenly felt resentful about being dragged into this situation. She glared down at the poem by their feet. "Why did Mark have to send that to me? Geoffrey's *his* ancestor, not mine. Why do I have to be involved with his problems?"

Di shuddered and hugged herself, eyeing the paper as if it were a poisonous snake. "W—well, you've been involved from the start. *Your* house is where the ghost showed up. To be completely fair, Mark didn't really have any more choice in the matter than you."

"*He's* the one who sent me this." Lara bent down and picked up the poem, folding it without reading the words. Grabbing Mark's letter from the table, she stuffed both sheets back into the envelope and threw the packet on top of Mark's book. "Well, if my mind wasn't made up before, it is now. I want nothing more to do with either of the Verekers."

Snatching up her breakfast dishes from the table, she stalked off into the kitchen.

Her friend followed closely behind her. "Wait a minute. You can't very well fight the . . . the supernatural. You've been saying so yourself for the past couple of weeks. The ghost has chosen to come to you for a reason. You have to let this thing play out."

"Not if I have any choice in the matter." Lara spun around to face her. "Would *you* want a ghost calling the shots in your love life? Trying to judge whether Mark and I might actually have something worthwhile between us is hard enough without wondering whether a ghost is meddling in our business. Maybe Geoffrey even contrived somehow for us to meet in the first place. Maybe he has other tricks up his sleeve. What sort of powers does a ghost have, anyway?"

"Oh, come on." Di tilted her head to one side. "No one but you is calling the shots. Whether Geoffrey Vereker is trying to influence you or not, you'll always have your own free will. In fact, if you let your fears take over now, you won't be living your life the way you want to, anyway."

The argument struck a nerve with Lara, but she

didn't want to admit it to herself. Turning back around, she began rinsing off her dishes in the sink.

"When Ron left," Di went on, "you said you'd never let anyone else hold you back again. Doesn't that include Geoffrey Vereker? Damn it, Lara, don't be afraid of him. Take hold of the reins yourself."

She stopped with her plate and sponge poised under the running water. Was it true that she was letting the ghost get the best of her?

Di rushed out into the hall and came back carrying the cordless phone. She held out the receiver. "Here. Call Mark and find out the whole story. Then you can determine for yourself what this all means and where you stand with him."

Staring at the phone, she considered her friend's arguments. Yes, Di was right. If nothing else, it was time to get everything out in the open. She might well end up telling both Verekers off, but then at least she'd have the satisfaction of knowing she'd faced up to them.

"Okay, I'll call him." She turned off the faucet and dried her hands on a dish towel. "But don't bother getting your hopes up. I want this thing settled once and for all—but not necessarily the way you'd like."

Di handed her the phone.

She punched the digits into the pad. The phone at the other end of the line rang. She took a deep breath, willing her jumpy stomach to calm down.

After only one ring, Mark picked up. "Hello?"

Hearing his voice again affected her more than she expected. The sound of his smooth baritone had always been enough to make her heart flutter—but after everything that had happened, she should have been immune to it. She swallowed her emotions. "Hi, Mark, it's me."

"Lara." Her name rushed out of him, almost like a sigh. He sounded relieved to hear from her, but she couldn't be sure what his motives were. Maybe he just didn't want to come off looking like the bad guy. That didn't mean he wasn't.

Steeling her expression and, she hoped, her tone, she said, "I agree with you that we need to talk. When would be a good time for you to get together with me?"

"I can be at your place in ten minutes—if that will work for you."

She hesitated, but saw no reason to put off the meeting. "That'll be fine. I'll see you then."

"See you—and thanks."

He didn't have cause to thank her, but she didn't bother pointing it out. Frowning, she hung up without responding. Di was watching her, so she said without excitement, "He's coming right over."

"Then I'll get out of your way—unless you need me to help you get ready."

She shook her head. "I'm not making any sort of fuss for him."

"Fair enough." Di retrieved her purse from the countertop. Hooking the strap over her shoulder, she said, "If you have a chance later tonight, please give me a call and let me know how things work out. I promise not to put any more pressure on you if you still think he's not right for you. Despite my penchant for matchmaking, I wouldn't want to see you stuck in another relationship that's less than you deserve."

"Thanks."

Lara saw her to the door and watched through the

window until her friend's car pulled out of sight. There was no sign of Mark yet. Only a few minutes had passed . . . though every second dragged.

She turned away and looked around the kitchen. What could she do to keep busy while she waited for him? Knowing she would need to discuss the ghost with him as well as their relationship, she acknowledged that she probably should read Geoffrey's latest poem.

Returning to the dining room, she sat down at the table and opened the envelope again. She took out both sheets of paper and placed the second page on top. Di had been right; it looked as new as the sheet Mark had written on.

She felt very cynical as she began skimming the lines. Geoffrey spoke about the past, and she supposed a ghost could claim some knowledge in that realm— but as for having much to say about the future, she hardly accepted *him* as an authority.

Di seemed to have been right about the reference to Mark and her, too. Lara presumed the ghost had written the verses in the last day or so—not that the belief convinced her to consider his advice. She wasn't about to stake her love life on guidance offered by the spirit of a man who'd probably never really known love himself.

When she read the final couplet, however, a wisp of cold air grazed the nape of her neck and sent a shiver down her spine. She thought of part of the poem he'd shown her yesterday: "But, cherished lady, sometimes I wonder/Whether to save myself or go under . . ."

He did love her, she thought. *He was just too afraid to admit it.* The intensity of her impression made her believe her perception was true. Furthermore, she imagined that Geoffrey must have had plenty of time to think about what he'd done to Mariah and how both of them had suffered because of his fear of commitment.

Of course, that still didn't mean that she and Mark were meant to be together.

A banging at the front door made her start, and she bumped her knee on the leg of the table. "Ow!"

He was here.

Standing up, she paused and looked around the room. Everything was perfectly still, and she didn't detect any further coldness.

"I'll talk to him," she said to the air, "but I'm not promising anything more than that."

Without waiting for a response from the ghost, she went to answer the door.

Chapter 19

GEOFF WAS RATHER shocked when Lara addressed him. She didn't say his name, of course, but no one else was in the room. He hadn't meant to make his presence known, but he was in such a state of anxiety that he must have been more detectable than usual. Though he'd been keeping his distance from her physically, he obviously emanated a chill strong enough for her to feel.

After his initial astonishment dimmed, he noted that she seemed to be outgrowing her fear of him. He thanked heaven for that. Now of all times, the last thing he needed was to upset her unwittingly. At this critical moment for her and Mark, he couldn't afford for anything to go wrong. He had a feeling this was the only chance he'd ever get to redress the worst of all he'd done wrong during his life.

As she turned to leave the dining room, he forced himself to hang back and add to his distance from her, just in case. He couldn't risk another mistake. Emotion charged through him like current through a wire, and if he got any more agitated, he might even become visible. He'd never materialized during daylight before, but there was a first time for everything.

When she'd moved out of sight he floated into the hallway after her, anxious to see how she would greet his descendant. As she progressed toward the door, he stayed back about two yards behind her.

To his surprise, she suddenly stopped and spun around. She rushed back toward him, forcing him to shoot up above her head, still afraid his touch might disturb her. He narrowly missed contact with her as she passed under him.

What in damnation was she doing?

He watched as she turned back into the dining room. Had she changed her mind about seeing Mark? Surely not after she'd just *said* she would talk to him!

Oh, but women are a fickle lot. Wringing his hands, Geoff flew after her. For generations women had claimed that changing their minds was their prerogative. What on earth was he going to do to get this matter back on course?

As he entered the room, she snatched up the two sheets of paper on the table. Immediately she turned back toward the hallway.

Good Lord! She'd only wanted to fetch Mark's letter and his own poem.

Once again he rocketed out of her way just before she crossed paths with him. Her gait had quickened now.

Geoff sighed and clapped his right hand over his

chest, where his heart had once raced under such circumstances. For a moment he'd thought all was lost. The stark terror he'd felt showed him more than ever how much he was depending on the mortals to save him.

Trying hard to calm himself, he glided into the hallway a second time.

Lara had stopped before the closed front door, glancing down at the papers in her hand. Recalling her lack of reaction to his poem, Geoff regretted how little his words had affected her. To break Mariah's curse, he needed to "advance" Lara and Mark's love, and he hadn't made any impression on her. Thank goodness his descendant had shown a far greater response upon finding the poem. Geoff only hoped the part he'd played in bringing about this meeting would be enough to serve his purpose.

"We shall see. . . ." an otherworldly feminine voice whispered, seemingly close by.

Mariah? He froze in place, darting looks all around the foyer. His former lover was nowhere to be seen—but this time he knew she was present. If he'd needed further evidence of the significance of the occasion, he had it now. Clearly this was the defining moment in his ghosthood.

He clasped his palms together and pressed his thumbs against his mouth, almost as if in prayer. If he'd thought any god would listen to a vile creature like him, indeed he would have tried praying. But at the moment he felt it was Mariah's forgiveness he needed—or he could never forgive himself.

Lara reached for the door handle, and Geoff sucked in his ethereal breath.

*   *   *

Despite her determination to talk to Mark, Lara didn't quite feel ready for the confrontation. With her hand on the door handle, she paused to gather up her courage. It was bad enough that there might be a ghost watching over her shoulder—but she actually didn't care much about that now. This might well be the last time she and Mark ever spoke to each other, and it was bound to be a rough conversation.

Even after all the trouble he'd given her, she would hate to say good-bye. Thoughts of better times with him ricocheted through her mind—the nice inscription he'd written for her in his book, the day they'd spent in the village upstate. . . . He had really worked his way into her heart.

Then she remembered their last encounter, when she'd realized she hadn't know him as well as she'd thought.

She pulled the door open and took in his appearance with a glance. With his face unshaven and his hair disheveled, he looked as though he'd had a bad couple of days—yet he still managed to come off as sexy as hell. The sight of him brought an unexpected lump to her throat.

"Hi," he said with an uneven smile.

"Hello." She swallowed down the lump, wishing he didn't look so self-conscious—so *seemingly* innocent. The worst thing she could do was feel sorry for him. She needed to be strong. Turning her gaze away from his, she said over her shoulder, "Come on in."

Without looking back, she led him through the parlor. Neither of them said a word. When she entered the studio, she glanced back and saw him looking at the couch—the spot where they'd first made love. The muscles in her abdomen tightened painfully.

Purposely avoiding the secondhand monstrosity, she sat at one of the stools at the drawing table. She tossed his letter and Geoffrey's poem on top of one of her sketchbooks, then turned around to face the center of the room.

He took the stool beside her, so they were now in the same positions where they'd been for their first argument. Since that day, they seemed to have come full circle.

She looked over at him and noticed his fists were clenched in his lap.

After a long moment he said, "I wish I knew where to start."

Again, she felt a tug of empathy. He looked so damned miserable—but looks could be deceiving, and going easy on him would definitely be a mistake. She had ignored the early signs of Ron's problems and wound up crushed by him. If she let Mark steamroll over her, too, she'd have no excuse for her stupidity.

She leaned back against the table and folded her arms across her chest. Reluctant to show him how deeply he'd hurt her, she thought the best approach would be to keep the conversation as impersonal as possible.

"Why don't we discuss your ancestor's poem?" she said without much interest in her voice. "I'd just finished reading it when you came to the door."

Meeting her gaze with surprising steadiness, he cleared his throat. "What did you think?"

While he waited for her to respond, he looked as though he were holding his breath.

She wondered what he expected of her—some sort of praise for the writing, or a show of awe about the ghostly phenomenon? At this point she didn't have that kind of enthusiasm for anything.

"I think Geoffrey should mind his own business," she said in an irritated tone.

He watched her for another moment, then looked away. Getting up from his stool, he wandered toward the back of the room. "I think he would, if he had a choice. He probably doesn't want to be mixed up with us any more than we want to be with him."

She thought about this point and frowned to herself. The idea hadn't occurred to her that the ghost was stuck with them, too—but she supposed he was. Thinking back on all she had learned about Geoffrey, she believed he must be sorry for the wrongs he'd done. He'd ended up marrying an insensitive woman who'd probably made his life miserable—and now he was doomed to unrest.

For the first time since she'd found out he was the one who'd deserted Mariah, Lara felt truly sorry for him. He would certainly have a long time to repent giving up the woman who might have shown him how to love. A chance for love didn't come that often.

Mark stepped closer to the back of the room, and his movement caught her eye.

She had thought she'd had a chance for love with him. A trickle of worry seeped into her head. Would she come to regret dismissing Mark from her life? Might she someday wish that she'd given him another chance?

When he turned around to look at the bookcases lining the wall his actions made her feel nervous, and she dropped her line of thought. The entrance to the secret room was closed—as well as it *would* close—but thinking about the ghost had brought back her eerie feelings about the spot.

He stooped and started to examine the area around the base of the entrance, and her uneasiness changed to annoyance. Even now, with their relationship coming to an end, he was more interested in her house than in her!

"What are you doing?" she snapped at him.

"Just checking out a few things." He stood back up, tiptoeing and stretching his neck to look around at the tops of the bookcases. "Would you mind if I opened up the entrance?"

"Yes, I would." She jumped off her stool. "I thought we were having a conversation—but, as usual, all you can think about is this house."

He turned around to face her. "I'm sorry. This has to do with my idea for your studio."

She pursed her lips, unconvinced.

"Please, Lara, just give me a few minutes, and then I'll explain everything."

When she didn't answer, his shoulders sagged, but he didn't give up. "Aren't you even curious about what I have in mind?"

She wasn't really, but since she'd said pretty much all she cared to about the ghost, she supposed they might as well move on to another topic. "Okay, check whatever you want to—as long as I don't have to go into the secret room with you."

"No problem."

While she stood back watching him, he triggered the mechanism and the case ground across the floor. He spent another moment looking at the perimeters of the area, then disappeared behind the wall.

The lump in her throat rose again.

Within seconds he popped back out and grinned at her. "It's exactly as I thought."

She felt another pang of resentment that he could be so happy when she felt like her world was crumbling. "What are you talking about?"

"The secret room isn't an original part of the house. This wall was added later. When the house was built, this area was one huge room—maybe a ballroom." He motioned toward the row of bookcases. "If you tore these down—or, preferably, moved them elsewhere— it would add an extra ten feet or so on to the studio. Once you unblock the window in there, you'll even have more light. I think this room could really be fantastic."

She stared at him, letting the idea slowly sink in. To her amazement, she agreed with him. Combining the secret room and the studio would give her loads of space to work in. The extra expanse even had another fireplace. The finished room would be beautiful—and she wouldn't have to destroy the house to get it.

"Wow," she murmured.

"When you tell the historical society you want to re- store the house to its original floor plan, I'm sure they'll approve your grant." His smile faded a little, and he looked at her more seriously. "As for the zon- ing board, I'm really sorry about that fiasco, but I promise you won't have any further problems with them. I've spoken to the board chairman about your studio."

"Really?" A new bud of hope opened inside her.

He nodded. "It was the least I could do. In fact, I should have done it weeks ago, when I inadvertently started up the rumor mill with my slip of tongue. It's just that with everything that's been happening between you and me, that conversation with Karen was the last thing on my mind."

He'd said what she wanted to hear—that she came first in his mind and Karen came last. She began to think she'd made a mistake in not hearing him out before this. A little embarrassed, she asked, "So what did the chairman of the zoning board say?"

"He agreed that your project isn't a commercial undertaking, and he regretted their misunderstanding. When you send in your revised application, they'll issue your permit as quickly as possible—assuming you don't plan to do anything in violation of town codes."

A soothing warmth flooded her body. He really was a good guy, after all.

She gave him a small smile and shook her head. "Mark, I don't know what to say. I know you wouldn't have gone to so much trouble if all you cared about was preserving that outside wall, which is what I was afraid of. Thank you for talking to the officials and for coming up with a new plan for me. I can't believe it— you seem to have thought of everything."

"Then you do like the idea about annexing the secret room?" he asked. "I mean, you don't think it would transfer the creepy atmosphere to this room, do you?"

She considered the possibility, but it seemed to her that anything creepy about the house *stemmed* from the secret it had held. With the space opened up again, she had a feeling her home would be more cheerful than it had been in over a century.

"No, I'm convinced all the creepiness will be gone."

"Then I'll move on to the most important point of discussion." He took a step toward her, then stopped again. Meeting her gaze squarely, he asked, "Lara, how can I apologize for mentioning your plans to Karen? I should have told you what had happened right away. I wish I could go back and do it over again. Since I can't, I want to make it up to you the best that I can. I'd really love to work on renovating your studio with you, if you'll let me."

She gave him a crooked smile, trying not to break into tears and make a fool of herself. "*I* should apologize to *you* for not listening to you before this."

"Your reaction was understandable."

Hardly able to believe how everything between them had turned around so quickly, she looked away from him, glancing around the room. A nervous laugh slipped out of her. "So, you don't mind stripping paint? We'll have to do something about all of the dark varnish in here."

He rushed forward and took both of her hands, warming them in his. Grateful, she met his gaze.

His eyes looked big and intent as he stared down at her. "I'll gladly strip paint. I only hope it will help make up for what an idiot I've been."

Her smile widened into a grin. "It would certainly be a good start."

"What else can I do?" he asked, his expression solemn. "Just tell me. Really."

She knew what she wanted from him more than anything else at the moment but, after their brief separation, she felt oddly shy asking for it. Looking up at him through her lashes, she asked, "How about giving me a kiss?"

"My pleasure."

He leaned down and met her mouth.

His kiss was tender, an expression of caring rather

than of hunger. Closing her eyes, she reveled in the relief that flooded through her. She hadn't realized she'd been holding her body so tensely until this second, when all of her muscles relaxed.

He deepened the kiss as the minutes passed until she grew almost dizzy with joy. Eventually they pulled back and looked at each other. She felt warm and content, and the soft look in his eyes told her he felt the same.

"I'd like to try to make up for my bad behavior, too," she said. "Maybe I could start by illustrating that book for you."

He gave her a brilliant smile—then all at once something behind her seemed to grab his attention. His brow furrowed as he stared over her shoulder.

"What's wrong?" she asked, turning around to see what was there. He seemed to be looking toward her drawing table, but she didn't notice anything unusual about it.

"Just one question and then I won't bring the topic up again," he said, meeting her gaze. "It's about the poem of Geoff's that I sent with my letter. Did you get the same feeling about it I did—that it was written for you and me?"

"I have no doubt it was." The reminder drained away some of her happiness. "I have to say I think it's really scary that he's had some sort of hand in bringing us together."

"Well, whatever his influence, I'm grateful for it." He reached up and grazed her cheek with the backs of his fingers. "I feel connected to you in a way that I've never felt with anyone before."

As he leaned down to kiss her again, a gust of chilly air blew past them, making them both look up. Geoff's poem flew off the drawing table and landed on the floor, near the entrance to the secret room.

Lara waited for more to happen, but the chill faded quickly, and the house stood silent—empty except for her and Mark. Hot tears gathered in her eyes. Somehow, she knew that Geoffrey and Mariah had finally found peace with each other.

Mark lifted her chin and gently turned her face toward him. He gave her a shaky smile. "I don't think we'll be hearing from Geoff again."

To her amazement, the thought made her sad. Through her tight throat she croaked out, "In a way, it seems a shame to lose him."

"I don't know about that. I think it's better than the alternative." He glanced down at her quivering lips, then gazed back into her eyes. "Please don't look so unhappy, Lara. After all, he's left us an important legacy."

"Yes." She looked off toward the bookcase. "We'll always have his poetry."

He laughed. "I meant our love."

Her gaze shot back to meet his. He'd used that word again and, for an instant, it took her off guard. Then she smiled and nodded. "Yes, there's that, too."

She reached up and wrapped her arms around his neck.

"I love you," she said, trying out the words. They felt right, and she wasn't surprised.

"I love you, too."

He bent down and kissed her again.

About the Author

JENNIFER MALIN ADMITS she was once a "literary snob" who read only classics. Then one day during her college years her mother lent her a Regency romance, telling her, "This is like those Jane Austen novels you read." The story captivated her so much she stayed up all night to finish it. When she started seriously writing, romance was the genre she chose.

She hopes her books bring readers some of the enjoyment she's found in the work of others. Some of her favorite romance authors include Mary Balogh, Laura Kinsale, and Joan Smith. Besides Austen, her favorite classic writers are Shakespeare, Eliot, and Hardy.

Eternally Yours is her second Jove romance. Her first, *As You Wish*, appeared in January 1999 as part of Jove's Time Passages series. She is a past winner of the Golden Heart award, presented by Romance Writers of America.

Jennifer lives outside of Philadelphia with her husband, Martin, an Australian national. Besides reading, the two of them love music and travel. She's been to Europe three times and Australia three times and plans to keep expanding her horizons whenever possible.

HIGHLAND FLING

Have a Fling...every other month with Jove's new Highland Fling romances!

January 2002
Laird of the Mist
by Elizabeth English
0-515-13190-3

March 2002
Once Forbidden
by Terri Brisbin
0-515-13179-2

All books: $5.99